**Readers and authors love *The Post Office Girls*:**

'I loved *The Post Office Girls*! It really captured what it was like for women at home during the war. And the ending had me on the edge of my seat!'
Johanna Bell, author of *The Bobby Girls* series

'A wonderful coming-of-age story, full of humour against such an emotional backdrop'
Jessica Ryn, author of *The Extraordinary Hope of Dawn Brightside*

'Brimming over with period detail, this coming-of-age story has an endearing heroine and an absorbing plot. A sparkling debut'
Maisie Thomas, author of *The Railway Girls* series

'A wonderful story of love, family and loss . . . I can't recommend it highly enough'
Reader Review

'Heartwarming and comforting, with wonderful, well-rounded characters'
Reader Review

'Read this book in a day and couldn't put it down'
Reader Review

'Entertaining, enlightening and thoroughly enjoyable'
Reader Review

# A Post Office Christmas

*Book Two in the*
*Post Office Girls series*

## POPPY COOPER

**HODDER**

First published in Great Britain in 2021 by Hodder & Stoughton
An Hachette UK company

2

A CIP catalogue record for this title is available from the British Library

Paperback ISBN 978  1 529 31031 3
eBook ISBN 978 1 529 31029 0

Typeset in Plantin Light by Palimpsest Book Production Limited,
Falkirk, Stirlingshire

Printed and bound in Great Britain by Clays Ltd, Elcograf S.p.A.

Hodder & Stoughton policy is to use papers that are natural, renewable
and recyclable products and made from wood grown in sustainable forests.
The logging and manufacturing processes are expected to conform to
the environmental regulations of the country of origin.

Hodder & Stoughton Ltd
Carmelite House
50 Victoria Embankment
London EC4Y 0DZ

www.hodder.co.uk

Dear Reader,

I've been *thrilled* to receive many wonderful messages telling me how much you enjoyed getting to know Beth, Nora and Milly in *The Post Office Girls* and how impatient you were to find out what happened next. Thank you so much for all your lovely feedback – and I'm so excited that the next instalment is finally here! *A Post Office Christmas* is told through Milly's eyes and has been a joy to write – I love the festive season and it has been great fun seeing the world from feisty, passionate Milly's point of view as she struggles to work out who she is in an ever-changing world and as her friendship with Nora and Beth (who Milly knows as Liza) comes under pressure.

As ever I've tried my best to stay true to the spirit – if not to every detail – of the age. There really was a royal visit to the Army Post Office's Home Depot just before Christmas one year; I've seen a couple of different dates suggested for this (and, in reality, it was probably a year or two after 1915) but, as in the book, it seems the Royal visit was planned to boost morale during the the hectic Christmas rush. And it really was a rush – at busy times, well over a million parcels were being sorted at the Home Depot *every* week! It's been fascinating to learn more about the Suffragette movement; I previously had no idea of the extent of their bombing campaign – targeting everything from the Bank of England to St Paul's Cathedral, from theatres to football clubs, from post-boxes to railway stations. And I'd never even heard of the separation allowance – a proportion of a soldier's pay, augmented by the government while he was on active service, to make sure dependents were not left destitute - let alone the fact that it could be taken away from women who 'behaved badly'. No wonder Milly was outraged!

I really hope you enjoy the story and thank you again for all your support.

Love, Poppy xx

# A Post Office Christmas

I felt like giving the game up,
But my conscience murmured then:
'Remember that you are carrying on
In the place of the brave A MEN!'

*Temporary Sorter, Home Depot, WW1*

# I

I don't need a sweetheart.

Milly repeated the five words over and over to herself as the train puffed its way back to King's Cross.

*I* don't need a sweetheart.

I *don't* need a sweetheart.

I don't *need* a sweetheart.

Wasn't it interesting, she reflected, how if she put the emphasis on different words, the meaning changed? But it was always true.

She, eighteen-year-old Milly Woods, from Bow, East London, absolutely, definitely – and whatever other fancy words her friends Nora and Liza might care to throw at the matter – didn't need a sweetheart.

Not now. Not ever.

Women were fine on their own, weren't they? They were proving that by doing all the jobs their menfolk used to do, before the men went off to war. Women were doing things that no one had dreamed possible even a year ago – just look at her own family! There was nothing women couldn't do and at some point – hopefully sooner rather than later – they were darned well going to get the vote as they deserved.

So, no, Milly didn't need a man. And she didn't *want* a man, for that matter. After what Pa had done to Ma, after what Maggie's husband had done to *her* – well, you couldn't trust any of them, could you? It was just better – easier – to stay away from the lot of them.

But last night had threatened to change all that. Liza, her best friend from the Home Depot, had invited Milly and their other best friend, Nora, up to her home in Hertfordshire for the annual Woodhampstead Fundraising Ball – and a very jolly occasion it had been too. James, another friend from the Home Depot, had been there too and – oh! – the way he had looked at Liza as he'd twirled her around the dance floor. Everyone at work knew that Liza and James had been getting closer and closer over the past few months, but last night it had been obvious the two were mad for each other; Liza was a sensible, no-nonsense girl and not given to wild displays of emotion, but anyone could see that she was positively *glowing*. And then Liza's brother, Ned, had asked Nora to dance – and even though Nora, for all her mansions and grand relatives and fancy ways, was a liability on the dance floor, Ned hadn't been able to tear his gaze away from her.

Part of Milly longed to be looked at like that. To be held and twirled and admired. To be handled as though she was a piece of that delicate china that was sold up the Roman, and that Ma always scoffed at because it wouldn't last five minutes at home.

To be desired.

To be *loved*.

There. She'd admitted it – if only to herself.

But she couldn't afford to think like that – even if men said they loved you and made you pretty promises, it didn't last. Men hurt you. They betrayed you. They let you down. She was much better off on her own.

Thoughts like this got Milly all the way to King's Cross, onto the Tube and accompanied her on her short walk home.

'Clear today,' came a voice, as Milly reached the front gate.

It was Ruth, their next-door neighbour, appearing in her doorway. Ruth was *always* appearing in her doorway – the more so since her husband had gone to France. Today she was nodding sagely up at the blue autumnal skies, and Milly knew exactly what she meant. Without cloud cover, there was unlikely to be a Zeppelin attack that night. Even though everyone was putting on a brave face, they'd all been on tenterhooks since the last silent, deadly attack barely two weeks ago and everyone was in desperate need of a good night's sleep.

'Thank goodness for that,' said Milly fervently, opening the gate and gently pushing away their tail-less mouser, Cat, with her foot. She was exhausted after the late night and not in the mood for small talk.

Milly walked up the black-and-red flagstone path to the front door, put her key in the lock and swung open the front door.

The house was so *tiny*.

At least, it was compared to Liza's. Oh, Liza wasn't rich – not by any means; her family were shopkeepers and ran Woodhampstead's general provision store. And Liza's house was hardly palatial – it was nothing compared to Nora's huge white house next to the Regent's Park – and it didn't even have running water, for goodness' sake! But it was very spacious – Liza actually had her own bedroom – and it all smelt deliciously of ham and tea and butter from the adjoining shop, and her clean, wholesome village was so different to Milly's crowded, dirty London neighbourhood with its starving animals and filthy tenements. Her road, at least, was clean and respectable, but go a couple of hundred yards in any direction and it was a very different story. Milly knew they were all one small step away from penury and the work-house . . .

Milly sighed as she stepped into the narrow passage. It was

no different to the other houses in the street – she had nothing to grumble about – but it was all so *cramped*. On the left was the parlour door – or, at least, what would be the parlour if the room hadn't been rented out to Gustav Wildermuth, with strict instructions on when he could use the scullery and the kitchen. Like many Germans, Mr Wildermuth's bakery and lodgings had been targeted after the recent wave of Zeppelin bombings. Milly knew Liza had been shocked when she'd discovered Milly had a German living in her home – such a thing would apparently never be allowed to happen in her little corner of Hertfordshire – but around here, it wasn't especially unusual. As Ma said, Mr Wildermuth paid his rent on time and a German man's shillings went as far as the next man's. Besides, he had moved to London fifteen years ago when he was twelve – longer than Milly's brother, Charlie, had been alive – so he wasn't really German any more.

Milly carried on down the passage and pushed open the door to the kitchen – the heart of the home – with its oilskin-covered table, its ancient sagging sofa and huge blackened range dominating the space. Today, though, the heart of the home was empty. They would probably all be at Victoria Park, letting Charlie sail his new toy boat on the lake. Milly took off her hat and coat with a sigh, flinging them onto the nearest chair. She should really make the most of having the house to herself – it so rarely happened. She should make herself a cup of tea and lay all her sewing things out on the table without anyone having a grumble at her, and finally get around to changing the buttons on that white blouse that Nora had given her. Instead, she lay back on the sofa with another sigh and shut her eyes . . .

'Hello, sleepyhead!'

Milly woke abruptly with a little snort. Goodness, how long had she been asleep?

It was fourteen-year-old Caroline who had greeted her and who was now good-naturedly kicking her outstretched foot. Milly kicked back at her with a grin. 'Hello, yourself,' she said, hauling herself up and rubbing her eyes.

And here was Ma, bustling in and waving Milly's legs off the sofa at the same time as she bent down to kiss her cheek. 'Good night?' she asked, moving away without waiting for an answer and, in a couple of deft movements, lighting the oil lamps against the gathering gloom and swinging the kettle onto the range.

'Did they have horses?' demanded Caroline. 'And dogs? They must have had dogs.'

'She's probably too grand to speak to us now,' said sixteen-year-old Alice with characteristic grumpiness as she swept past Milly.

'Oh, hush, Alice.' Milly's older sister, Maggie, was jiggling her grizzly toddler and gave Milly a warm smile. 'Did you dance with anyone *nice*?'

Milly's twelve-year-old brother, Charlie, totally ignored her. 'I'm hungry,' he announced to no one in particular.

It was only then that Milly saw the bulging bags. Ma had brought home fish and chips! Such a rare treat. Only now did Milly register the salty tang that had followed her family through the kitchen door. Throwing a cushion to one side, she scrambled to her feet and hurried to set the table. There were even pickled eggs!

Ten minutes later, tucking into their hoard, washing it down with hot sweet tea and listening to the animated chatter, Milly looked around at her family with affection. They may not be the richest. They may not even be vaguely well-to-do. But they were *hers*.

When Pa had died and left them with nothing – well, nothing but memories that were more bitter than sweet, and a whole host of empty bottles – there had been many who'd whispered that it was only a matter of time before his family was scattered between workhouses. But look at them now! Milly had left her hated live-in position as a maid-of-all-work in Hackney, and now had a coveted job at the Army Post Office's Home Depot on the Regent's Park. That alone had shut the naysayers up: plain old Milly Woods, the slightly wayward daughter of John Woods, landing herself such a plum posting. And it hadn't stopped there. Alice had landed herself an equally well-paid job at one of the new munitions factories further east, and then Ma – *Ma!* – had amazed everyone by taking a job there as well. Pa had never let Ma take any sort of job – and that might have been all right had he not drunk away much of the money he'd earned as a docker – but he'd barely been cold in his grave before Ma had completed her first shift. You had to seize these opportunities when you could, she said. You had to think on your feet and stay one step ahead of poverty. Two Canaries in the family was nothing to be sniffed at, and, if both were in danger of getting the tell-tale yellow tinge to their skin, it was worth it for money they brought home. Even Maggie – who'd never much liked reading and writing – was earning a pound a week at the toy factory set up at the start of the war by the East London Federation of the Suffragettes, and which even provided a nursery to care for her toddler son, Arthur. Poor Maggie – her husband had upped and offed just after Pa died and she still lived in the rooms she'd shared with him, her reputation in tatters. So, the Woodses were hardly wealthy, but neither were they living hand to mouth and there was enough left over for treats like tonight's fish and chips.

Ma clapped her hands together, cutting across Milly's thoughts. 'Right, everyone,' she said. 'It's Hallowe'en and time to have some fun!'

When Pa had been alive, there had been no marking All Hallows' Eve – and woe betide anyone who tried. But Ma's family were Irish and she loved all the old traditions. And so, as soon as the fish supper was cleared away, out came the jack-o'-lantern that Charlie had carved from a huge turnip the day before and the candle was lit with much merriment and high spirits.

And then it was time for the games.

They started with apple bobbing, kneeling on chairs around the table and trying to remove apples floating in a large tub of water with only their teeth. Everyone took a different approach; Milly and her siblings might all have had the trademark Woods dark hair but they were so different in temperament it was a wonder they had the same parents. Alice went first and, with a characteristic frown, approached the challenge quietly and methodically, pushing the chosen apple over to the side of the tub to get some purchase and remaining virtually dry throughout. Milly went second; she used much the same technique but was quicker and less considered in her approach, and her unruly curls already escaping from her topknot got decidedly wet. Caroline spent quite a lot of time shrieking and tossing her hair about before cheerfully plunging her whole face into the water without apparent strategy, and emerging empty-mouthed. Charlie brought the war into it – of course he did – by declaring that he was going to 'defeat the Hun' and then produced a veritable tidal wave that soaked the floor, before running around the kitchen, arms stretched out, in imitation of an aeroplane. Maggie said that she didn't want to get water in her eyes – it would sting something dreadful – and anyway, Arthur was grizzling and she couldn't put him down, and then Ma tutted and took Arthur, and said that you got out of life what you put into it and Maggie should have a go. So, Maggie made a pathetic attempt and emerged saying she'd known she couldn't do it, and she didn't know why she'd tried. And then Ma – lovely Ma, the brown paper, glue *and* string of the family – patted her daughter on the arm and said Maggie was far too young to lose all her confidence in herself just because *he* had upped and offed and left her, and then Ma leaned over and plucked an apple from the water as effortlessly as if she was picking it up with her hands.

'One more game,' said Ma, as she lugged the tub of water through to the scullery. 'I don't think we played "blindfolds" last year, but let's give it a try.'

She returned to the kitchen and put half a dozen saucers onto the table. Milly and her siblings watched, intrigued, as Ma carefully placed an item on each – her wedding ring and rosary beads, a penny, a dried bean, some water and some soil from under the hedge bordering the front garden.

'What are these for?' asked Milly, intrigued.

'A prediction for the year ahead,' said Ma. 'We take it in turns to be blindfolded, then we "choose" a saucer and whatever it contains gives us a clue as to what will happen next year.'

'What do they all mean?' asked Caroline, with a little twirl of delight.

'Well, the ring means you will find true love soon,' said Ma, tapping the first saucer. 'Water means you will emigrate; rosary beads that you will take holy orders. The coin means you will be rich; the bean that you will be poor.'

'What about the mud, Ma?' asked Charlie.

Ma paused. 'The clay means you might be poorly,' she said. 'But it's all just a bit of fun; no need to take it too seriously.'

Ha! The clay clearly meant you would die, thought Milly. But who cared? Nobody believed this sort of thing. Not nowadays, anyway. It was, as Ma had said, a bit of fun from her own childhood to cheer up a cold autumn Sunday evening before they all went back to work or school.

Charlie went first. The scarf tied around his eyes, he was

spun around three times and positioned in front of the table. Reaching out, he touched the saucer containing the water.

'Ooh, you're going to travel, Charlie-boy,' said Maggie, ruffling his hair as she untied the blindfold.

'Hurrah!' shouted Charlie. 'Maybe I'll be able to join the war.'

'Over my dead body,' muttered Ma. And then, a little louder, 'The only place you're going to travel to any time soon is up to bed to get your beauty sleep.'

Caroline went next and chose the rosary beads. Everyone erupted into laughter. There was no one less likely to become a nun than Caroline; she would far rather roam the streets tending injured animals than go to church.

Maggie chose the coin. 'Ooh, you're going to be *rich*, Maggie,' said Milly, rubbing her older sister's arm.

Maggie gave Milly a sardonic glance. 'Fat chance of *that*,' she said, and she suddenly looked close to tears. 'How, pray, can an abandoned wife with a baby son get rich? I can't get married again whilst I'm still bleeding married. I'm stuck! Why, only yesterday, Ruth next door reminded me that until we know where Leo is, I'm doomed to be an old maid – even though I'm still married—'

'My turn,' interrupted Alice impatiently, pushing the others aside and tying the scarf over her eyes. Caroline and Charlie spun her around – once, twice, three times – and then she reached out, her finger jabbing the clay. She pulled the blindfold off, her face like thunder.

'Oh, rotten luck, Alice,' said Maggie. 'Anyway, we all know it's not true. As if Caroline's going to be a nun!'

'It's a horrid game,' said Alice, stamping her foot. 'Why is it funny to say I'll get poorly?'

'It's meant to be that you'll die,' said Milly. She couldn't help it. 'Ma was just being kind.'

Alice gave Milly a look, made a loud huffing sound and stormed out of the room, slamming the door behind her.

'Milly!' said Ma, shaking her head in exasperation before leaving the room in pursuit of Alice.

Milly sighed. Alice always overreacted like that and there would be hell to pay in their shared bed that night. She'd have to fight for her share of the eiderdown . . .

'Your turn, Milly,' said Maggie, holding out the scarf.

Milly smiled at her gratefully. Even though Ma and Alice had gone, Maggie always wanted to see fair play. Milly tied the scarf around her eyes, let her younger siblings spin her around and reached out. The cold, sharp rim of a saucer and inside . . . a ring.

Now Milly knew the game really was nonsense. As long as she had her family, she really didn't need anything else. Let Liza keep her fancy middle-class trappings; let Nora keep her mansion. She had all she needed.

And she most definitely *didn't* need a man!

# 2

'Oh, Lordy! That *stink*!'

Milly had intended a more conventional greeting as she arrived at work the next morning – but the stench assaulting her nostrils couldn't be ignored. It had been a couple of weeks since the terrible fire in the new extension had destroyed hundreds of sacks, but the ghastly smell showed no sign of abating. The parcels in the sacks had contained everything from meat to clothes to cocaine, and the combination almost made Milly gag.

Nora and Liza were sitting together in the returned letters office, their blonde heads bent over a copy of *The Day*.

'Morning,' said Liza, looking up with a smile. 'It's a ghastly smell, isn't it? And all that hammering and sawing is giving me a dreadful headache. It's so noisy you can't even hear the lions!'

Milly smiled as she hung up her hat and coat. The Home Depot had been hastily erected only a stone's throw from London Zoo, and the working day was often punctuated by the lions demanding their next meal.

'Hopefully the ash will be better today,' added Nora. 'The usual sack dust is bad enough, but Mummy asked why I'd gone quite grey last week and if it was the stress of the work! But the smell is definitely the worst. Maybe I should bring in a couple of pegs tomorrow – if I can wrestle some off Ada.'

'Ada?' asked Milly idly, sitting down at her own desk.

'New daily,' said Nora. 'Let's hope she lasts longer than the last one. Mummy is going round the twist.'

Liza grinned, swinging her plait over her shoulder. 'Well, I hate to tell "Mummy", but I think Ada will scarper once she's worked out she can earn a lot more working here.'

Nora made a face. 'You're probably right,' she said. 'Maybe I should do a good deed and tell her. Goodness knows we'll need all hands on deck in the run-up to Christmas, although Mummy would have my guts for garters if I encouraged Ada to leave.'

The three girls laughed easily together, and Milly – for about the thousandth time – thought how strange the world had become. Liza and Nora were the best friends she had ever had, but she would never have had an opportunity to make friends with either of them before the war. On the contrary; if Milly had met Nora before the war, she would have been curtseying and yes-missing and minding her Ps and Qs. And, yet, here she was, talking to both girls as an equal – doing exactly the same job as Nora, for goodness' sake (although Liza had already been promoted and was working as a supervisor in the broken parcels department). Who knew how long this strange state of affairs would last, and what would happen when the war was finally over?

Anyway, never mind about *that* at the moment.

'What about the weekend?' Milly exclaimed. 'The dance!'

To her amusement, both Nora and Liza flushed crimson.

'Wasn't it pleasant?' mumbled Nora.

'Pleasant?' demanded Milly. '*Pleasant!* You spent all evening being twirled around the floor by Liza's brother – her very *dashing* brother, might I add? – and you call it "pleasant"? For shame!'

Nora giggled and the blush showed no sign of abating. 'He *is* very dashing, isn't he?' she said.

'I've never seen him quite in that way,' said Liza, her

expression deadpan. 'But I can attest that he is the most marvellous person alive. And he certainly seems to have taken a shine to you, Nora! It's just so awful that he's going back to France tomorrow and goodness only knows when he'll be back again.'

'He's asked me to write to him,' said Nora, her blush deepening.

'How marvellous!' Milly clapped her hands together delightedly. 'Yet another reason to make sure that the post runs smoothly. And, as for you, Liza Healey. At one point, I thought James Blackford was going to kiss you right in the middle of the dance floor.'

It was Liza's turn to flush bright pink. 'I can assure you that we did not,' she said mock-primly. 'But he *has* asked me to step out with him!'

The loud squeals that ensued were cut short as the door swung open and their supervisor swept into the office.

Liza glanced at the clock on the wall and got to her feet. 'Nearly nine o'clock,' she said. 'I'd better report for duty. Men to trenches; women to benches.' And she was gone.

'At least the fire means there's less post to process,' said Milly, as the girls settled down to work.

It had been meant as a joke. It was what she was known for: bringing a bit of fun into the rough and ready days, and cheering everyone up. Like the time she had introduced the 'Alphabet Packing Game' – the loser buying everyone else jammy buns from the canteen at break time. *That* had got them all giggling.

But Nora didn't laugh. She didn't even smile.

'Don't even joke about it,' she said.

Milly was surprised. It hadn't been the funniest joke, but it was unlike the usually easy-going Nora to be quite so po-faced. Of course, her uncle, Major Benham, was in charge of the whole depot, but Nora had always been one of the girls – one of the gang.

'Come on, grumpy,' said Milly, feeling hurt. 'Why shouldn't I make a joke about it? It was an accident, for goodness' sake, and it ain't as if anyone got hurt. Oh, I know James hit his head, but it's not as though anyone died.'

Liza and James had been the only two in the warehouse when the fire had started. There had been no suggestion of foul play and the official story was that matches in one of the parcels had ignited and started the blaze. It had happened elsewhere and would continue to happen until they stopped matches being sent through the post. Anyway, Liza and James had attempted to extinguish the fire, but a stack of burning sacks had fallen onto James and he'd been knocked out. By all accounts, Liza had been very brave and, disregarding her own safety, had dragged James to safety but, in the meantime, the fire had taken hold. Thank goodness the warehouse hadn't been full. Imagine if it had been a few weeks later in the run-up to Christmas.

Nora glanced at their supervisor and then turned back to Milly. 'Sorry,' she said. 'It's just Liza told me earlier there's going to be an investigation into the fire and that, in the meantime, James has been suspended. It really isn't a laughing matter.'

'Oh.' Milly sighed. That put quite a different slant on proceedings. 'Then I'm sorry for being flippant. Why have they suspended him?'

'They suspect him of smoking in there.'

To be fair, Milly had wondered much the same. It wouldn't have been the first time James had had a secret – and illicit – ciggie in the extension. Loads of people had done it. She had done it. And goodness knew that James had had a lot on his mind, losing both his father and his brother in quick succession.

'That's terrible,' said Milly. 'I wonder if it's true.'

Nora just pursed her lips and gave a tiny shrug of her

shoulders, and Milly suddenly wondered if she knew something Milly didn't. After all, Nora and Liza did seem to be particularly close at the moment and, on more than one occasion, Milly had felt a little edged out. Only yesterday, for example, she had assumed Nora would be heading back to London on the same train as her when, at the last moment, Nora had announced she'd be staying an extra night. Milly hadn't been invited to stay an extra night . . .

'Sorry to be a grump,' Nora was saying. 'It's not your fault. It's just all so horrid for James and Liza and, on top of everything else, Ted Wilmington's written a beastly article in *The Day* this morning.'

Keeping a beady eye on the supervisor, she passed Milly the paper, jabbing a finger at an article on an inside page. Milly read it surreptitiously. The Home Depot fire had, of course, featured prominently in the papers. 'Fire in the Army Post Office' and 'Parcels for Our Boys Go Up in Smoke', the headlines had screamed. But the story had been off the front pages by the next day and, since then, it had all but disappeared completely. But now, here it was again. An opinion piece by the paper's editor, no less. Milly scanned it. The gist was that the 'accident' was most unfortunate, and the Home Depot couldn't afford any more bad publicity without it permanently affecting public morale and the outcome of the war itself.

'Ain't that marvellous,' said Milly, folding the paper and thrusting it back at Nora. 'One mistake and no one can trust us anymore!'

'He's got a point, though,' said Nora. 'It might not have been arson or sabotage but, at the very least, it was carelessness with the nation's post.'

'I think Ted Wilmington just likes to have something to complain about,' said Milly. 'I don't very often read *The Day* – I can imagine Ma's face if I tried to bring it home – but

Sylvia Pankhurst was having a right moan about him a few
weeks ago. He wrote an article saying that the suffragettes
should pipe down and go away until the war is over – and
preferably forever! Right old hoo-ha there was at the meeting
about that!'

'Maybe he's got a point there.' Nora said this quietly, almost
under her breath.

'Less chatter, please, ladies,' said their supervisor mildly,
and both girls turned back to work.

No time for idle chit-chat.

Working in the returned letters department was less physically
tiring than many of the roles at the Home Depot, but it was
emotionally draining.

When a soldier died, any letters that had been addressed
to him were returned to sender – but only after the official
telegram from the War Office had been released. The Home
Depot had to hold on to all returned letters until they had
confirmation the telegram had been delivered, because who
wanted to find out a loved one had been killed by your letter
to them being returned marked 'killed in action'? Plans were
in hand to send all the returned letters directly to the War
Office precisely to make sure mistakes didn't happen but, in
the meantime, it was down to the men, and particularly the
women, of the Home Depot to keep things on track. Every
day the War Office sent over a list of the telegrams that had
been dispatched, and Milly and Nora checked off the returned
letters before they allowed them to go on their way. Milly had
already seen first-hand the misery that could be unleashed
should they make a mistake, and had vowed that she would
never again let her concentration falter – not even for a
moment.

That day, there were only a couple of sacks of letters waiting
to be sorted, but Milly knew that more – many more – would

be added throughout the day. The Battle of Loos had resulted in horrendous casualties and, even though the fighting had finished, the injured were still succumbing to their injuries. Sighing, Milly reached for the first letter. It was addressed to Private Andrew Millar and sent from Stella Millar. Poor Stella, thought Milly, flicking through the list of telegrams. Did she already know that her husband, son or brother had been killed, or was she blissfully unaware that a young telegram boy or girl was about to knock on her door . . .?

'Good morning, Miss Woods.'

Milly looked up. It was Miss Parker, supervisor of all the female employees at the Home Depot. As the number of women at the Army Post Office had grown, so too had Miss Parker's role and importance but Milly had got to know her in the early days several months ago when she, Liza and Nora had been part of the 'advance guard'. Miss Parker was a firm but fair supervisor, and Milly liked her enormously.

'Good morning, Miss Parker,' Milly replied.

'Would you come with me, please?' said Miss Parker.

'Of course,' said Milly, standing up and smoothing down her skirts.

Giving Nora a nervous glance, Milly followed Miss Parker down the corridor. Whatever could Miss Parker want with *her*? She'd only just been moved to the returned letters department, so she couldn't be being moved again. And she hadn't done anything wrong – well, not as far as she knew. She hadn't cheeked the sergeant major, been late reporting for duty or lost another admission card – so it was unlikely she was to be reprimanded.

Milly trailed Miss Parker through the centre of the huge wooden building. There were literally hundreds of people working here now, but everyone seemed quiet and subdued. Really, the very worst thing about the fire had been the effect on everyone's mood. Despite the best efforts of the humourless

Sergeant Major Cunningham, who had been given an honorary army rank for the duration of the war and who ran the Home Depot with a rod of iron, it was usually a jolly place to work. There was always *something* going on with plenty of opportunity for japes – like the time she and Liza had wheeled Nora home across the Regent's Park in a 'borrowed' wheeled basket after she had fallen and twisted her ankle. How they – and everyone else – had laughed. But today, you really couldn't imagine anything like that happening at all.

Now, they were skirting the broken parcel department. There was Liza, a newly appointed supervisor, bending over a table and subjecting one of the repackaged parcels to the drop test whilst the young woman who had done the repackaging looked nervously on. Liza didn't look up and Milly couldn't help but feel relieved she hadn't been spotted meekly following Miss Parker like a naughty schoolgirl. Liza was lovely, but she could be a bit of a goody two-shoes and she was a real stickler for the rules. This whole business with James would have hit her hard . . .

Milly followed Miss Parker into her office and sat down as directed in front of her desk.

'Well, I won't beat around the bush,' said Miss Parker, resting her elbows on the desk and making a steeple of her hands. 'We'd like to reassign you within the Home Depot with immediate effect.'

Oh.

That was very abrupt. Where was Miss Parker moving her to? The censoring department? The honour letter department? The parcels for prisoners of war department? There were more than a dozen possibilities, and all of them quite exciting.

Miss Parker was still talking. 'I'd like you to move to the main sorting-room floor,' she said. 'I've arranged for someone to show you the ropes this afternoon together with a couple of other new recruits, and I'd like you to be at your new post tomorrow morning. We're seriously understaffed on the main floor as it is and we're expecting things to get ten times busier as Christmas looms. And now the Battle of Loos is over, we are – thankfully – expecting less pressure on the returned letters department . . .'

Milly's thoughts were in turmoil. *The main sorting-room floor?* That couldn't be right. She couldn't have heard correctly.

Oh, it was never specifically acknowledged, but everyone knew the general sorters were the bottom rung of the ladder. There were hundreds upon hundreds of them, and they stood all day throwing letters into sacks slung from wooden frames and slotting letters into pigeon holes.

It wasn't the skilled work she'd been doing ever since she'd joined the Home Depot. It wasn't the same thing at all. She was being demoted!

With great effort, Milly concentrated on what Miss Parker was saying. 'Despite pleas to the contrary, we are expecting the volume of letters and parcels to the various fronts to soar in the run-up to Christmas. I'm sure you will make yourself very useful to your new supervisor there.'

Milly didn't reply. She just sat there, blinking at Miss Parker, overwhelmed by shock.

'Why?' she wanted to demand. 'Why me?' But she was too proud to ask, and too frightened of the answer.

'Is Nora moving with me?' was all she ventured.

'No,' said Miss Parker. 'Miss Benham is staying put. It's just you who's moving and you'll report to your new department after lunch. Dismissed.'

Milly stumbled from Miss Parker's office in a daze. Instead of returning to her duties, she slipped outside. It was an overcast and drizzly day, and she stood under a plane tree on a small grassy knoll and lit a cigarette. She had stood under that same plane tree on her first day at the Home Depot, the day she had first met Nora and Liza. The tree had been in full leaf then, shielding the three girls from the blazing early summer sun. Today, it was a mere shadow of its former self, the few leaves remaining no match for the elements. How different things had been back then. How full of hope everything had seemed – the very air alive with the promise of new friendships and exciting escapades. Things had gone so swimmingly for the first few months. There had been ups and downs, of course, but her work in the returned letters department had felt important and worthwhile. She had thought she was doing *well*.

And, now, everything had changed. The plane tree had turned brown and orange, and its leaves were beginning to fall into a soggy mass on the ground. And it was cold; bitterly cold. Milly shivered as she took a deep drag from her cigarette. She didn't even have her coat.

Why had she been demoted?

She couldn't help wondering if Liza and Nora had reported her for accidentally returning Liza's sister's letter before the official telegram about her husband's death had been dispatched. Milly had volunteered to own up but Liza and Nora had told her not to; the damage had already been contained and no one was going to tell tales. But maybe they hadn't kept their word. Maybe they had gone behind her back, after all. Now she thought about it, on the night of the fire, they had virtually accused her of being up to no good after she'd lost two admission cards.

No. She was being silly.

Of course her very best friends wouldn't do that to her!

It was time to go back inside. She really didn't want to get in trouble for going AWOL. She also didn't want to contemplate the other – and perhaps more likely – possible reason for her demotion. Maybe she'd been banished to the sorting floor because she was plain old Milly Woods from the East End of London. She wasn't Nora Benham, niece of the major

in charge of the Home Depot. She wasn't even clever, depend-
able, middle-class Liza Healey, darling of Miss Parker.

She was just Milly Woods.

And maybe being Milly Woods just wasn't enough.

Milly knew she was unlikely to warm to whoever was training
her in her new role. But Miss Rich really was awful. While
not exactly rude, she was brusque and impatient with them
all, and Milly couldn't help feeling there was something derog-
atory in her tone – a slight sneer perhaps – whenever she
addressed Milly directly. Miss Rich must have known Milly
had been transferred from another department unlike the
other three nervous-looking girls, who were raw recruits. She
must have known Milly had been demoted. Because she had.
Milly had seen it in Liza and Nora's eyes when she'd told
them she was moving departments over jammy buns at break-
time. Oh, they had tried to hide their surprise and shock, had
muttered about it being a nice change and much jollier than
processing letters that had been sent to dead soldiers, but the
truth hovered just below the surface. It was a public humiliation and everyone knew it. And now she had to sit and listen
to Miss Rich, who had, no doubt, been at the Home Depot
a darn sight less time than Milly.

She glanced round at the other three girls and suppressed
a grin. Those hobble skirts wouldn't last long here! There was
no way they'd be able to brace for the heavier sacks on the
uneven floors in those. And as for those funnel sleeves! They
might be fashionable but they would get horribly in the way
when sorting letters. Milly wagered both would have been
altered before the week was out – if the girls even survived
the initiation period, that was.

'Do I have your attention, Miss Woods?' asked Miss Rich,
cutting across her thoughts.

Milly could feel herself blushing. 'Yes, Miss,' she mumbled.

The training was taking place in the same office Milly had received her initial induction in all those months ago. Then, the room had been almost unbearably hot and stuffy, but now it was distinctly chilly and Milly hugged her shawl tighter around her shoulders. Miss Rich was pointing things out on the blackboard with a long cane, and Milly was reminded of being at school. She'd better mind her Ps and Qs or she may well be on the receiving end of the cane's biting sting.

'Every morning, Whitehall tells us the latest positions of each battalion so each item can be dispatched to the right place,' Miss Rich was saying. 'It's a huge, and obviously highly confidential, operation.'

Next to her, the other three recruits looked at each other with wide, shining eyes. This was important! Top secret! Milly stifled a yawn. Exciting and impressive it might be, but she had heard it all before.

'Our job is to assemble bags of mail for every unit,' Miss Rich continued. 'We label them with a code to show which field post office they need to be forwarded to. Then the army lorries – you will have seen them outside – take the bags destined for the Western Front to the south coast to be loaded onto ships and sent to the three Army Postal Service depots in France. Does anyone know where they might be?'

'Calais, Le Havre and Boulogne,' Milly rattled off.

Everyone in the returned letters office knew that – it was where their sacks of mail originated from. But the other recruits turned to her, clearly impressed. As Miss Rich wrote the names of three ports on the blackboard, Milly began to relax. If nothing else, at least she could bask in being the resident expert.

'How long does the mail take to get there?' asked the recruit with spectacles.

'It depends on where the unit is located,' replied Miss Rich.

'Usually a day or two for the Western Front. Sometimes as little as twelve hours . . .'

'Twelve hours?' The recruit shook her head in amazement. 'Fancy!'

'It's really quick,' said Milly, suddenly animated. 'Plenty quick enough to send perishables. I worked in the broken parcels department and, believe you me, people send *everything*. One family sent a portion of their roast dinner! Tatties, greens . . . all of it. Of course, it leaked everywhere. The peas got everywhere! We was picking them off the floor for days!'

'Thank you, Miss Woods,' snapped Miss Rich over the laughter.

'Sorry, Miss,' said Milly, risking a surreptitious wink at the bespectacled girl. Maybe she'd be able to have some fun.

'The transit time for other fronts depends on how far it has to travel, but it usually takes weeks,' said Miss Rich. 'A good deal is sent by sea, although there are now some military-mail rail routes through France and Italy to serve the new Mediterranean and Middle Eastern fronts.'

'In other words, don't go sending your Sunday roast to the Dardanelles,' added Milly. 'It'll arrive covered in a nice blue mould.'

'Miss *Woods*,' exploded Miss Rich. 'I don't want to officially reprimand you for disrespect on your first shift, but I won't hesitate to do so if you carry on like this. Let's move on to how we sort the mail. It's firstly sorted by theatre and then—'

'Theatre?' interrupted the third recruit, wrinkling a snub, freckled nose.

Milly laughed. She couldn't help it. 'Yes,' she said. 'The Theatre Royal, the Savoy, the Adelphi . . .'

Milly found herself in front of Miss Parker for the second time that day.

'I know it's difficult, Milly,' said Miss Parker. 'And I do

know that Miss Rich can be a little . . . dry. But there is no excuse for disrupting her induction session.'

'I were just trying to lighten the atmosphere,' protested Milly. 'And them new girls didn't even know what a theatre of war was. I mean, as if it were the Savoy!'

Milly knew that Miss Parker had a good sense of humour and she looked for a twitch of amusement in her supervisor's mouth. Miss Parker's countenance, however, remained grave.

'You were trying to be disruptive, Milly, and I'm disappointed in you,' she said. 'You could be a real asset to the sorting department, but you've made a very poor start. And if you're hoping I'll assign you elsewhere or keep you in the returned letters department, you're out of luck. You've been reassigned to the sorting floor and I'm afraid that's that. Now, please accept this as a warning and let that be the end of it. If I see you in here again, I'll have no choice but to mark your file for misconduct. Understood?'

'Yes, Miss Parker,' said Milly, cheeks flaming. She hated disappointing Miss Parker. Miss Parker really was a bit of a heroine to Milly: she had managed to carve herself out a hugely responsible role in a man's world; she was firm but fair; and she was invariably supportive to the women in her care. Milly wanted Miss Parker to respect her. To admire her, even.

She *hated* being rebuked by her.

'Now, I'm going to ask Rita Briggs to informally take you through the rest of the training,' Miss Parker was saying. 'Rita has worked in the department for many months, and I trust you will listen attentively. And then, when training is complete, you can take up your place on the sorting-room floor with the other new recruits. Understood?'

'Yes, Miss Parker.'

'Dismissed.'

★

Milly had learned her lesson.

Much as she didn't want to be reallocated to the sorting floor, she really didn't want to be dismissed. Not like this.

So, she listened attentively while Rita explained that outgoing mail from the Home Depot was sorted first by military theatre – France, Balkans, Egypt – and then by military unit – artillery, infantry, cavalry – and after that by division and regiment. Milly had to concentrate hard to take it all in. Although she'd already worked at the Home Depot for several months, she had thus far had no need – no wish – to get to grips with how the British Army was structured. And it was *complicated*.

Worst of all, there seemed to be acronyms for everything. Given there were thousands of units operating in France and Belgium alone, that made for an awful lot of initials to get to grips with. Milly looked at the key-list she was given with something approaching panic: pages long, it was a veritable encyclopaedia! How on earth was she going to get on top of all that?

Rita – a much more sympathetic type than Miss Rich – was laughing.

'Look at your expression, Milly,' she said. 'Don't worry. You'll soon get to know the ones that relate to your road.'

'Road?' asked Milly with a mock grimace. 'What on earth is a road?'

Rita grinned. 'It just means a section,' she said. 'If you're working on the G-road, you're sorting mail for the Gloucestershire Regiment. Easy!'

'So, nothing to do with a real road?'

'Nothing at all,' said Rita.

Milly sighed, suddenly feeling a lot more sympathy for the hapless recruit who'd asked about theatres earlier. Why on earth had she assumed that the sorting floor was the easy option?

'Do you know how to address an envelope to someone in the army?' asked Rita.

'Of course,' said Milly. Everyone knew *that*. 'Name, rank and regiment.'

'It's actually a little more complicated than that,' said Rita.

'Of course it is,' said Milly ruefully.

Rita unfolded a piece of paper and smoothed it on the table between them. 'This is the sheet we return to sender if an envelope hasn't got enough information on it,' she said. 'It's surprising how often it happens.'

Milly pored over the piece of paper. Entitled 'How Letters to Soldiers Should be Addressed', it was densely typed with multiple steps. Letters or parcels needed to include the recipient's rank followed by his initial and name; the number or letter of his squadron or company; the number and name of his regiment, battery or battalion; or the name of any special appointment he might hold. It also had to include which expeditionary force the soldier was serving with, or, if not serving with an expeditionary force, the country he was stationed in.

'Clear?' asked Rita.

'Crystal,' Milly replied woefully.

'Let's try a couple of examples,' said Rita, putting a stack of envelopes on the table. 'Take a look at this one. Why do you think it would be returned to sender?'

Milly stared at the buff-coloured envelope, waiting for inspiration to strike. The letter had a penny stamp in the top right-hand corner; it had a name and a rank – *Private C. Travis*; it had all sorts of unfathomable letters and numbers on it; and it was addressed to the British Expeditionary Force in France.

Surely that was enough?

Milly looked at Rita and shook her head. 'I ain't got a clue, I'm afraid,' she said.

'Well, it's got a platoon, an infantry brigade and a division on it, but it hasn't got a *regiment*,' said Rita, as if it was the most obvious thing in the world. She pulled out a little stamper and pressed it firmly onto the envelope. When she lifted it again, bright red letters proclaimed 'Inappropriately addressed: name of regiment required'.

'There you go,' she said, 'Easy.'

Milly made a face at the envelope. 'Right,' she said. It didn't seem easy to her at all. In fact, now she came to think about it, she really didn't know the difference between a brigade, a regiment, a platoon and a company. And what on earth was a battery?

'Let's go and get a cup of tea in the canteen,' said Rita. 'It doesn't do to stare at these things for too long. And I suggest you take a copy of the key-list home and try to familiarise yourself with some of the abbreviations. I'm sure all will be clear in the morning.'

But as she looked down at the seemingly endless list in her hand, Milly wasn't so sure.

She really wasn't so sure at all.

# 3

She didn't have to stay, Milly reminded herself on the Tube journey home that night. She was still repeating the words to herself as she alighted at Bow Road Station and started the short walk home.

She didn't have to stay.

It was already dark and chilly – a real winter nip to the air – and Milly wrapped her coat more tightly around herself as she acknowledged she could leave. She could hand in her notice and move on. People did it all the time – because they were getting married, or moving further away, or because they just didn't like the work. Over the past few months, thousands of new opportunities had opened up all over London and there were plenty of other things that she could do. She could become a Canary like Ma and Alice; she could work on the trams; or in a bakery like Mr Wildermuth. And, yes, it might take her a little longer to find a new job because injured soldiers were beginning to return from the war in search of employment, but she didn't *have* to stay at the Home Depot and be humiliated. She didn't have to see the pity in her friends' eyes – if indeed, Liza and Nora would still want to be associated with her. Maybe they would start avoiding her.

Milly sighed. She really didn't want to go straight home after the day she'd had. Not given the way she was feeling that evening.

Milly knew she'd been dismissive about the sorters to her family on more than one occasion, and now she was going to have to eat humble pie and admit she'd been moved there herself. Ma would be short-tempered because she always was on Monday – what with work at the factory and wash-day to contend with – and Alice would be sneery because she was always sneery, and it would all be too horrible and humiliating for words.

It was Monday night so she could go to the East London Federation of the Suffragettes' meeting just up the road. That way she could put off going home – if only for a couple of hours – and hopefully she would be feeling calmer and more composed by then. The trouble was, that she hadn't been to ELFS for weeks. There'd been a time when she wouldn't have dreamed of missing a meeting – they had been the highlight of her week – but then she'd invited Liza and Nora along and all hell had broken loose. She could feel herself going hot (as well as dusty!) under her collar just thinking about it! Liza and Nora had taken great exception to ELFS' anti-war stance and it had resulted in Nora stomping out of the room in high dudgeon, and Liza – polite, mild-mannered *Liza* – on her feet and giving the entire meeting a piece of her mind.

Oh, it had been dreadful!

Since then, Milly had been unable to face going back. There was the embarrassment, certainly, but it was more than that. If Milly was being totally honest with herself, it had unnerved her to see the issues from Nora and Liza's perspectives. Milly still firmly believed in women's suffrage and the rights of the poor – of course she did – but she had since wondered if ELFS shouldn't be wholeheartedly supporting the war effort rather than stoking the flames of division.

But, at the end of the day, why shouldn't she go along to the meeting tonight? Hopefully everyone would have forgotten about the rumpus, and, if not – well, when had Milly ever backed away from a fight?

★

The meeting was held in the Mother's Arms, a former pub that ELFS had requisitioned at the start of the war and which now served as a nursery, baby clinic, milk-distribution centre and meeting place. Self-consciously, Milly climbed the stairs to the meeting room on the top floor. She often helped with the refreshments, but today there seemed to be a lot of young women pouring out the tea and cocoa, so she left them to it and slipped into one of the chairs at the back. She'd keep a low profile for this meeting. Only speak if she was spoken to . . .

Goodness! Was that Miss Pankhurst heading in her direction?

Yes, Sylvia Pankhurst – founder of ELFS, no less – seemed to be making a beeline for her. Was she going to take Milly to task? Ask her to leave? Maybe Milly should get up and make a dash for it . . .

But Miss Pankhurst was already slipping into the chair next to her.

'It's Milly, isn't it?' she said.

Milly was surprised. *Shocked.* Fancy Miss Pankhurst knowing her name. Oh, a few weeks back, Miss Pankhurst had dubbed her and Liza the 'Dusty Elves' because of the tide marks of sack dust around their collars and cuffs. But to actually know her Christian name . . . Things must be worse than she'd thought.

'Yes,' said Milly, realising that Miss Pankhurst was waiting for an answer. 'I'm Milly. And I'm so sorry about—'

Miss Pankhurst held up a hand. 'Please don't apologise,' she said. 'I'm very pleased to see you back here.'

*Oh!*

'Thank you,' said Milly. 'But . . . my friends! Nora storming out like that! It was . . . mortifying!'

Miss Pankhurst smiled. 'Firstly, you are not responsible for your friends' behaviour,' she said. 'And, secondly, we pride ourselves on being a broad church at ELFS and discussion is always good.'

Milly couldn't help thinking that neither Nora nor Liza had really been 'discussing' the matters in hand, but thank goodness Miss Pankhurst wasn't holding it against her.

'Thank you, Miss,' she said, feeling her shoulders return to their normal position. She hadn't even realised she'd been hunching them.

'Your friends obviously hold their beliefs very passionately,' Miss Pankhurst continued. 'And, just between us, the debate they prompted was extremely useful to me. It cast a light on the breadth and depth of support for more radical action within the organisation. It needed to be addressed because no such action will be tolerated by me or ELFS while the war continues. I've made that very clear over the past couple of weeks, and I will remind our members again this evening. So, you see, Milly, you did me a favour by bringing your friends along and I'm very grateful to you.'

*Well.* That put a rather different spin on events. Miss Pankhurst touched Milly lightly on the shoulder before walking to the front of the room. Milly felt a warm glow of happiness and couldn't help smiling.

She would never miss a meeting again.

Milly was still smiling as she skipped down the steps outside the Mother's Arms after the meeting. She set off down the quiet backstreets, thinking how lovely it was to really belong somewhere. The East End was her home and these were her people. She must never forget that. Her family would understand about her being moved to the sorting department; in fact, they wouldn't give two figs about it. She would still earn the same money and, more importantly, she was still the same Milly. Their Milly.

''Ello, darling.'

Milly started out of her reverie.

There was a man walking up the road towards her. From the way he was listing from side to side, Milly could tell he was drunk and, as he got closer, she could see he was wearing an army greatcoat. A soldier, either home on leave or discharged from the army. The East End was full of them and hopefully this one wouldn't be any trouble. Milly stepped into the road, planning to skirt the man and continue on her way.

'That's not very friendly,' slurred the soldier. 'A chap risks his life fighting for King and Country, and when he gets home a lass won't even give him the time of day.'

He moved into the road so that he was blocking her way, close enough that Milly could smell the alcohol on his breath. She glanced up and down the deserted street with the first prickle of alarm.

Why hadn't she stuck to the main road as Ma always told her to?

'Good evening,' she said, politely but firmly. 'Now, if you'll allow me on my way, my ma is waiting for me.'

Hopefully that would do the trick.

The soldier stepped backwards with a belch. 'Give us a kiss, sweetheart,' he said.

Milly's unease ratcheted up a gear. There was no point in trying to talk to him – he was far too drunk. She would have to make a dash for it and hope that he wouldn't try to follow her or that she could outrun him to the busy Roman Road. Milly darted back onto the pavement, hoping to undercut the soldier, but he was too fast for her. Grabbing Milly by the arm, he half frogmarched and half dragged her into the alleyway running between two wood merchants. Milly – under no misconceptions as to what the soldier was after – let out a strangled cry, her breath coming in raggedy little gasps.

'Help,' she shouted, but her voice sounded helpless and hopeless even to herself.

'Hush.' The soldier pushed her roughly against the alley wall, bricks hard and unforgiving against her back. It was all happening so quickly – too quickly. Milly tried to kick up with her knee, to lash out with her nails, but the soldier was always one move ahead of her. His mouth pressed down heavily on hers . . . teeth clashing . . . pulling at her coat . . . her blouse . . . hands on her breasts . . . traitorous buttons popping . . .

No.

*No!*

'No!'

It took Milly a moment to notice that this was a different voice.

It was someone else, not her own internal cry of distress. And then, thank the Lord, the hands and the mouth and the weight were gone.

Milly straightened up, gasping for breath and wiping her mouth with the back of one hand while she pulled her coat tightly around her with the other. It took her a moment longer to register what was happening. Her assailant had been ripped off her and was being restrained – with a good deal of effing and blinding – by two young sisters Milly recognised from ELFS. They were all flailing around like a grotesque three-headed monster, but the man – despite his advantages of bulk and gender – was so drunk he didn't really stand a chance.

'Help's coming,' one of the girls panted.

Milly was about to attempt a furious targeted kick at the struggling soldier when she heard the sound of running feet and two policemen appeared at the mouth of the alleyway. The fight suddenly went out of the soldier and, in a couple of moments, he was cuffed and docile.

Milly suddenly found she was shaking and that her legs felt like lead. One of her rescuers put an arm around her.

'You're safe now,' she said, and Milly sagged against her in relief.

The soldier was led away by one of the policemen and the other came over to Milly.

'Can you tell me what happened, Miss?'

To Milly's surprise, it was a woman. A female bobby! But Milly reminded herself, why shouldn't it be? Over the past year, women had proved they could do just about anything . . .

'The bastard!' Shock rendered Milly incapable of moderating her language. A female police officer would surely understand. 'The . . . bastard! Tried to have his way with me, he did. If it wasn't for these two stepping in, he'd have succeeded too. I wish I'd been able to give him a good kick where it hurts the most!'

'Good on you, girl,' said one of the ELFS girls, handing her a handkerchief. Milly tentatively wiped her bruised and tender mouth, and the hanky came away spotted with blood.

'Bastard,' she said again with venom.

'I quite agree,' said the policewoman, mildly. 'A first-class, gold-plated example to boot.'

Despite the circumstances, Milly gave a bark of delighted laughter. Fancy an officer of the law agreeing with her like that!

'I don't know why fellas like him think they can get away with it,' she said.

'It's my job to make sure that they can't,' said the bobby briskly, pulling out a notepad. 'Now, if you'd like to give me a statement, I'll let you get on your way.'

Milly nodded and, teeth chattering, gave her details together with a brief summary of what had happened.

'We'll be in touch,' said the policewoman, snapping her notebook shut. 'Now, will you be all right getting home?'

'We'll make sure she does,' said one of the girls.

The policewoman nodded. 'Then I'll bid you good evening,' she said, and walked away.

Milly turned to her rescuers. 'I can't thank you both enough,' she said, meaning it from the bottom of her heart.

'It were lucky we saw you,' said one of the girls, steering Milly gently out of the alleyway. 'A few seconds later or earlier and we wouldn't have done. We just happened to be walking past the bottom of the road and saw him pulling you away—'

'Didn't your ma ever tell you about walking down quiet roads on your own?' interrupted her sister. 'You should have come down St Stephen's with the rest of us.'

'Oh, hush now, Hilda,' said the first girl. 'It were doubly lucky the police were patrolling the Roman and the girl we was with ran to get them.'

'Well, thank you! All three of you. If you hadn't come along, Lord only knows what might have happened.'

'Yes,' said Hilda. 'He might have been happy with a fumble, but who knows? Lord, sometimes I really hate men. What makes them think they've got the right?'

'I wish I had kicked him,' said Milly fervently. 'Right where it hurts, an' all.'

'The important thing is that he's been nicked,' said the other girl, briskly. 'Now, shall we pop to the Nag's Head so you can get yourself cleaned up, or would you rather go straight home?'

Milly hesitated. She didn't really like pubs. Pa had been a drinker – Maggie's husband too – and look where that had got them all. Oh, Milly had been into a couple of pubs with her colleagues at the Home Depot to celebrate a promotion or a birthday, but somehow that had felt different. There were always so many people from the Army Post Office in the local hostelries, they almost felt like an extension to the canteen. But this was different. Surely three girls wandering into a pub in the East End was asking for trouble. But neither did she want to go home dishevelled and bleeding. That would upset Ma. It would upset *all* of them, and that would never do. It might even prompt Ma to insist Milly came straight home from work in future . . . and that would never do, either.

'Our uncle's the landlord of the Nag,' Hilda said, as if reading Milly's mind. 'We'll be quite all right in there. He'll wave us to a quiet corner; no questions asked. And I've got a sewing kit in me bag if you want to patch your blouse up before you go home. I think I've even got some buttons!'

Well, that solved the problem.

Milly looked from one sister to the other in gratitude. 'The Nag would be lovely,' she said.

And it was.

In fact, it was just what Milly needed. As soon as she got inside, she started shaking uncontrollably, but the saloon bar was warm, comfortable and surprisingly genteel. Hilda had a word with the man behind the bar and the three girls were shepherded over to a quiet table by the fire. The man asked kindly after Milly's welfare and reappeared seconds later with brandies – on the house – for them all.

Milly took a warming glug and then heaved out a huge sigh of relief. 'I really can't thank you enough,' she said again.

'It's nothing. Us girls have got to stick together, haven't we? Ain't that what Miss Pankhurst is always saying? Ain't that the whole point of ELFS? I'm Elsie, by the way. Elsie Collins. And this is me younger sister, Hilda.'

Milly smiled from one to the other. The two sisters were in their early twenties, and were very similar with their straight dark-blonde hair, wide-set blue eyes and snub noses. In fact, had Elsie not pointed out that she was the elder, the two might almost have passed for twins. In repose, their faces were serious – almost grumpy – but when they smiled, they were prettiness itself: Hilda displaying dimples and Elsie an endearing gap between her front teeth. Milly had a feeling that one of them – she couldn't recall which – had been very outspoken at the meeting Nora had stormed out of. In fact, if she remembered rightly, hadn't one of them enraged Liza by suggesting foodstuffs were being deliberately stockpiled at the docks to drive up prices? Still, it wasn't for Milly to pass judgement – everyone was entitled to their opinion and everyone knew that profiteering did happen. Besides, you had to take as you found – as Ma was wont to say – and both Elsie and Hilda had been kindness personified.

'Why don't you pop to the lavvies and take your blouse off?' Elsie was saying. 'If you fasten your coat back up and put your scarf around your neck, no one will know. Then Hilda can pop the buttons back on and fix the buttonholes before you go home. Hilda's a whizz with the needle.'

Hilda, rummaging in her bag, looked up and smiled at her sister, and Milly felt a stab of envy at their easy camaraderie. She couldn't imagine Alice complimenting *her* like that. More to the point, she couldn't imagine Alice and herself out for an evening together at all – least of all to ELFS. Alice scorned the suffragettes, thought them a bunch of hysterical women likely to put *back* the cause of women's suffrage . . .

Still, now wasn't the time to dwell on things like *that*. Milly nipped to the lavvies out the back and wriggled out of her blouse. Wrapping her coat back around her, she inspected her face in the cracked mirror above the basin. Her bottom lip was thickening rapidly – there was no way she'd get that past Ma's eagle eye – but at least it had stopped bleeding and there was no other obvious damage. She carefully washed her face and smoothed her hair down as best she could. The brandy had already brought high spots of colour to her cheeks, and her eyes were glittering brightly. She gave herself a cheerful smile in the mirror – chin up, old bean! – bundled her shirt under her arm and went out to join the others.

By the time she re-joined her table, Hilda had emptied most of the contents of her bag over the polished wooden table. Milly blinked in surprise: there was such a breadth and depth of sewing paraphernalia that it put Ma's workbox to shame. There were scissors, thimbles, threads and needles galore, and a choice of small white buttons, if you please.

'Goodness,' said Milly. 'You've enough to open a shop there!'

Hilda grinned at her. 'Sewing's what I love to do,' she said, simply. 'But the one thing I don't have is any cream thread. I used it all on a nightdress recently and I haven't replaced it yet. Do either of you have any?'

Milly shook her head. The most she carried around was a selection of safety pins to deal with any wardrobe mishaps. Elsie picked up her own bag and started emptying the contents on the table.

Cigarettes . . . Matches . . .

Milly grinned to herself: so far, so like her own bag.

Powder . . . Rouge . . .

Yes, it definitely looked as if she had much more in common with Elsie than Hilda.

Cream thread . . . Half a brick . . .

*Half a brick?*

Milly let out a snort of surprised laughter. 'Why on earth have you got half a brick in your handbag?' she asked.

Elsie smiled wryly. 'You never know when you'll need one, do you?' she said lightly. 'And I like to be prepared. Seriously, don't you wish you'd had one today?'

'I certainly do,' said Milly fervently.

Although whether she'd have had the forethought – or the ability – to pull it out of her bag and brandish it at the soldier earlier on was a different matter altogether. Still, Elsie had a point. It was best to be prepared – and it was something she wasn't very good at. She vowed she would do better in future.

Meanwhile, Hilda had started repairing Milly's torn shirt with small, exquisite stitches. And, while she did so, the three girls talked. And talked and talked. They chatted about their jobs and families, and all the coincidences that seemed to link strangers in the East End. It turned out Elsie worked at the ELFS' toy factory with Milly's older sister, Maggie, and hadn't it been dreadful when Maggie's husband had upped and offed leaving Maggie all alone with a baby? And their mother's friend used to work at the Home Depot and Elsie's sweetheart used to drive one of the lorries that delivered the post there. It was a small world, they agreed, as one brandy turned into two and Milly began to forget that her mouth hurt and that that horrible man's hands had been all over her body. She discovered that Hilda worked for a textile company – of course she did – and that, while she had been engaged the year before, she was now single like her sister. 'And the least said about *that*, the better!'

By the time they left, Milly was feeling almost like herself again.

'Same time next week?' asked Elsie as the two girls walked Milly home through the quiet streets.

'Same time next week,' replied Milly with a smile.

Oh, it was so lovely to have found her people.

It was ten thirty by the time Milly finally got home.

As she put her key in the lock, she wondered if everyone would be in bed. By 'everyone', of course, she meant Ma; her siblings would have turned in hours ago – as soon as Mr Wildermuth took possession of the kitchen to cook his evening meal. In the summer it was different, but with the nights drawing in, bed was the warmest place to be. But tonight, Ma was still up, standing in the doorway to the kitchen, lines etched into her forehead. She'd obviously been waiting up for Milly – worrying about her – and Milly felt a stab of guilt.

She hadn't even told her mother she was going to the ELFS meeting.

'I'm so sorry, Ma,' she said, hanging up her coat and hat. 'I had an awful day at work and I decided to go to the ELFS' meeting off the cuff and then a few of us . . . stayed around chatting afterwards. I should have let you know.'

Would Ma notice her blouse? Would Hilda's needlework pass muster?

'What on earth's happened to your mouth?' asked Ma.

Milly's hand flew self-consciously to her swollen lip. She should tell Ma the truth. She really should. But Ma might overreact; curtail her freedoms.

She should . . .

She couldn't . . .

Milly let out a silly little tinkling laugh, which sounded false even to her own ears. 'Would you believe one of the men swung a sack off the lorry at work and hit me in the face with it?' she said, crossing her fingers behind her back. 'I *said* I'd had an awful day!'

Milly held her breath. She'd never get away with it. But, to her relief, Ma threw back her head and let out a great big belly laugh.

'And here I was thinking your job were the safe one,' she said. 'No chemicals, no explosives, no machinery to speak of – and yet our Milly manages to get smacked in the face with summat. Dear, oh, dear—' She broke off in a volley of coughs and Milly looked at her in concern.

'Are you all right, Ma?' she said.

'Just a cold starting.' Ma patted her chest. 'Next time, tell me where you're going, please. And no funny business with the suffragettes.'

'Yes, Ma. Sorry, Ma.' Milly stood on the bottom stair, her hand on the newel post. 'Love you, Ma.'

And she scampered up to bed.

# 4

Milly really wasn't at her best as she set off for work the next morning. Her body ached, her lip throbbed and she was so tired she could hardly keep her eyes open. Her temper was short and, even though she wasn't really one for crying, easy tears felt only a heartbeat away.

Milly found her legs slowing as she walked up the side of the Regent's Park towards the Home Depot. What was today going to hold? Hopefully she would have another day of gentle training with Rita, slowly getting her head around the complicated sorting protocols. After all the drama the night before, she hadn't really had a chance to look at the complicated key-list she'd taken home. Still, Rita seemed the sympathetic sort; once Milly had told her about the attack, surely she would allow lots of time to go through everything again.

But, to Milly's surprise – her *shock* – she was put straight on the sorting-room floor. No more patient Rita plying her with tea. No more slowly learning the ropes. Now she thought about it, neither Rita nor Miss Parker had said that there would be more training. She had just assumed that there would be. But now she was being plonked straight into it all! Worst of all, her new supervisor was Miss Rich — the woman she had cheeked the day before.

It all felt rather like being in one of those nightmares where you were totally out of control. At least she had all her clothes on and her teeth weren't crumbling away!

'Right, Milly,' barked Miss Rich. 'This is Mary, this is Eloise and this is Belle, and they are part of the Mediterranean Expeditionary Force team. The mail here has already been through one round of sorting, and this is where we further subdivide it by brigade and regiment. You'll need to sort quickly but accurately – there's a huge backlog of letters already, more are arriving all the time and we need you up to speed as quickly as possible. The girls will show you what to do.'

'Yes, Miss Rich,' said Milly.

Now probably wasn't the time to admit she didn't know the difference between a brigade and a regiment. Or anything at all about the Mediterranean Expeditionary Force.

Miss Rich bustled off and Milly turned to the three girls – one blonde, one redhead, one brunette. 'Hello,' she said with a smile.

The three girls smiled back at her, but their smiles were perfunctory and disinterested.

'Hello,' the blonde one with an immaculate up-do and a haughty expression imitated Milly's accent. Milly couldn't remember whether she was Belle, Mary or Eloise, but decided she was a stuck-up little miss whoever she was. 'Welcome to Team Incomparable,' the girl added, before trilling with affected laughter. 'Get it?'

Milly had absolutely no idea what she was talking about. But there was no way she was admitting that. There was no way she was putting herself at a disadvantage right from the get-go. So, she affected a little trill of her own and said, 'Of course. Very clever!'

To her relief, the girl just gave Milly a self-satisfied smile and turned back to her sorting. Then the one with wavy dark hair and a face that looked like she was sucking lemons stepped forward.

'Grab yourself a sack from the pile over there,' she said. 'And then start sorting into these sacks in front of us – they're all clearly labelled by regiment. Use your key-list if you get stuck – and shout if you really have to.'

And that seemed to be all the briefing she was going to get, because Lemon-Face had also resumed her sorting, flicking letters into the sacks in front of them.

'Right you are,' said Milly to no one in particular. Certainly no one seemed to be listening to her. Nervously, she dragged a bag of unsorted letters over to the little circle. She looked at the sacks she would be sorting into. They were held upright and open by the wooden frames, and each frame had a county name attached to it.

*Gloucestershire* . . .

*Worcestershire* . . .

*Herefordshire* . . .

Deep breath. How hard could it be?

Milly reached into the sack for the first letter. Small, spidery writing, but that was no problem: Milly was used to deciphering the most illegible of handwriting. There was a name, lots of letters and numbers, and – yes! – there it was. *2/ Hampshire*. She plopped the envelope triumphantly into the sack marked *Hampshire*. Phew! And here was another. *1/Essex*. She was on a roll.

The third was trickier. There was no obvious county. Nothing at all! Only the letters *NSSR*, which didn't correspond to any of the labelled sacks. *Blast*.

She didn't want to interrupt the other girls. Not now. Not so soon. She wanted to prove that she could do this on her own. After all, she had almost certainly been at the Home Depot a lot longer than they had, and she didn't want them thinking she was a complete novice. *Surely* she could work it out for herself?

The others carried on flicking letters at an impressive rate of knots and idly discussing whether the pond in the Regent's Park might freeze over that winter.

'Are you all right, Milly?' asked Lemon-Face finally. 'You've been staring at that letter for about five minutes!'

The girl didn't say it unkindly, but Milly knew she wasn't imagining the slight snigger from the others. And it smarted. It really smarted – partly because it seemed so unfair. She hadn't been staring at the letter for anything like five minutes and everyone had to start somewhere.

'I'm perfectly all right, thank you,' she said stiffly. 'I'm just trying to work out what NSSR stands for.'

The redhead glanced at her. 'It's this one,' she said, kicking one of the hanging sacks with her boot. Milly looked at the label, *Prince of Wales's (North Staffordshire Regiment)*.

'But that doesn't make sense!' said Milly indignantly. 'How are we supposed to work *that* out?'

The redhead shrugged. 'Use your key-list,' she said, and turned back to her chatter.

The morning dragged on, Milly perhaps sorting one letter to every half a dozen of the other girls. She noticed, though, that even they had to stop fairly often to rifle through umpteen pages of the key-list until they found what they were looking for. It was all so tedious. And her fingers were freezing. She noticed the other girls were wearing light cotton gloves, but all she had with her were her woollen mittens and they would make her fingers impossibly clumsy.

And where the Dickens was *this* letter meant to go?

Without meaning to – without really thinking about it at all – Milly reached out and plopped the letter into the nearest sack. And then she stopped and held her breath, half expecting Team Incomparable to swing round as one and call her out. One of them would produce a whistle and three shrill toots would summon Miss Rich, Miss Parker or Sergeant Major Cunningham – possibly all three. There would be a public dressing-down and then the slow walk of shame out of the Home Depot.

In fact, nothing happened. Nothing at all.

Team Incomparable carried on twittering among themselves and no one paid Milly a blind bit of attention.

Milly exhaled slowly. She'd got away with it.

Of course, the misfiled letter would be discovered sooner rather than later, but there was no way for anyone to know who had put it there. There were four of them in the group and any one of them could have made the mistake. And, of course, there were umpteen such groups sorting letters for the Mediterranean Expeditionary Force and, with a bit of luck, the letters would be amalgamated before anyone got around to checking them. Thank goodness for that.

Milly carried on sorting. The next dozen letters made perfect sense and she was able to sort them without difficulty – but then there was another that was totally incomprehensible. Milly made a show of consulting her key-list . . . and then chucked it into a random sack. This was easy! Almost too easy.

'The strangest thing happened yesterday,' said the blonde girl. Eloise? Or was it Belle? 'We were in Dorset this summer and I was minding my own business sketching Lulworth Cove, when a soldier confiscated my sketchpad. He was ever so polite about it, but apparently sketching is prohibited near the coast at the moment. Anyway, it's been returned to me, all present and correct and accompanied by a charming little note. Apparently, my little doodles aren't a threat to national security after all!'

Everyone laughed. 'I wonder they bothered to take it at all,' said the redhead.

Milly flicked a letter in the direction of the nearest sack. It missed and, self-consciously, she picked it up and deposited it safely. 'It's in case pictures of the coast fall into enemy hands,' she said. 'It could help plans for an invasion.'

The redhead tinkled with laughter. 'Oh, I know that,' she

said. 'But surely it should have been obvious Eloise wasn't up to no good.'

Milly felt her temper rising. 'Why not?' she asked, mildly enough. It wouldn't do to make a scene on her first morning.

Was it because Eloise was a woman or because she was obviously well-to-do?

The redhead looked nonplussed. 'Well, a lady's sketchbook isn't exactly a threat, is it?' she said.

Milly took a deep breath. 'But that's not the point,' she said. 'If we're demanding equality, the rules should be the same for everyone.'

'Goodness me! Look at you getting all hot under the collar,' said the redhead. 'If you must know, I'm not demanding equality.'

'What! Not even the same pay as men doing the same job?' demanded Milly indignantly. It never ceased to outrage her that that wasn't the case at the Home Depot. Everyone knew that men were paid far more – although how much more she had no way of knowing. To be fair, the picture was the same everywhere women were doing war work, but that didn't make it any more acceptable. It was so blatantly unfair.

'You sound like a suffragette,' said Eloise, with an indulgent smile. 'Next you'll be saying Edith Cavell deserved to be shot!'

Edith Cavell had been a nurse working in Belgium, who had been found guilty of smuggling hundreds of Allied troops back to Blighty. Despite an almighty outcry, she had been executed a few weeks previously and the papers were full of it.

'She didn't deserve to be shot,' said Milly, carefully. 'Of course, she didn't. No one did. But should she have been spared *just* because she was a woman?'

Team Incomparable took a sharp intake of breath.

'I don't think we should talk about this if we want to work together cordially,' said Eloise coolly.

Milly opened her mouth to argue, but she could tell there was little point. With a great effort, she bit her lip and lapsed into silence, letting the conversation ebb and flow around her. Belle, Mary and Eloise were the worst kind of girl, she decided. The kind who had been born with silver spoons in their mouths and yet were doing their utmost to stop other women from being given a chance. Oh, Milly knew that she was probably being unfair as Nora was even more la-di-da – even Liza had her moments – and yet Milly had become fast friends with both of them. But somehow that was different. The three of them had been pioneers – the advance guard – at the Home Depot and learning the ropes together had forged a bond that transcended class and status. And that was before their various adventures had strengthened the bonds.

The whistle finally went for lunch and, all around Milly, people started drifting away. No one asked her to accompany them to the canteen or to have a ciggie under the plane trees or to go for a stroll in the park. In fact, no one said anything at all to her and Milly suddenly felt horribly left out. *Exposed.* She wasn't used to feeling like that – she was used to being the one in the thick of the action, the one making everyone else laugh, the one issuing the invitations – and she didn't like it.

Keeping a determined smile on her face and her head held high, Milly walked over to the canteen by herself. Her ears were ringing, her eyes could hardly focus and every muscle ached. She wasn't used to standing still for that length of time – she'd been able to sit down in both the broken parcel department and the returned letter department – and her legs, in particular, were protesting very loudly. This was hard work – the hardest morning's work she'd yet had in the Home Depot – and she was longing for several cups of strong, sweet tea as well as something comforting to eat. And if she had to sit by herself, then so be it. Worse things happened at sea.

She opened the door to the canteen and scanned the rooms for a free table.

'Cooee! Milly!'

It was Nora and Liza, sitting together at a corner table and beckoning to her enthusiastically. Milly's spirits soared. She hadn't seen either girl all day – she'd stayed on the sorting floor at break time with everyone else but had hoped they might come over to say hello – and she'd begun to wonder if they had been avoiding her. Yet, here they were, friendliness personified. Maybe it was going to be all right.

Milly went over to their table and touched the spare chair tentatively. 'Is this free?'

Liza burst out laughing, long blonde plait jiggling. 'Of course, it is, you clot,' she said.

'We won't take offence if you'd rather sit with people from your new unit, though,' added Nora, mouth full of bangers and mash.

Milly looked from one to the other, but there didn't seem to be any edge to their voices. No points being made. No sneering. They were just being their usual friendly, thoughtful selves. She pulled out the spare chair and sat down.

'They're a really unfriendly lot on the sorting floor,' she said sadly. 'I don't want anything to do with them.'

'Give them a chance,' said Nora. 'You've only been there a morning and there will be times when our shifts don't coincide.'

Milly shrugged. How could she explain? On one hand, she felt vastly superior because of the length of time she had been at the Home Depot and, on the other, she felt hugely, humiliatingly out of her depth. To her shame, she felt tears pricking at her eyelids.

'It's so *hard*,' she whispered.

'Oh, Milly. It will get better,' said Liza. 'Just keep your head down, learn the ropes and you'll be the darling of the department in no time.'

Milly nodded and dashed the tears from her eyes.

Nora patted her hand. 'I've got something that will cheer you up,' she said. 'But it's really, *really* secret and you must promise not to tell anyone.'

Milly perked up immediately. 'Ooh, don't tell me! Miss Parker is stepping out with Sergeant Major Cunningham?' she suggested.

Liza let out a squeal of laughter. 'You are a one, Milly,' she said. 'Oh, do tell, Nora!'

Nora leaned forward. 'It really is secret and you mustn't tell *anyone*,' she said.

'We promise,' said Milly and Liza, as one.

'All right,' said Nora. 'Well, Uncle Alf – Major Benham – was round for dinner last night and, afterwards, he was chatting with Daddy in the library. And I didn't mean to eavesdrop – I really didn't – but I'd left my book in there and I was dying to carry on reading it. I was just working out whether it was a good time to interrupt or whether I should creep away when I heard them.'

'Heard *what*, Nora?' said Liza. 'Spit it out!'

'Promise you won't say?'

'*Promise.*'

'All right. Well, I heard him say that the King, Queen and Princess Mary – the *royal family*, if you please – are going to be paying a visit to the Home Depot just before Christmas.'

Liza rattled her cup back into her saucer, clapped her hands together and said 'No!' so loudly that several faces at neighbouring tables turned to look at her curiously.

'Shh!' hissed Nora.

Milly took a moment to think it all over.

Sometimes she resented the King and Queen; of course, she did. She resented them and everybody else in power – the establishment – for the blasted war and for poverty in the East End, and for a world in which men held all the cards.

Because it was all so damned unfair. But, then again, there was no doubt that a royal visit to the Home Depot was hugely exciting. A thrill, a once-in-a-lifetime experience, something to tell her grandchildren about . . . Suddenly she found she was grinning at Nora like an idiot. Wait until she told Ma and Alice and the rest of them about *this*.

'They're planning a big reception and a speech and a tour and *everything*.' Nora's eyes were shining as she looked from one to the other. 'It's to thank us all after the big Christmas rush and to restore public trust and confidence after the fire. Princess Mary is going to be there because of the Christmas tins she sent to every soldier last year, and it's all going to be a huge celebration of women and the role we're playing here. Oh, it's going to be magnificent. But we mustn't tell anyone yet. Not until the official announcement.'

'I wonder who will show them around?' mused Liza. 'And who will do the presentations?'

'I'm sure Nora will do something, since she's the major's niece,' said Milly, matter-of-factly.

Like it or not, that was just how things were. It wasn't Nora's fault.

'Not likely,' said Nora with a giggle. 'I'm so clumsy, I'd probably trip over and trip them over in the process.'

'True,' said Liza, giving Nora a friendly nudge. 'Well, it won't be me,' she added. 'I'm caught up in the extension fire investigation and have well and truly blotted my copybook.'

'Yes, I heard about that,' said Milly. 'I'm so sorry. How's James?'

To her consternation, Liza's eyes filled with tears. 'Physically, he's getting better,' she said. 'But he's still reeling from losing his father and brother so quickly, and he's just discovered he's been suspended pending the investigation.'

Nora reached out a hand and covered Liza's. 'I'm sure it's just a formality,' she said.

Liza nodded her head. 'I'm sure it is too,' she said. 'Still, I think it's safe to say that I won't be presenting any bouquets to the royal family. So, it's all down to you, Milly!'

'I think it's more likely that Miss Parker will start stepping out with Nora,' said Milly with a snort. 'It'll probably be the very annoying miss in my new department who won't shut up about how she doesn't want the vote.'

Nora rolled her eyes. 'I think the most important thing is that we all make sure we're on duty that day,' she said. 'And they're about to ask for volunteers for the Christmas party planning committee, so we all need to sign up for that too.'

Milly suddenly felt much happier. Oh, it was lovely to be back among her friends again. She was daft to have doubted them.

'What happened to your mouth, Milly?' asked Liza suddenly.

Milly touched her lip and the memories – the fear – of the night before came flooding back. Suddenly she was dying to tell her friends all about it. They would sympathise. They would understand.

'A horrid thing happened last night,' she began. 'I was walking back from the ELFS meeting, minding my own business when—'

'Wait!' interrupted Liza. 'You went to an ELFS meeting?'

'Yes. I wasn't planning to, but—'

'You went back after they said it was a good idea to set fire to the post?' added Nora.

'The people in charge didn't say that,' said Milly coolly. 'And Miss Pankhurst specifically made a point of saying . . .'

But Liza and Nora were standing up.

'I need to get back on duty,' said Liza, putting some money down on the table. 'There are some new girls in my section and their repackaging has more holes than a sieve.'

'And *I'd* better get back to those returned letters,' said Nora, adding her money to Liza's. 'They won't process themselves.'

Milly sat staring after their retreating backs.

After her solitary bowl of soup, Milly headed back into the Home Depot. Without much enthusiasm, she threaded her way back towards 'Mediterranean' and tried to remember where Belle, Mary and Eloise actually were. The sorting floor was huge and it was very easy to get lost. Ah, there they were – on the other side of a huge pile of sacks. That afternoon's quota, no doubt . . .

'Hold your horses!'

A man in soldier's khaki had stepped out in front of her. Milly stumbled backwards, hand to rapidly thumping heart. The alleyway . . . bricks against her back . . . teeth crashing against hers . . .

*No.*

'I'm so sorry,' the man was saying. 'I didn't mean to frighten you.'

Milly took a deep, deliberate breath and looked up at the soldier. He had a black patch over one eye and looked quite scary. Not that she was going to let that show.

'You almost frightened the life out of me,' she snapped.

'Sorry,' the man repeated. 'Although, strictly speaking, *you* barged in front of me.'

Milly ignored him. She had no wish to exchange pleasantries. She wanted nothing to do with soldiers for the time being. Perhaps for ever.

'I've not seen you here before,' the soldier persisted. 'First week?'

Oh! That was too much.

'If you must know, I've been here since June,' Milly replied coldly. 'I were one of the very first recruits.'

And, with that, she swept past him, and went over to join her team.

# 5

Miss Parker called for Milly the very next day.

'I'm getting reports – no, *complaints* – about inaccurate sorting,' she said, as soon as Milly had sat down. 'Miss Rich says there were an unfeasibly high number of wrongly sorted letters from your group yesterday, and she asked me to have a word with you.'

Milly flushed to her roots. How embarrassing. How *humiliating*. And damn Belle, Eloise and Mary for ratting on her.

Miss Parker must have read her mind. 'Let me assure you there's been no tale-telling,' she said. 'In fact, the rest of your team have no idea why I've called you in today. But the letters are checked at the next station and the proportion of wrongly sorted letters was particularly high yesterday. I can't believe it's a coincidence?'

There was no point in arguing.

'No, Miss. Sorry, Miss,' said Milly, staring down at her hands.

Miss Parker sighed. 'I'm not even going to ask if you're making genuine mistakes or deliberately putting letters in the wrong sacks for reasons best known to yourself,' she said. 'Either way, it's got to stop. I expect an immediate – and vast – improvement to your performance or I'm going to have to take disciplinary action. Understood?'

'Understood.'

'Dismissed.'

Milly stumbled from Miss Parker's office on the verge of tears. A matter of weeks ago, she had been a well-respected and hardworking member of the Home Depot. Yes, she had made mistakes – who hadn't? – but she'd always genuinely tried her best. She hadn't cheated. She wouldn't have dreamed of it!

What on earth had happened to her?

Soberly, she re-joined Mary, Eloise and Belle. Time for a fresh start. If she couldn't work out where a letter went, she would consult her key-list and, failing that, she would swallow her pride and ask the other girls for help. It didn't matter that they disliked each other. It didn't matter that their political beliefs differed. The important thing was to do the job to the best of her ability and not to let herself or Miss Parker down again.

Fired up with renewed enthusiasm, she reached into her sack for the next letter and . . .

Ouch! A slice of liquid pain shot across her thumb.

Milly pulled her hand out of the bag and inspected the damage. There was a long, deep cut right across the pad and it really stung. Everyone knew that paper cuts were a hazard of the job, but who knew an innocuous little letter could cause so much damage. And, as Milly stood looking stupidly at the wound, the blood started; a thin red line bubbling and oozing down her thumb and onto the palm of her hand.

'Ooh, nasty,' said Belle.

'I'd get to the surgery if I were you,' added Eloise.

'It's not that bad,' said Milly, trying to extract a handkerchief from her bag with her 'good' hand. 'It won't stop me sorting.'

'It's not that,' said Eloise. 'If you get even one drop of blood on the letters, Miss Rich will have your guts for garters.'

That put quite a different complexion on matters.

Milly couldn't afford to get in any more trouble that day, so, clumsily wrapping her thumb in her hanky, she set off for the surgery on the other side of the Home Depot. Hopefully she would be back on duty before anyone had even noticed that she'd gone.

The little surgery was packed!

All three booths were occupied and there were about half a dozen people sitting waiting their turn. The red-headed nurse who checked Milly in told her she was looking at a good twenty minutes before she was seen to. So much for a quick-in, quick-out. Worse still, the only empty chair – the one the nurse was directing her to – was next to the soldier she had bumped into the day before, now nursing a badly grazed forearm.

Had she been *very* rude to him the day before?

'We must stop meeting like this,' the soldier said good-naturedly. He nodded at her thumb. 'Paper cut?'

Milly nodded ruefully as she sat down.

'Occupational hazard, I'm afraid,' the soldier continued. 'Some people say that cotton gloves help, but I'm not convinced.'

'What have *you* done?' asked Milly, indicating the soldier's bleeding, oozing grazes.

The soldier made a face. 'Listen and learn,' he said. 'I was jumping between piles of sacks in the extension, lost my balance and put my arm down to break the fall. I'm just hoping I haven't broken it.'

Despite herself and the situation, Milly laughed. 'I am listening and I am learning,' she said. 'If I'm ever called upon to climb a pile of sacks in the extension, I won't start jumping between them.'

'Very wise,' said the soldier. 'And especially don't do it if you ever find yourself without an eye. Makes it rather difficult to judge distances.'

Milly wasn't sure what to say to that. She wasn't used to

soldiers discussing their war wounds so openly. So, instead, she said, 'I wonder what everyone else is in here for.'

'Ah,' said the soldier in a quieter voice. 'I've been eavesdropping, so I can fill you in on that if you like.'

Milly nodded. 'Yes, please,' she said, rather warming to him.

'Well, in the left-hand cubicle is one of the kitchen staff, who's cut herself grating suet. In the middle is a chap who was perching on one of the large baskets when it most inconveniently moved, causing him to fall and injure his hip. And in the right-hand cubicle is a lady who has hurt her back carrying a particularly heavy sack.'

'Fancy,' said Milly. 'Who knew the Home Depot was such a dangerous place to work?'

'Indeed,' said the soldier with a grin. He turned to Milly and offered her his left hand. 'Jack Archer.'

Milly took his hand and shook it. 'Milly Woods,' she replied.

The soldier's one good eye was green with surprisingly dark lashes, and he really was very handsome – if a girl cared to notice that sort of thing. He had short golden-brown hair – slightly ruffled – a broad face, a determined chin and a wide, curving mouth.

'So, how are you finding the sorting department?' asked Jack.

'I think it's awful,' said Milly honestly.

For some reason, she didn't feel the need to keep up appearances with this man. She had nothing to prove to him and so she could say exactly what she thought.

The one good eye blinked at her. 'Why?'

'I were in the returned letters department,' said Milly simply. 'I didn't want to move.'

Jack laughed. 'We aren't *that* bad,' he said. 'And I'd have thought you'd have been pleased to find yourself in the thick of the action – at the heart of the operation, so to speak.'

Milly made a face at him. 'What do you mean?' she said.

'Well, sorting the mail is what this whole building – the biggest wooden building in the world, as they're always telling us – was built for. All that money to get letters out to Tommy. The sorting department is the nerve centre, the beating heart. Everything else is . . . peripheral.'

Milly screwed her face up while she considered this. She had never thought of it quite like that. And maybe, just maybe, Jack had a point.

'I still hate it, though,' she said.

'Why's that?'

'It's so confusing. All those names and initials and acronyms – I can't get my head around them. And then I panicked and put a few envelopes I couldn't make head nor tail of in any old sack just to get rid of them, but Miss Parker found out and gave me a right old ticking off. And now I've cut my thumb!'

There! She'd admitted what she had done out loud. She stole a glance at Jack and, to her surprise, found that he was laughing.

'Oh, Miss Woods,' he said. 'Please don't think for a moment that you're the first person to have done that.'

Milly's mouth gaped open. 'You too?' she asked.

'Yes!' said Jack. 'I maybe didn't do it as enthusiastically as you did because I was never hauled over the coals for it. But I think everyone's done it at one time or another. Especially at the beginning.'

Milly grinned ruefully at him, beginning to feel better. 'It's just so difficult,' she said.

'Not when you get used to it,' said Jack. 'What's particularly confusing you at the moment?'

'All of it!' said Milly vehemently. 'Starting with why the girls I work with call themselves Team Incomparable and expect me to know what they're talking about!'

Jack snorted with laughter. 'You've been put in with Eloise and her sadly vacuous friends, haven't you?' he said.

'Yes,' said Milly. 'They're awful. They don't even want women's suffrage. I think if I said I were a suffragette, they'd chase me out of the Home Depot!'

She had no idea why she was telling Jack this, but some instinct told her he would understand.

'Women with the vote?' said Jack with a grin. 'God forbid! Anyway, Eloise and her chums call themselves Team Incomparable because the 29th Division – the one that comprises the Mediterranean Expeditionary Force – is nick-named the Incomparable Division.'

'Aha!' said Milly. 'Now I understand! Although the sad thing about the Mediterranean Force is that they're incomparable in how many men they've lost.'

The disastrous campaign at Gallipoli had been in all the newspapers, of course, but Milly had more reason than most to know how bad the casualties had been. The returned letters department had been inundated by letters sent back because their intended recipients were dead. It haunted them all.

'It's awful,' agreed Jack. 'I had it pretty bad in France, but what those poor saps are going through with the heat and flies doesn't bear thinking about. The sooner this war is over the better.'

'Amen,' said Milly. And the two locked eyes for a moment longer than was strictly necessary.

'Apart from Team Incomparable, what else is confusing you?' asked Jack.

Milly shrugged. 'The key-list is so long. It takes me ages to look anything up. How can you possibly learn it all?'

Jack laughed. 'You don't need to learn it all,' he said. 'You just need to know the regiments, that make up the 29th Division. There are about fifty of them – but some are bigger than others and crop up much more often. You'll soon get the hang of it.'

'Really?'

'Really. I remember when Eloise and her gang started. They couldn't get to grips with it at all, and now they can do it in their sleep with enough energy left over to bore us all senseless with tales of their sketching trips and new ice skates.'

'Jack Archer?' The pretty red-headed nurse was standing in front of them. 'Come with me, please.'

As Jack stood up, Milly's thoughts started going nineteen to the dozen.

'Private Archer,' she said. 'If you don't need to go to the hospital, would you meet me in the canteen at lunchtime?'

Jack looked completely taken aback – as did the nurse – and Milly suddenly realised how it must have sounded. Oh, goodness – she was such a clot! Private Archer and the nurse must think her incredibly pert – and she hadn't meant it like that at all.

'I'm formulating a plan,' Milly said, in an attempt to clarify matters. 'And I wondered if you wouldn't mind helping me out?'

'I see,' said Jack, looking like he didn't see at all. 'Well, I'd be happy to help. Just as long as whatever you're planning is ethical and legal?'

'Both the above,' said Milly, with a grin. 'Thank you. And please bring your key-list.'

Jack left, smiling over his shoulder at her, and Milly suddenly noticed that, despite soaking her handkerchief in blood, her thumb hadn't been hurting her at all.

Jack was as good as his word.

He came to find Milly in the canteen at lunchtime, key-list in hand.

'It's not broken,' he said, waving his bandaged hand at her. 'Just some grazes and a sprained wrist.'

Milly waggled her bandaged thumb in reply. 'We live to fight another day,' she said.

Jack sat down. 'I'm intrigued to hear what you've got in mind,' he said, good eye crinkling in merriment.

Milly paused. 'First of all, I wanted to say I'm sorry I were rude to you the first time we met,' she said. 'I hope I didn't upset you?'

Jack looked at her levelly. 'Miss Woods, I spent endless days with the enemy trying to blow me to kingdom come,' he said. 'I think I can cope with a girl who was a trifle sharp because I'd appeared from nowhere and scared the living daylights out of her.'

His words were tempered by a lopsided grin, which creased his face in a most disarming way.

Careful, Milly.

'Well, nonetheless, I am sorry,' said Milly. 'And now for my plan. I'm going to make a new and improved key-list, which only contains the information relevant to the Mediterranean section. I've "borrowed" some supplies.' She opened her bag and produced scissors, string, glue and some blank sheets of paper. 'Mabel in the broken parcels department was most obliging.'

Jack rocked back on his chair and started laughing.

'You're making fun of me,' said Milly crossly.

'No, I'm not,' said Jack. 'I think it's marvellous. I only wish I'd thought of it myself! Now, what can I do to help?'

'I need you to tell me the names of all the regiments fighting with the Mediterranean Expeditionary Force,' said Milly. 'I'll find them on the official key-list, cut them out, glue them onto these sheets of paper and, hey presto! A key-list that is ten times shorter and is actually helpful.'

'Miss Woods, you are a marvel. Let's make a start!'

The two worked companionably, totally absorbed in their task and food all but forgotten. They only looked up when the lady superintendent in charge of the canteen bustled up to their table.

'Away with you now,' she said. 'I've no idea what you're up to, but you can't be using one of my tables for hours on end when there's honest folk waiting to be fed.'

'I'm so sorry,' said Milly. 'We're about finished though!'

And she waved her new key-list – two pages long rather than the usual ten – around with a flourish.

'Ta-da.'

And it worked.

It really worked. In fact, to say it totally transformed things for Milly wouldn't have been an exaggeration. Now, if there was an abbreviation or some initials on a letter that she didn't understand, she could find which regiment or battalion it related to quickly and easily, pop the letter into the right sack and move on.

No more time-wasting. No more mistakes. No more *cheating*.

Even Team Incomparable – despite a modicum of initial sneering – was impressed. In fact, the next day, Eloise quietly asked if Milly would mind if they copied the idea for the new recruit who was about to join their team. Milly said she didn't mind at all and that, if Mabel from the broken parcels department would be happy to lend them the wherewithal, she would be happy to help Eloise pull another modified key-list together in their breaks.

And, from there, they went one stage further and introduced another of Milly's initiatives: adding the most common abbreviations for each regiment under the official name on the sack – so that more often than not, there was no need to look anything up at all.

Slowly, slowly, Milly began to feel she belonged. Soon she was pretty much matching Team Incomparable letter for letter, helping to train the new recruit and even joining in some of the chatter and the occasional sing-song. Perhaps this wasn't so bad after all.

And then Miss Parker called for her.

'Well done on your first week, Milly,' she said. 'I hope you're beginning to learn the ropes?'

'Yes, Miss Parker. It ain't so bad after all. The other girls are all right and . . .'

'Good. Good,' said Miss Parker. 'But I hope you haven't got too comfortable because I'm afraid I'm going to move you again. This time, you'll be sorting parcels destined for France . . .'

Milly stared at Miss Parker in dismay. Surely her efforts at customising the key-list weren't in vain? Surely she wouldn't have to start all over again with a whole load of new regiments and new abbreviations to get to grips with?

'Have I done something wrong?' asked Milly in a small voice.

'No, no, not at all,' said Miss Parker. 'Well, cheeking Miss Rich at the beginning of the week probably wasn't the best start and neither was the high volume of wrongly sorted letters. And then word got to me that some of your topics of conversation might have ruffled some feathers. But, mainly, I want to give you experience of the different sections and types of work on the sorting floor. You will start your new duties on Monday, and I suggest you restrict your chatter to what you've seen at the cinema.'

Milly sighed. 'Yes, Miss Parker,' she said, and turned to leave.

No one else was rotated between different sections to get more 'experience'. Miss Parker was just being kind. The other girls had clearly complained – she was too radical, too militant, not one of them – and she was being moved on.

The simple truth was that being Milly Woods from Bow sometimes wasn't enough.

# 6

'Do you know an Elsie at the toy workshop?' Milly asked Maggie on Sunday evening.

The weekend had passed in a blur, as it always did. With the whole household either working full time or at school, chores had to be crammed into Saturday. Sunday was kept free for church, visits to the park and family games, and then Ma and Alice had left for a night shift at the munitions factory and Maggie had hung around to help Milly with the younger children.

Maggie stopped stirring the pan of oxtail stew. 'Elsie Collins, do you mean?' she said, distractedly. 'Arthur, do not put things you find on the rug in your mouth. That's coal and you will not like it.'

'Yes,' said Milly, taking the piece of coal from her nephew's chubby fist and marvelling at how it looked like he had an elastic band around each wrist. 'She goes to ELFS and she was very helpful to me last Monday night.'

'Yes, that's Elsie Collins,' said Maggie. 'Can't read nor write for toffee, but she's very good with the manes.'

'Very good with the manes?' echoed Milly with a grin. 'Whatever do you mean?'

'On the rocking horses,' said Maggie. 'It's really fiddly getting them just so. Most of us manage to get glue everywhere, but she's ever so neat and tidy. And she's a whizz with the jack-in-the-boxes too.'

'A useful skill to have!' said Milly, setting out bowls and cutlery. 'Caroline, Charlie, wash your hands. It's time for dinner.'

The four clustered around the kitchen table, and Maggie started doling out the stew. There was plenty to go round, which was just as well as it was proving more and more difficult to get bread. That weekend they hadn't been able to buy any for love nor money.

There was a cough behind her. Milly glanced around to see Mr Wildermuth standing in the doorway.

'Would you like to pop through?' she said politely. Ma was a stickler for Mr Wildermuth only setting foot in the kitchen during the allotted hours, but Milly thought that was silly. After all, sparing everyone's blushes, when a man needed to use the privy, he needed to use the privy – and it seemed daft to make him use his chamber pot unnecessarily.

'I've brought you some bread from the bakery,' said Mr Wildermuth, his fair hair highlighted by the gas lamps. 'It's slightly singed but I thought you might enjoy it with your dinner.'

'Oh!' exclaimed Milly. 'How did you know we didn't manage to get any?'

'I am a very clever man!' said Mr Wildermuth with a wink at the younger children.

He handed over two loaves in a brown paper bag, and turned to leave.

'Thank you so much, Mr Wildermuth,' said Maggie.

And there was something in the way she said it and the way she was looking at Mr Wildermuth that made Milly suddenly say, 'Why don't you join us, Mr Wildermuth? After all, we have plenty of stew – even if we didn't have any bread.'

Maggie turned to Milly, trying not to display her shock in front of Mr Wildermuth. Ma would have a *fit* if she was here. One didn't invite the lodger to dine with you – even if he had just gifted you bread.

It simply wasn't done.

But, then again, reasoned Milly, why *shouldn't* she extend a simple invitation? After all, Mr Wildermuth had been wonderful during the Zeppelin raids and had sheltered Charlie – and sometimes Caroline – under his table because there wasn't room for them all under the kitchen table. And Ma wasn't there, so what could be the harm? Men and women were fraternising far more nowadays than had been the case before the war – take her and Jack – and so they were just keeping up with the times!

And she had a sneaking feeling Maggie was sweet on Mr Wildermuth. Maybe that was why her sister spent so much time round at the house. Why had she never noticed before?

As if to confirm her suspicions, Maggie was smiling at Mr Wildermuth.

'Yes, please do,' she said. 'You've shared your bread and we'll share our stew.'

And suddenly they were all shuffling around and clearing a place at the table and beckoning Mr Wildermuth in, the younger children tickled pink by the unexpected turn in events.

'Are you sure?' asked Mr Wildermuth hesitantly.

'Completely sure,' said Milly, before Maggie could change her mind.

'And afterwards maybe you can help me fix my catapult?' added Charlie.

'Cheeky,' said Maggie, ruffling his hair. 'Now, Mr Wildermuth, how hungry are you?'

'Ravenous,' said Mr Wildermuth.

Milly wondered if she was the only one to notice the two bright spots of colour that had appeared on her older sister's cheeks.

What a strange evening it had turned out to be.

Mr Wildermuth proved to be the perfect dinner guest. He really was most attentive, asking them about their work or about school. Milly found herself opening up to him, explaining all about her new role and how it had seemed totally daunting to begin with, and, just as she was getting used to it, she'd been moved on again. And Mr Wildermuth seemed fascinated by it all – asking her all about how the Home Depot was organised and laid out – and exactly what went on in the various departments. Milly basked in all the attention – her family was wonderful, but they had little interest in what she actually did all day.

'The King and Queen are coming to see Milly at Christmas,' said Charlie, when there was a break in the conversation.

'*Charlie!*' said Milly, ruffling his hair. 'That's meant to be a secret. And they're certainly not coming in to see me!'

Milly had, of course, told her family about the royal visit the very day she'd heard about it. The King and Queen visiting the Home Depot was too exciting a piece of news *not* to share – and the look of pure jealousy on Alice's face had made it more than worthwhile. Besides, when Nora had told her and Liza not to tell anyone, she hadn't meant their families. Everyone told their families everything. It was just how things were. But Charlie telling Mr Wildermuth . . .?

Mr Wildermuth gave her a reassuring smile and touched the side of his nose.

'Mum's the word,' he said. 'But make sure you practice your curtsey.'

When Mr Wildermuth turned his attention to one of her siblings, Milly carried on watching him out of the corner of her eye. He might have been born in Germany, but his English was faultless – virtually no trace of an accent at all. Anyway, it was hardly his fault the two countries were at war. He was as much a victim of it as everyone else.

He was handsome. He was generous. He was kind.

He might do very well for Maggie.

If only she wasn't already married.

# 7

Milly would have loved a chance to produce a modified key-list in advance of starting her new position on Monday. But, without any detailed knowledge of which regiments were involved, that had proved impossible. She started her new role feeling just as much a fish out of water as she had done the week before. Dealing with parcels meant there was no risk of paper cuts, and thank goodness for small mercies because the work was back-breakingly hard.

By the time her shift was over, Milly was exhausted, but she was still looking forward to the ELFS meeting that evening. She'd given Ma advance notice of her intentions this time, and she really wanted to see Hilda and Elsie again. She missed spending time with Liza and Nora, and longed to have some more female friends. Besides, she had yet to confide in anyone about the attack and, as the days marched by, she found she was thinking about it more rather than less . . .

So, Milly arrived at the Mother's Arms full of anticipation. To her pleasure and relief, Hilda and Elsie looked just as delighted to see her.

'You came!' said Hilda, giving Milly a dimpled smile as she sat down. 'I'm so pleased!'

'And your lip has healed nicely, an' all,' said Elsie, sitting down on Milly's other side and giving her a gap-toothed grin.

'Bloody soldiers,' said Hilda, taking a sip of her hot chocolate. 'They're all the same – thinking they can do what they want because they've taken a pop at the Germans.'

Milly was tempted to point out that this wasn't quite fair. Not all soldiers were the same. She certainly couldn't imagine Jack drunkenly wandering the streets at night waiting to drag unsuspecting girls into alleyways. The thought was preposterous!

'Have they charged him?' asked Elsie, before Milly had a chance to answer. 'I hope they're going to throw the book at him!'

Milly turned to Elsie in surprise. 'I haven't heard a thing,' she said. 'Should I have?'

'Too right, you should,' said Hilda.

Milly wondered how the police would contact her. She really didn't want them arriving at the front door . . .

'Tell you what,' said Elsie. 'Let's all pop down the nick after the meeting.'

'Oh no, there's really no need . . .'

'Yes, there bloody is,' said Elsie firmly. 'You was *assaulted*. And, if we hadn't been passing, who knows what might've happened.'

'All right,' said Milly.

All her encounters with the police had thus far been negative: a night in the cells for throwing stones with the suffragettes before the war; a caution for nicking sweets when she was younger. She had always thought it best to stay well away from the law, and leave them to seek her out! It had never crossed her mind to actively go into a police station and ask for information. But . . . why not? It would be better than the awkward front doorstep conversation with Ma.

'And afterwards, if you wouldn't mind, you could help us carry some stuff from here round to Nan's,' Elsie was saying. 'She lives round the corner.'

'Nan?' asked Milly. Who the heck was Nan?

'Family friend,' said Hilda. 'And a member of ELFS. You'll recognise her. Reddish hair? Specs?'

Milly could just about picture who they were talking about. A quietly spoken woman, Nan took three sugars in her tea, sat at the back of the room during meetings and rarely contributed to discussions.

'Why are you visiting her?' she asked. 'Why ain't she here?'

'She's poorly,' said Elsie, dropping her voice as Sylvia Pankhurst walked to the front of the room. 'Her chest is proper bad and she ain't looking after herself. We thought we'd take her some bits and pieces, and check she's doing OK.'

Milly looked from one to the other of her new friends with new found respect. 'It will be gone nine o'clock, by then,' she said. 'Won't she mind?'

Hilda shrugged. 'She ain't got anyone else helping her.'

'Then I'd be pleased to come,' said Milly firmly.

How kind her new friends were.

And how pleased she was she had found them.

That evening's meeting centred on the Distress Bureau ELFS had set up to help local women obtain the separation allowance they were entitled to when their son or husband joined the army. The separation allowance generally consisted of a contribution from the soldier's pay, which was augmented by the government, to ensure those left at home were not left destitute. The whole system seemed fraught with errors. Miss Pankhurst ran through some of the recent cases they had taken up, where forms and legal documents had gone missing or the wrong amount of money had been granted.

Milly listened with half an ear. It wasn't an ELFS initiative she had ever got involved with. She'd been more taken with helping at the mother-and-baby clinics (to say nothing of enthusiastically creating public mischief before the war!) and it all sounded rather dry and tedious. So, for once, Milly was clock-watching during the meeting and found herself quite relieved when it finally drew to a close.

'Ready to pay a visit to the old nick?' said Hilda, turning to her with a smile.

'Too right,' replied Milly.

She *was* ready. But nervous too.

If the soldier didn't admit his crime – and why would he? – what would happen next? Would she have to identify him in a line-up? Face him across a courtroom? Have her own past misdeeds shared with all and sundry?

Was it worth it?

It was, she decided resolutely. It was up to all women to call out inequalities and injustices whenever they could. She had no excuse not to.

Bow Street Police Station was large and imposing – several storeys high with more columns, balustrades and statues than you could shake a stick at. Milly's heart was thumping as she followed the others through the main door. The outer office was quite empty with just a couple of drunks slumped disconsolately on benches. Milly glanced to see if any of them might be her attacker, but then checked herself. No, he'd be banged up inside, waiting for his trial.

At least, she hoped he was.

Hilda had walked straight up to the front counter, and Milly hurried to stand beside her. Hilda was a kind and supportive person, but Milly didn't want anyone speaking for her.

Milly could speak for herself, thank you very much!

'How can I help you?' asked the duty sergeant.

There was something in his tone which immediately put Milly on the defensive. She drew herself up to her full height – still a good six inches below the sergeant's – and lifted her chin.

'I were attacked last week,' she said, trying to keep her voice steady. 'I reported it at the time but I've not heard nothing since.'

'Name?' The sergeant sounded supremely bored.

'Milly – Amelia – Woods.'

The sergeant rifled through some papers. 'Nothing here,' he said, as if that was that.

'But there must be,' insisted Milly. 'I gave a statement an' all.'

'Sorry, love.'

'*Listen*,' said Milly. 'He were taken away by a policeman. He were arrested.'

'I recognise you,' said the duty sergeant, peering at Milly more closely. 'Was this incident near St Stephen's Road?'

'Yes!' cried Milly in relief.

She hadn't recognised the sergeant; she'd been shocked and in distress, and one bobby in uniform looked much like another. But at least he remembered *her*.

'Bit of a drunken kiss in an alleyway that went too far, was it?' said the sergeant with a sneer.

*What?* How dare the sergeant even suggest that?

'No,' said Milly, trying to keep her temper. 'He dragged me in there.'

'That's not what he said,' countered the sergeant. 'Said you were ready to drop your drawers for him and then, at the last minute, you changed your mind and started kicking up a fuss.'

Rage – pure rage – crackled through Milly.

'He's lying!' she cried. 'You can't let him get away with it!'

'No case to answer, I'm afraid.'

'But I made a statement . . .'

'Not worth the paper it was written on.'

'But the policewoman *said* . . .'

'She's new,' said the sergeant condescendingly. 'Still learning the ropes.'

'That doesn't mean anything. She saw what happened. She believed me.'

'Oh, away with you,' said the duty sergeant. 'Or I'll book you for wasting police time.'

The fact he was almost laughing made the whole thing ten times as bad, and Milly stepped forward to give him a real piece of her mind.

Hilda grabbed her arm. 'Don't,' she whispered urgently. 'Don't do or say anything you'll live to regret. That bastard ain't worth it.' Then she turned to the duty sergeant and said, with great dignity, 'There will come a time when women are believed and taken seriously, and then you'll be laughing the other side of your face.'

'Yes, and let me tell you, that day ain't far away,' added Elsie. 'You're denying this woman justice and you know you are.'

The duty sergeant put his hand to his heart. 'Oh, Lordy,' he said. 'A slag and a couple of suffragettes. What a combination. Careful you don't go putting any stones through windows on the way out or all three of you will be feeling the full force of the law.'

Eyes blinded by stinging tears of humiliation, Milly stumbled from the police station, Hilda and Elsie in tow. Behind her, Milly could hear cackles of laughter. She put her hands over her ears and set off along the pavement at full pelt . . . slap bang into a young female bobby.

Milly recognised *her* straight away.

'They're not pressing charges,' Milly blurted out without preamble, stepping forward until she was nose to nose with the policewoman. She was about to stab an accusing finger for good measure, but thought the better of it and let her hand drop to her side. Behind her, she felt Elsie or Hilda lay a restraining hand on her shoulder.

The policewoman started backwards. She peered at Milly,

Ma was waiting up for Milly again.

'You're very late,' she said, as soon as Milly walked through the front door.

Milly felt a stab of guilt. Lovely Ma; how pale and pinched she looked – and how inconsiderate Milly had been to give her even a moment of worry.

'I'm sorry, Ma,' she said, hanging up her hat and coat. 'I've had such a night of it.'

'You're not in some sort of trouble, are you?'

Guilt shifted to annoyance.

Why did Ma immediately have to assume she was in trouble? All right, sometimes she *could* be pert and sometimes that *did* land her in sticky situations. But not always. Not even most of the time! At least she'd the sense not to get herself knocked up like Maggie. After all, Milly wasn't the one who'd had to get married to some ne'er-do-well, who'd then proceeded to bugger off at the earliest opportunity.

Milly opened her mouth to remind her mother of this, but then stopped. Ma was bent almost double in a fit of coughing that seemed to go on and on.

*Just like Nan.*

'What's wrong, Ma?' asked Milly in alarm, rubbing her mother's back.

'Nothing,' said Ma, straightening up, hand to mouth. 'A little cough. Let's have a cuppa – just you and me – and you can tell me all about your evening.'

Milly followed her mother into the empty kitchen. Her younger siblings were already in bed, so Milly had Ma all to herself. That didn't happen very often and Milly was determined to make the most of every minute. She settled down on the sofa with a little sigh, and Ma brought her over a hot, sweet cup of tea.

'So, where's my girl been tonight, then?'

obviously trying to work out who she was and what on earth she was talking about. Then the penny dropped and she let out a deep sigh.

'I did try,' she said. 'Believe me. I tried my best.'

Milly's shoulders slumped in defeat. 'Don't tell me,' she said bitterly. 'I were asking for it. I egged him on and then I changed my mind. Was that how it went?'

The policewoman gave a rueful shrug. 'Something like that,' she said. 'They kept him in until he sobered up and then they let him go on his way.'

'Not even a caution?' asked Hilda.

The policewoman shrugged. 'Busy night,' she said. 'I'm really sorry.'

'But you *saw* what he did,' Milly burst out.

And then she remembered that by the time the police had arrived, Elsie and Hilda had already pulled the soldier off her.

It was her word against his.

She had no way of winning.

She turned away, defeated. But she couldn't help thinking if it had been Nora who had been assaulted – or even Liza – the outcome would have been very different.

They would have been listened to.

They would have been believed.

They would have *mattered*.

# 8

After that debacle, Milly was in no mood to go and visit Nan.

She wanted to go home, lick her wounds and be with her family, but she knew she was just being churlish. Hilda and Elsie had given up their time to accompany her to the police station – it wasn't *their* fault she hadn't had the outcome she'd wanted – and the least she could do was help them out in return.

Although why they needed her was anyone's guess.

A quick visit back to the Mother's Arms and all became clear. Elsie and Hilda were bringing provisions to Nan – and not just bits and bobs, either. There was a small – but surprisingly heavy – sack of coal, some bags of potatoes and carrots, a couple of blankets, some eggs and a veritable little hoard of tins and jars. All far too much for two people to comfortably carry on their own.

'We had a whip round for Nan last week and people have been ever so generous,' explained Hilda.

'Well, you're being ever so kind to her now,' replied Milly.

'She were really good to our ma before she died,' said Elsie. 'And now she's poorly herself, so we want to do our bit. Our ma would've expected it.'

Oh! Elsie and Hilda had lost their mother. Milly didn't know how she would cope without Ma.

'I'm so sorry,' she mumbled.

'It's been a year now,' said Hilda. 'Still, others have it much worse. Here we are . . .'

It looked like the topic was closed.

They had arrived at a tenement block. Red-bricked and several storeys high, it was identical to dozens of others in the neighbourhood. For the second time that evening, Milly felt her heart rate ratchet up a gear. These blocks housed some of the poorest in the East End, and were known as a hotbed of crime and depravity. Ma would have a fit if she knew Milly was wandering around an area like this after dark.

She took a deep breath and followed Elsie and Hilda through the open archway and into the large courtyard in the centre of the building. All was still and quiet. During the day it would be full of children playing and clothes drying and women gossiping, but now there was just a cluster of men – boys really – peering slyly out of the shadows.

'Help you, Miss?' one of the bolder ones asked Hilda, appearing at her side and pointing at the bag of coal she was struggling with.

'Do we look daft?' Elsie replied. Her voice was amused rather than frightened, but there was a definite edge of steel to it. Milly wasn't surprised when the boy melted away to his friends.

Milly adjusted the weight of the bag she was carrying and followed the other girls over to one of the staircases where a stooped woman was filling buckets at the communal tap. Up and up the stairs they went, and Milly's heart was going nineteen to the dozen by the time they stopped outside a black door, identical to all the others.

'Yoo-hoo!' called Elsie softly, rapping lightly on the door and then pushing it open. 'It's only us.'

The door entered straight into a largeish room. It was dark; one small candle vainly battling the gloom. It took Milly's eyes a while to adjust – and then she noticed the woman lying on the sofa. She was so still and so small that, for a horrible moment, Milly wondered if she might be dead. But then she stirred and said, 'Hello girls,' in a quiet voice.

'This is Milly,' said Elsie. 'She's one of us.'

Milly smiled. 'One of us' sounded nice.

Like she belonged. Like she *mattered*.

And, after the horrid experience at the police station, it was exactly what she'd needed to hear.

'It's cold in here, Nan,' said Elsie. 'Icy cold. You've not got your fire lit!'

'I ain't got no coal,' said Nan, breaking into a paroxysm of coughing.

Nan didn't sound particularly distraught or panicked by this. She was just stating how things were, and Milly realised she was probably too tired and too poorly to do anything else.

'We've bought you coal,' said Elsie cheerfully. 'We'll get this room toasty and warm in no time. Then we'll get a brew down you and then we'll get you something to eat.'

'Bless you, dear,' said Nan.

Hilda was lighting the gas lamps and Milly could now see that Nan was in her forties, with strands of dark-red hair escaping a messy bun, sunken cheekbones and hooded blue eyes. Her skin was pale and pallid, her lips were cracked and she really didn't look at all well. How had she got herself into this situation? How had she ended up all by herself in the cold and the dark with nothing to eat or drink? Oh, Milly knew this little tableau was echoed umpteen times over throughout the East End – but Nan was a member of ELFS for goodness' sake, and Milly remembered her looking hale and hearty only a matter of weeks ago.

How had things gone so wrong for her and so quickly? If it could happen to Nan, surely it could happen to anyone.

No, Milly. Don't think like that. Nothing good could come of it.

'Have you got anything I can use to light the fire, Nan?' Hilda was saying.

'There's some paper on the table,' Nan rasped through more racking coughs.

'I'll do that,' said Milly quickly, anxious to be helpful. She went over to the table under the window and picked up a little pile of papers. 'This?' she asked Nan.

'That's right, dear,' said Nan. 'All rubbish.'

Milly sat down at the table. She was about to start twisting the first three sheets into a firelighter when something caught her eye. The top sheet was a letter from the Bow Street Police Station – the very station Milly and the others had been in earlier that evening – and the words *Separation Allowance* and *terminated* leaped out at her. Intrigued and concerned, she took the letter over to one of the lamps and scanned it more fully. It seemed Nan's separation allowance had been terminated *with immediate effect* because of a *disturbance of the peace*. Milly stared at the words, puzzled. What on earth did they mean? And what 'disturbance of the peace'? From what – admittedly little – Milly knew of Nan, she was a quiet, mousy woman, not given to violent or noisy outbursts.

'Ain't you getting your separation allowance anymore, Nan?' she ventured. She knew she was being unforgivably nosey – that it was none of her business – but something about the letter had piqued her curiosity.

Hilda, rump in the air, clearing old ash out of the range, made a tutting noise. 'Oi, Milly,' she said. 'Stop reading Nan's letters and hurry up with those firelighters, will you?' She said it lightly enough, but Milly didn't miss the definite edge to her voice.

Elsie looked up from peeling potatoes and carrots. 'Yes, come on,' she said. 'We need to get the fire going so we can get some food inside Nan this side of midnight.'

Milly returned to her task. 'Sorry,' she said, twisting some of the other papers into firelighters and passing them to Hilda.

'If you want to be helpful, can you pop downstairs to the tap in the courtyard and fill a couple of buckets?' said Elsie. 'Nan needs some water and we need to get the brew and the stew on.'

'Of course,' said Milly. She picked up the metal buckets stacked near the front door and clattered down the stairs with them, thoughts a-whirr. Even though she had only scanned the letter, she knew what she'd read. Nan had lost her separation allowance and it was something to do with the horrible police station she'd been at earlier that evening. Maybe it even had something to do with the horrible duty sergeant who'd openly sneered at her and then laughed behind her retreating back . . .

It was quiet and a little eerie by the tap at the bottom of the stairs. Milly turned the tap on, wondering how full she should fill the buckets given she had to climb three flights of stairs with them.

''Ello, love!'

Milly glanced up. A man stood at the entrance to the next flight of steps around the courtyard – the red highlights in his auburn hair illuminated by the solitary lightbulb.

The right height. The right build.

'No!' she blurted out. '*No!*'

She shut the tap off as quickly as she could – never mind she'd only filled one bucket – and set off back up the stairs as quickly as she could.

'That's not very friendly!' The man's voice – his laughter – rang in her ears. 'Something I said?'

Milly carried on running upstairs, buckets clanging, water sloshing everywhere. It took two flights for her to realise the man wasn't following her – there were no running footsteps closing in up the stairwell behind her. It took the final flight to realise that, of course, it wasn't her attacker. This man was too short, too slight and his voice was higher. And hadn't her attacker had jet-black hair?

How could she have got so confused?

How could she have got so *scared*?

Milly stood on the landing outside Nan's flat for a moment to give her heart a chance to return to normal. Then she pushed the door open with her foot. Warm fingers of heat wrapped around her, the chill from the air already dissipating.

'I'm sorry,' she said, indicating at the one half full and the one empty bucket. 'There was a man downstairs and . . .' She trailed off, embarrassed.

Hilda took the full bucket. 'It's all right,' she said. 'There's enough here to be getting on with. Why don't you give Nan a glass of water? She's coughing something awful.'

Hilda dipped a – rather grubby – glass into the water and handed it to Milly. Milly carried it across the room and sat down next to Nan. 'This should help you to feel a bit better,' she said, proffering the glass.

'Thank you, dear,' said Nan, shuffling to a sitting position. 'So silly I've allowed meself to get into this situation. No water. No fire . . .'

'Not at all,' said Milly.

How close they all were to allowing themselves to get into 'this situation'. At least Milly had Ma and her sisters and brother. And Mr Wildermuth, she supposed. Together they should be able to help each other through the harshest winter. But it looked like poor Nan had no one. Well, no one but Hilda and Elsie. And now her. Milly decided she would knit Nan a blanket for Christmas. One in the brightest colour wools she could find. Something that would help to brighten up the dull, drab room.

She waited while Nan took a sip of water and then leaned towards her. 'Did you lose your separation allowance?' she asked.

To her consternation, Nan's bloodshot eyes filled with tears. 'I did,' she said. 'And now I ain't got no money.'

And she started to cry in earnest.

Elsie came over to join them. '*Of course* you're still getting your separation allowance, Nan, love,' she said. 'Why wouldn't you be? Even though your son's been killed – God bless his soul – your husband's still out there, ain't he? Don't you be worrying about that.'

Milly's hand shot to her chest. Poor, poor Nan. Her son dead. Her husband still at the front.

Was it any wonder the woman was in such a state?

Then she noticed Nan was struggling to speak.

'Police . . . so ashamed . . .' she croaked.

'What was that, Nan?' asked Elsie, suddenly alert.

Nan took another sip of water. 'The night I heard Sam had been killed, I were stopped by the police. And, well, it all kicked off then.'

'What happened, Nan?' asked Hilda.

Nan buried her head into rough, work-sore hands. 'The bobby asked what I were doing out all by meself at that time of night,' she said. 'Accused me of being out on the game, he did. And I couldn't help meself! I hitched me skirts up, flashed me drawers, and told 'im there weren't no one who wanted it, but maybe he'd like to be the first to 'ave a go.'

Despite the circumstances, Milly found herself swallowing a giggle and she could have sworn Hilda and Elsie's lips had twitched too. She just couldn't understand the woman in front of her saying something like that. It was, she reflected, absolutely devastating what grief did to people.

Suddenly she didn't feel like laughing at all.

'Oh, Gawd, Nan,' said Elsie. 'What happened, then?'

'Well, I ended up in the old nick, didn't I? They let me go without charge a few hours later and I thought that were that.

But then, a couple of days later, I got a letter saying they were stopping me separation allowance.'

'What?' exploded Hilda. 'They can't do that.'

'They did,' said Nan flatly. 'And it would have been all right if I hadn't then lost me job at the Home Depot. And now I ain't got nothing!'

Milly started with shock. She'd had no idea Nan used to work at the Home Depot.

'I work there too, Nan,' she said.

Nan fixed her pale blue eyes on Milly. 'You work there *now*,' she said. 'But don't you go getting too comfortable there, girl! All us women is on temporary contracts and they can get rid of you quick as they can click their fingers. You arrive late or you miss a day and you're out! Me son died and I was out, just like that! And now I've got no money to live on, me only child is dead and I wish I were dead as well.'

'Oh, Nan,' said Elsie. 'Don't talk like that. You've got to keep the home fires burning for Ted.'

'With what?' said Nan bleakly. 'I've got through all me savings, such as they were! I ain't got no money left.'

'Why didn't you tell anyone you'd lost your allowance?' asked Hilda. 'Why didn't you tell us?'

'I were ashamed,' wailed Nan. 'I deserve it! I deserve it all.'

Milly hadn't said anything – she was reeling.

Reeling from the fact Nan had worked at the Home Depot.

Reeling from the fact Nan had lost her job there.

Because that wasn't how Milly saw her job at the Army Post Office at all. Oh, she knew that every woman had a temporary contract – of course she did – and no one knew what would happen when the boys came back from the war. But surely things wouldn't go back to how they had been before and, in the meantime, if she kept her head down and did her best, surely her job was secure. Indeed, she *hadn't* always done her best – not recently, at least – and she'd got away with *that* without even a rap on the knuckles. And yet. And yet. Here was Nan, sacked after her only son had been killed.

That seemed positively heartless.

'You don't deserve it,' said Milly firmly. 'You was acting out of character because you was grieving.' She got up from the sofa and went over to the table. Picking up the letter she'd read earlier, she scanned it quickly. 'Listen to this,' she said. 'The police have been granted powers by the Home Secretary that can lead to discontinuance of the separation allowance . . . acting to relieve public concern that, without the restraining influence of their husbands, women will be out of control, leading to a rise in drunkenness and immorality . . . an incident on Alfred Street, Bow when an officer of the law was propositioned . . . Allowance will cease with immediate effect. Cecil Bell.'

Of course, a man had signed the letter, thought Milly. Of course, it was a man who was telling a woman she couldn't have something she was perfectly entitled to. It was enough to make your blood boil!

Hilda slammed down the pan. 'I've never heard of such a thing,' she said. 'I know the Soldiers' and Sailors' Families Association used to monitor how the allowances were being used, but I thought they'd stopped all that.'

'Have a look,' said Milly, passing her the letter.

Hilda waved it away. 'Wouldn't mean much to me,' she said. 'Reading and writing were never me strong points at school.'

'Mine neither,' said Elsie, passing Nan a cup of tea. 'But it sounds like the police have taken over where the Soldiers' and Sailors' Families Association left off. Bloody men. Is there to be no end to it?'

'Surely we can *do* something, though,' said Milly. 'Surely if we explain the reason Nan was drunk, they'll let her have her money back. Surely if they knew her son had just died . . .'

'You've more faith in the police than me, Milly,' said Elsie. 'But, maybe the ELFS Distress Bureau could help. They could write to this Cecil Bell, whoever he is.'

'*I* could write to this Cecil Bell,' said Milly. 'I write letters all the time at work . . . or at least, I did when I was in the returned letters department. We was always having to write to the War Office, checking up on this and that, and I know how it all works. Let me do it.' Suddenly Milly was all fired up, anxious to do her bit to make things better for Nan. Maybe it was the fact Nan had fallen foul of the same police station she had. Maybe it was because Nan had worked at the Home Depot and had – it seemed – been very unfairly treated by the Army Post Office. Maybe it was a combination of the two things but, whatever it was, there was no doubt the whole thing suddenly felt personal. 'May I take the letter, Nan?' she added.

Nan nodded. 'Be my guest,' she said. 'But I shouldn't think you'll get very far. I reckon once they've made up their mind, they've made up their mind . . .'

And she broke off in another paroxysm of coughing.

'Ask ELFS to get involved, Milly,' said Hilda. 'They'll know the best way to go about it. In the meantime, Nan, we'll look after you. Look, I've made you some dinner. It's only carrots and tatties and a tin of pressed meat, but get that down your gullet and you'll start feeling better in no time.'

'You've got enough food and coal to keep you going for a few days,' added Elsie. 'Don't let your fire go out again, and carry on sleeping in here like you are now. The bedroom will be freezing. We'll empty your chamber pot, bring you up some more water and get your neighbours to check in on you too. We'll come back in a couple of days. All will be well. You'll see.'

★

'Do you think she'll be all right?' said Milly as the three girls finally left, clattering down the stairs together.

'I hope so,' replied Hilda over her shoulder. 'I had no idea things were that bad. If we hadn't turned up when we did, Lord only knows what would have happened.'

'Isn't anyone else helping?' asked Milly. 'Her family? ELFS?'

'Her family are all down Eastbourne way,' said Hilda. 'And she left ELFS a couple of months ago. She fell out with a couple of people and I think it were all getting a bit much for her. Me ma's friend Val had been visiting her, but she's hurt her leg and can't get up the stairs no more. It were Val who told us Nan were getting into a bad way and asked us to start checking in on her, but we had no idea she were getting this bad.'

'Where were her neighbours, that's what I want to know?' added Elsie. 'Poor Nan, all on her own.'

'The woman next door said she hadn't seen her for a couple of days and assumed she'd gone to her sister,' said Hilda. 'She were really sheepish when I knocked on her door, and she promised she would look in from now on.'

'Do you think we should write to the sister, just in case?' asked Milly. They had reached the courtyard now and Milly kept a sharp eye out for the man who had shouted to her earlier, but he was nowhere to be seen.

'Let's keep an eye on Nan and make a decision in a few days,' said Elsie. 'If her cough clears up and her money starts coming back through, she should be all right.'

'Yes,' said Hilda. 'Let's visit her again on Wednesday and have a drink in the pub afterwards. Are you sure about looking into the separation allowance thing, Milly? One of us could do it, if not.'

'I'll do it,' said Milly. 'And I'll come along on Wednesday, an' all.'

And she meant it.

★

'Well, first I went to the ELFS meeting,' said Milly, and Ma nodded. Ma had little interest in ELFS herself – 'not enough time, not enough energy' – but she was happy with Milly going as long she stayed on the right side of the law.

'I remembered it were your suffragette night,' she said. 'Did it go on this late?'

Milly paused. She didn't want to lie to her mother. But surely not mentioning she'd been to the police station didn't count as lying. After all, Ma didn't know she'd been attacked in the first place.

And there was no point in upsetting her.

Milly took a deep breath. 'After the meeting, we went to visit one of the members who's fallen on hard times,' she said. 'She's lost her job, her husband is at the front and her only son's been killed.'

Ma shuddered. 'The poor soul,' she said.

'I know,' said Milly. 'And the worst thing is that she used to work at the Home Depot and they sent her packing. Her son had died, Ma! How could they be so awful? I thought they were better than that and I hate them all for doing that to her! I hate them!'

Ma patted her hand. 'Don't go getting so upset on behalf of someone you don't know, love,' she said. 'It won't help anyone, least of all yourself. And I dare say the Army Post Office is no worse than anywhere else. These places are run by men; there's no place for sentiment and don't you be forgetting that. Just do your work and take the money because it's good money and it won't last for ever.'

Milly sighed. Maybe Ma was right. The Home Depot was just an extraordinary job in extraordinary times.

She turned back to Ma. 'To make things even worse for this poor woman, she got a bit disorderly after her son died and the police have taken away her separation allowance. She's nothing – *nothing* – to live on.'

'Oh, Milly,' said Ma with feeling. 'Never ever rely on a man. They bring nothing but misery.'

'I don't ever intend to,' said Milly. 'But I am going to do all I can to get Nan's separation allowance back to her. I don't care if I have to write a hundred letters. She's entitled to that money and I'm to make sure she has it.'

'My lovely, clever girl,' said Ma, pulling Milly close and kissing the top of her head. 'That's the way it's done. But don't do it all by yourself. We women are stronger together.'

# 9

The next morning, Milly sat on the Tube to work, mentally composing the letter to Chief Inspector Bell. It was far and away the most important letter she'd ever written, and she had to get it absolutely right. She knew the facts but the tone was, of course, crucial too, and she wasn't sure which way to go. Should the letter be indignant? That, at least, was her natural inclination. Should it be conciliatory? That wasn't her natural inclination at all, but perhaps it would be wiser. Or maybe it should be very matter of fact – no emotion at all.

Oh, why was it all so *difficult*?

Milly wondered if she should ask Liza and Nora for help. They'd be good at this; she knew they would. They'd know all the right sort of things to write, all the long words to impress. And Nora might even be able to give her a couple of names to throw in – names that would make even Chief Inspector Cecil Bell sit up and take notice.

But, on the other hand – *no*.

Liza and Nora wouldn't understand. They might say they did, but they wouldn't. Not really. Oh, Nora might moan about how awful it was that her father wanted her to settle down with the first suitable chinless wonder that crossed her path – but that wasn't exactly in Nan's league of suffering, was it? And Liza had been distraught a few months earlier when her family had thrown her out for lying to them and taking the job at the Home Depot behind their backs. But

Liza had a sister who lived down the road and who had taken her in – and Milly knew Liza's parents would never have let her sleep in the gutter. Or even in a freezing tenement like Nan's. Neither girl would understand. They wouldn't understand that men in power could take away your separation allowance simply because you'd done something daft when you were beside yourself with grief – and that this simple act could leave you without enough money to feed yourself and keep yourself warm. And they wouldn't understand that if you were assaulted, the police could simply dismiss the case – and dismiss you too. As if you didn't matter . . .

No, she wasn't going to ask Liza and Nora for anything.

What about ELFS? Hilda and Elsie had made a point of telling her to ask the organisation for help – and even Ma had warned her not to strike out on her own. And, after all, the Distress Bureau had been set up for exactly this eventuality.

But that would take time – too much time.

She would have to wait until the next meeting and get referred to the relevant people. And Nan needed help *now*. There was no time to mess around. It would be much quicker and much simpler if Milly did it herself.

It wasn't until she was almost at Portland Road Station that Milly suddenly realised she had been barking up the wrong tree. She shouldn't write to Chief Inspector Cecil Bell at all! No, she should present herself at the Bow Street Police Station and ask to see him in person. That was the right thing to do – of course it was. For one thing, it would be much quicker than writing a letter and waiting for a reply – to say nothing of the possibility the letter could go astray. And, once she was sitting opposite Chief Inspector Bell, she'd be able to be much more persuasive than in a letter – and a little charm might not go amiss. Milly would be able to explain exactly why Nan had been behaving as she had, and why the decision to remove her separation allowance had been so wrong. (Not, of course, that *any* woman should have her allowance removed because of how she chose to behave – but that was an argument for another time.) Milly would lay out the facts simply and clearly, and hopefully Chief Inspector Bell would be able to make a decision there and then.

Yes. Definitely the right thing to do.

She would go there tomorrow. With any luck, Nan's money would be reinstated immediately and all would be well.

'How's the new key-list working out?'

Jack fell into step with Milly as she was returning to her station after her break.

Milly turned to him with a smile. 'Oh, it's marvellous, thank you,' she said. 'It's made things so much quicker and easier.' Her face fell. 'Or at least it would have done if Miss Parker hadn't reassigned me last week. I've got the Western Front now and I've got to start all over again.'

'Oh, rotten luck!' said Jack. 'I wonder why she moved you.'

Milly gave a rueful shrug. 'I don't think Team Incomparable appreciated my views on female emancipation,' she said.

Jack gave a low whistle. 'You're a braver lady than me,' he said. He hesitated for a moment and then said, 'Fancy a turn around the park at lunchtime? I hear there's a stall selling rather good meat pies over by the lake.'

It was Milly's turn to pause. She had planned to quickly grab something and then spend the rest of her lunch hour pulling together a modified key-list for her new section. But . . . to hell with that! Yesterday's events had made her realise the Home Depot didn't deserve any extra effort on her part. If they could dismiss staff like Nan so blithely and so callously, why on earth should she give up her lunch hour in a bid to work more efficiently?

And a turn around the park might be fun. Even though she had every reason to be wary of soldiers, she instinctively trusted

Jack. She liked him too. He was warm and friendly and funny – and really rather handsome. His patch somehow only added to his devil-may-care look. Besides, the newspapers were full of how returning soldiers resented the women who had taken 'their' jobs, but Jack didn't seem like that at all. Maybe it was because they were still urgently trying to recruit to cope with the Christmas rush – and so no one was actually taking anybody's job. Either way, there didn't seem to be any edge to him at all.

'That would be lovely,' she said lightly.

The rest of the morning skipped by, and at one o'clock, Milly met Jack by the perimeter gate.

'This might warm us up, an' all,' she said, by way of greeting.

It was a clear November day and, while it was cold, it actually wasn't much worse outside than in. In fact, over the past couple of weeks, the Home Depot had become distinctly chilly – all those bodies inside doing little to warm up what was essentially a cavernous, uninsulated barn. Goodness knew what the King and Queen were going to think about it when they made their – as yet unannounced – visit. She couldn't help thinking the powers-that-be might find some way to warm it up *then*.

Jack laughed. 'Let's pray for a mild winter,' he said. 'This place is going to be hell if we have a really cold snap.'

'I'm already bringing in an extra woolly to work,' said Milly. 'In fact, I'm thinking of setting up a stall outside.'

'I'm not sure they'll suit me,' quipped Jack, and the two laughed easily as they set off across the Regent's Park.

'Do you mind if I ask about your eye?' asked Milly.

She had been tempted to ask ever since she'd met him. After all, there weren't many people – even soldiers – who wore a black patch. But, as soon as the words were out, she could have bitten her tongue. Was that terribly impertinent? It was certainly none of her business!

Her and her big mouth.

But, to her relief, Jack didn't look the slightest bit put out. 'Ah, you mean my Blighty wound?' he replied cheerfully. 'Bit of German metal – straight in the eye.'

'I'm sorry,' said Milly. She'd suspected something along those lines. 'Doesn't it work anymore?'

'Doesn't it work?' echoed Jack with a lopsided grin. 'It isn't there!'

Milly wasn't sure how to reply. 'Then . . . what's . . . I mean?'

'What's there, instead?' asked Jack and, when Milly nodded, he added, 'Would you like to see?'

'Well . . . I . . . yes, please.'

Jack stopped walking. He turned to face Milly, and, very matter-of-factly – no shyness, no dramatic 'ta-da'– lifted his patch. Milly steeled herself not to flinch or turn away, but it was . . . nothing really. No gaping wound. No hideous mutilation. Just a closed eyelid and some scarring, already turning to silver.

Milly exhaled noisily, not realising she'd been holding her breath.

'Surgeon did a marvellous job,' said Jack. 'Of course, it's been a few months now.'

'What happened?' asked Milly, resisting the temptation to reach out and smooth the slightly puckered skin.

'Booby trap in an abandoned German trench,' said Jack. He was staring into the middle distance over Milly's shoulder. 'Our job was to make the damn things safe. Trouble was, no sooner had we learned to stabilise one type, than Jerry would change or add parts. It was a bloody game of cat and mouse, and it usually felt like we were losing. In this case, the thing went off before we had a chance to disarm it and the poor sap I was with was killed outright. I was lucky.'

'I'm so sorry,' said Milly. She was saying 'sorry' so often, she was beginning to feel like one of those stuck gramophone records. 'Is it a dreadful nuisance?'

What a thing to say, she thought. How could it *not* be a nuisance only having one eye?

'Let's just say I wouldn't trust myself to defuse a bomb anymore,' said Jack. He replaced his patch and the two carried on strolling slowly across the park. 'But I can still have a stab at most things. And at least I can still take pictures. I'd be lost without my photography.'

'Photography?' echoed Milly. How terribly exotic. She didn't know anyone who took pictures as a hobby. Photography was something people did for a living – plastering your picture all over the papers when you least wanted or expected it. 'What kind of photography?'

'Anything, really,' said Jack. 'People, mainly. In fact, I'd love to bring my camera into work sometime. I'd take pictures of people on the Tube if they'd let me – everyone always looks so miserable – and then I could get some inside the Depot. Maybe you'd let me take some of you too.'

'Fancy!' said Milly, giving a little twirl. 'But wouldn't all that equipment be a bit heavy on the Tube? And surely it'd hardly be practical to set up a tripod with all those people coming and going.'

Jack started laughing. 'Things have moved on a bit from Victorian times,' he said. 'Cameras are really small and portable nowadays. Or, at least, they can be. The Kodak I've got is nicknamed the "soldier's camera" because so many boys brought them out to the front. Oh, the tales they tell . . .'

'Was it really awful?' Milly asked.

Somehow, she had to ask.

Had to *know*.

There was a long pause, and Milly assumed Jack either wasn't going to answer or was going to come out with some platitude. But then he simply nodded and said, 'Hell.' He shook his head and then continued. 'It was almost – *almost* – worth losing an eye to come home. At least I *came* home.

That's all I'm going to say about it and I am never, ever going to mention it to you again. Now . . . lunch!'

They were nearly at the boating lake. A series of jaunty little stalls had been set up along the path, and the smell of roasting chestnuts drifted delightfully over to them. There was a pie stall, another selling toffee apples . . . and it was all so festive and happy and *unwarlike* that Milly clapped her hands together in glee. She had needed this, she realised. After the stress and misery of the police station and then Nan's last night, she really needed a bit of fun and frivolity.

Minutes later, she and Jack were sitting on a bench over-looking the lake, tucking into slices of flaky beef pie.

'Not frozen yet,' said Milly, nodding at the lake. She wasn't sure why but she didn't care for silence just then.

'Thank goodness for small mercies,' Jack said, nodding solemnly. 'At least we won't be treated to the lovely Eloise doing her twirls just yet.'

Milly burst out laughing in a most unladylike fashion. Even though she'd had Eloise in mind when she made her comment, she hadn't expected Jack to pick up on it and certainly not so marvellously.

She was still laughing loudly and with gay abandon when a voice behind her said, 'Hello, Milly.'

Milly swung around. It was Liza, arm in arm with James. Milly hadn't seen James since the dance in Woodhampstead a couple of weeks ago – she hadn't even realised he was back in London. Milly wondered where he was living. Was he still in the hostel on Gloucester Gate reserved for staff from the Home Depot, or had he lost that too? She felt a twinge of guilt for not having asked Liza.

'Hello,' she said. 'And hello, James. Good to see you back.'

'Thank you,' said James. 'Despite everything, it's good to be back in London. At least, I think it is!'

Milly laughed. She'd always liked James. There were many

who gave him a wide berth because he was vehemently opposed to the war, had no intention of ever signing up and didn't care who knew it. But none of that fazed Milly. After all, she was ambivalent about the war herself and she had had many congenial ciggies in the extension with James, putting the world to rights.

'Are you back living here?' asked Milly. James had stayed with Liza's family in Woodhampstead after being injured in the extension fire.

'I am,' said James. 'I'm allowed back in the Gloucester Gate hostel – even if I'm not allowed back in the Home Depot. I've spent the morning reading to the blind soldiers at St Dunstan's. Poor buggers! Yet another reason to avoid signing up at all costs.'

Jack, who had remained seated with his back to the little party, chose that moment to stand up and turn around. There was a sudden awkward pause as James and Liza took in both his soldier's khaki and his eyepatch. Their gazes returned to Milly, and the silence stretched until it threatened to become awkward.

Oh, Lordy! They were obviously waiting to be introduced.

'Sorry,' said Milly. No one bothered with things like that in Bow and it was sometimes difficult to remember the 'rules' were different here. 'This is Jack Archer, who works in the Mediterranean sorting section and who's been a great help showing me the ropes. Jack, these are my friends – Liza Healey, who's a supervisor in the broken parcels department, and James Blackford who – er – was a supervisor in the honour letter department.'

There was a brief flurry of hellos and how-do-you-dos.

'How long have you been stationed at the Home Depot, Private Archer?' asked Liza. There were two high spots of colour in her cheeks: justifiable embarrassment, presumably, at what James had just said.

'A couple of months,' said Jack, politely enough. He wiped some stray pastry crumbs from the side of his mouth with an immaculate, white hanky and then asked, 'You?'

'The girls are very proud they've been here since June,' said James. 'They never tire of telling me they were part of the advance guard.'

'Well, in June, my Blighty wound was still being patched up,' said Jack.

'You were injured at the front?' asked Liza, and Jack nodded. 'I'm so sorry,' Liza added.

'Ah, well,' said Jack lightly. 'We've all got to do our bit for King and Country.'

There was the tiniest edge to his voice and the merest flicker of a glance towards James. Milly noticed James's eyes narrow slightly in response. Nothing more was said – nothing needed to be – and, after a little inconsequential chit-chat, Liza and James set off back towards the Home Depot.

'Oh, Milly,' said Liza, over her shoulder. 'I've signed you up for the Christmas party planning meeting. Tomorrow lunchtime . . .'

And they were gone.

Jack grinned at Milly. 'Quite the little joiner-in, aren't you?' he said. 'I would never have guessed it.'

Milly paused. Should she tell him the only reason she was getting involved with the party was because she had insider information the royal family was attending? No. Best not. It was one thing telling her family; it was quite another to tell someone who actually worked at the Home Depot.

Instead, she dipped a little curtsey and said demurely, 'Just trying to do my bit, sir.'

Jack rewarded her with a bark of laughter. 'I'm pleased to hear it,' he said. 'It's time we were heading back too,' he added, holding out his arm.

Milly linked her arm in his. Should she mention what had

just happened with Liza and James? What it *meant*? Because she liked Liza and she liked James but, boy, that situation had been awkward . . .

'Damn, those pies were good,' said Jack, before she'd decided whether to say anything. 'Definitely worth walking across the park for.'

'They ain't as good as the ones up the Roman,' replied Milly lightly. 'You can't beat an East-End pie. But, even so, they weren't bad.'

'Agreed,' said Jack. 'Pies from the Roman Road are the undisputed gold standard. But I'd say today's were a definite A minus.'

Milly turned to him in surprise. 'You know the Roman?' she said.

Somehow, she had imagined Jack would know as little about the East End – let alone Bow – as Nora and Liza.

'Yes,' said Jack. 'I live in Hackney and I have been known to walk across Victoria Park just to get a slice of pie between meals.'

'Well, I never,' said Milly.

Hackney was a mere couple of miles north of where she lived. Even though it had some quite well-to-do parts, somehow Milly had imagined him living somewhere . . . different. Somewhere grander. Jack was a class above her – that much was obvious. But, if he lived in Hackney and walked across Victoria Park to the Roman, then, maybe, just maybe, he wasn't totally out of her league.

Milly! For shame!

It didn't matter where Jack lived. It didn't matter at all. He was just a friend from work; a nice man and good company during a lonely lunch hour.

Nothing more, nothing less.

And she definitely didn't need a sweetheart.

# 10

The next morning, Milly dressed with extra care.

At least that's what Nora and Liza would have said. For Milly, with a limited wardrobe at her disposal, it simply meant she put on the best of her three white blouses – the one with the mother-of-pearl buttons – and made sure her naturally unruly dark hair was twisted tightly into its bun with no messy tendrils springing free. She also dispensed with powder and blush – along with many of the girls, she was wearing it daily to work nowadays, although if Ma was around, she would tut and try to blot it off. But even Milly agreed it wouldn't give quite the right impression at the Bow Street Police Station. Anyone over the age of twenty-five still associated it with ladies of loose morals – and that wouldn't do at all.

For once, everyone had gone for the day well before Milly judged it was a good time for her to leave for the police station. She walked round the empty kitchen, plumping up cushions, wiping the table, enjoying the solitude and the silence. Milly was very rarely alone and she decided that it was strangely lovely. It was also the perfect opportunity to rehearse what she was going to say when she was in front of Chief Inspector Bell. After all, she only had one chance to impress the man, and she needed to get it right.

She stood and addressed a point right in the middle of the scullery door.

'Chief Inspector Bell,' she declared theatrically. 'I believe there has been a great miscarriage of justice.'

*No.* That wasn't right at all. There was no 'I believe' about it.

Nan was entitled to her money, and that was that. It was an open-and-shut case.

She tried again. 'Thank you for seeing me, Chief Inspector. I'm afraid there's been a great miscarriage of justice.'

Yes, that was better.

'Miss Amelia?'

Milly swung around, startled. Mr Wildermuth was standing in the doorway to the hall, looking startled. Milly had completely forgotten he would be home.

'Can I help you?' she said. 'Do you need to come through?'

'Not at all,' said Mr Wildermuth. 'But – are you in some kind of trouble?'

'What?' Oh, goodness. She'd been speaking out loud and she'd been overheard. How embarrassing. 'No, it's not about me. I'm helping . . . a friend.'

Mr Wildermuth didn't look particularly convinced. 'I see,' he said. 'But, er, Milly, if you ever are in any trouble, I hope you know you have a friend in me.'

That was so unexpected Milly almost burst out laughing. Mr Wildermuth was about the last person she would go to if she needed help. Not because of . . . well, anything really – he was a nice man – but it simply wouldn't cross her mind to confide in him. He was just there, lurking in the shadows. But it had been very kind of him to offer and, again, she found herself thinking he might do very well for Maggie.

'Thank you, all the same,' said Milly. 'But I really ain't in any trouble.'

Mr Wildermuth sidled closer into the room. 'I'm afraid you may be in a little trouble,' he admitted sheepishly.

Milly raised her eyebrows at him. 'Am I?' she said. 'Why's that?'

Mr Wildermuth gave a rueful smile. 'Your mother discovered I joined you for dinner the other night,' he said. 'It's fair to say she was most unhappy.'

'Oh dear.' Ma really did have the most ridiculously old-fashioned ideas sometimes. But, if she really *had* been that upset, why hadn't she mentioned it when they'd chatted a couple of nights before? 'I'm really sorry, Mr Wildermuth. I didn't mean to get you in trouble – I'd just wanted to thank you for bringing us the bread. And I promise it wasn't me that told tales on you to Ma.'

'No, no, I think it was one of the younger children. In any case, I would not encourage you to keep secrets from your mother and I'm only sorry I got you in trouble for accepting your invitation. It was – inappropriate – of me. Most pleasant but inappropriate, and I assure you, with regret, that it will not happen again.'

He gave her a formal little bow and disappeared without another word.

Milly sighed. If Maggie really had set her cap at him, it was all going to be more difficult than she might have hoped.

For the second time in almost as many days, Milly found herself standing in front of the duty sergeant at the Bow Street Police Station. To her dismay and consternation, it was the same sergeant who had been on duty on Monday evening. Didn't he ever get any time off? To make matters even worse, he clearly recognised Milly – right at the very moment that she recognised him.

Milly's heart dropped, but she tilted her chin and approached the counter with a confidence she didn't feel.

'I'd like to see Chief Inspector Bell,' she said firmly.

'Wouldn't we all?' drawled the duty sergeant. 'Got an appointment, have yer?'

'Well, no. Not as such,' admitted Milly. 'But I'd like to discuss this letter he sent to my – er – friend.'

She took the letter out of her bag and unfolded it on the counter that separated her from the duty sergeant. Hopefully, he would read it, realise its importance and summon Chief Inspector Bell immediately.

He didn't even look at it.

'Would you now?' he said, waggling his brows. 'Well, I'm afraid Chief Inspector Bell isn't here.'

'Not here today, or not here at all?' asked Milly, with her most beguiling smile. He must have a sympathetic and helpful side – she could turn this around.

The duty sergeant pointed to the ceiling. 'Chief Inspector Bell is upstairs – many floors upstairs – and is not to be disturbed by the likes of you. Not now. Not ever. Understand?'

Milly understood all too clearly.

But she couldn't give in. Not without a fight. But how on earth was she going to get him to change his mind? Realise the urgency of the situation?

'I do need to see Chief Inspector Bell, I'm afraid,' she persevered. 'My friend, Nan Reid, has had her separation allowance discontinued and it's essential that . . .'

'Oh dear. Another woman getting drunk and dropping her drawers in a public place?'

The duty sergeant crossed his arms over his chest and laughed down at her. This was clearly sport to him. And it was too much. Too, too much. Milly felt her cheeks growing hot and her hands curled into fists by her side.

'I was not drunk and I did not flash my drawers,' she hissed, her rage rising in waves.

'If you say so, love,' said the duty sergeant. 'But if your "friend" has lost her separation allowance, I'd hazard a guess she's done one or the other.'

Milly swallowed an urge to scream.

'The reason Mrs Reid acted out of character was that she'd discovered her son . . .'

The duty sergeant leaned across the counter until his face was very close to Milly's. 'I don't care,' he said. 'Scram!'

Milly could feel it all slipping away from her, although, to be honest, she knew the odds had been stacked against her since the beginning.

'What about if I make an appointment?' she asked, trying to keep a note of increasing desperation from her voice.

'Scram,' repeated the duty sergeant.

'Because you've taken away her separation allowance, she has nothing to live on,' cried Milly. 'Nothing. Don't you understand?'

'Plenty of jobs around for you women nowadays.'

'She's *poorly*,' said Milly. 'She has no one. What if it was your mother? Your sister?'

'Scram,' said the duty sergeant for the third time. This time there was a definite note of menace in his voice. 'Unless you want to be arrested for wasting police time, I suggest you leave. Right now!'

'No!'

The duty sergeant swung open the hinged counter and stepped through it. Taking Milly firmly by the upper arm, he frogmarched her down the front steps to the street.

'Count your lucky stars I'm in a good mood today,' he said, before disappearing back inside.

For the second time in as many days, Milly found herself on the pavement outside the police station shaking in rage and impotence, the sour taste of failure in her mouth.

It was all so bloody unfair. He hadn't taken her seriously. He hadn't even listened to what she had to say.

In fact, he'd written her off as soon as she'd walked through the door.

Milly was tempted to pick up the nearest thing to hand

and lob it through the police-station window. That would wipe the smirk off the duty sergeant's face. Unfortunately, it would also result in her being arrested and – even given the state she was in – Milly knew it simply wasn't worth the risk. Taking a deep breath, and with great effort, she turned and walked towards the Tube station.

Surely her day couldn't get any worse.

'You're late. Your shift started two hours ago.'

Her new supervisor was standing over Milly, hands on hips. Milly bit her lip as she thought of how best to reply. After all, it was nearly eleven o'clock and she was guilty as charged. Not that she'd tried to sneak in undetected, or to pretend she'd been in the whole time. She'd been upfront about it. And it was the first time she'd been late in a long, long while.

'I'm sorry. I've had an emergency.'

The supervisor looked unimpressed. 'What sort of emergency?' she said with a sniff.

'I had to go down the police station. It were . . .'

The supervisor held up a hand. 'On second thoughts, don't tell me,' she said. 'You're late and that's that. You're to stay after your shift today and make up the lost hours.'

Milly stared at the supervisor in dismay. She was, of course, fully prepared to make up the lost hours – it was, after all, much better than having her pay docked. But Miss Parker always let them make up lost time during breaks and at lunchtime, and, if Milly stayed after work today, she wouldn't be able to go round to Nan's with Elsie and Hilda as she had promised.

'Please, Miss,' she said. 'I have ever such an important appointment after work today.'

'Another trip to the police station?' The supervisor said this in a louder voice than strictly necessary and curious heads craned in their direction.

Milly shook her head, embarrassed. 'No, Miss,' she said.
'Then you're to stay for two hours after the others have
gone home. Is that clear?'

'Yes, Miss.'

What was left of the morning passed in a blur of anger, misery
and a counting down of the time until lunch. And, yes, even
though Milly had only been in work for a couple of hours, she
was damned well going to enjoy her break if she had to stay
after work. Every single minute of it. She'd go for a leisurely
stroll around the park, and have another slice of that delicious
pie. Maybe she'd even ask Jack to accompany her again . . .

And then she remembered she was expected at the inaugural
meeting of the Christmas party planning committee. That was
the last thing she felt like, but she could hardly back out now.
At least it would give her a chance to see Liza again after the
rather awkward encounter the day before . . .

The training was taking place in the same room Milly had
received her induction in all those months ago, and where
she had had her ill-fated training for the sorting floor with
Miss Rich. Liza and Nora were sitting together at the back
of the room – blonde heads together; thick as thieves – and
something about the little tableau brought Milly up short. On
their very first day, it had been her sitting next to Nora, and
Milly remembered watching Liza – with her solemn expression
and her no-nonsense blonde plait – nervously coming to sit
in front of them. Now, the roles had been reversed and she
wasn't sure she liked it.

Could Liza and Nora sense her discomfiture?

'Afternoon,' she said cheerfully, twisting round in her seat.

Liza and Nora both smiled and answered in kind. Was Milly
imagining it, or were their smiles somewhat strained? And
was she inventing the glance they gave each other? It was tiny
– a mere flicker – and it might not have been there at all.

The meeting was actually great fun.

This time, she wasn't having to impress either Sergeant Major Cunningham nor Miss Rich. Miss Parker, who was leading the meeting, was in relaxed and expansive mood, and made it clear that the women – and it was *all* women – who had volunteered to help with the party organisation were not on duty. There was even a plate of little pies and another of jammy buns to share in lieu of lunch. Miss Langham talked a little about the 'dignitaries' who would be attending, and the presentations and speeches that would start the party off. Milly was amused by how impatient people seemed by this part of the proceedings, obviously assuming the 'dignitaries' would be insufferably dull. If only everyone knew it was actually the King, Queen and Princess Mary – that would wipe the bored looks off their faces. How she wanted to exchange glances with Nora and Liza.

But she couldn't. She *wouldn't*. She could sense the unfriendliness oozing from them.

Milly stayed determinedly looking forward with a neutral expression on her face, and dutifully volunteered to help head up the decorating sub-committee with Nora and Liza. Most of her spare time in the next few weeks would be spent making paper chains and bunting – but at least she could do it with her friends.

At the end of the meeting, Nora and Liza seemed in no hurry to leave and Milly waited with them as everyone else filed out.

'Aren't we going?' asked Milly eventually.

This time, the two girls definitely *did* exchange a glance.

'Nora's been waiting to tell me something,' said Liza awkwardly.

'Oh,' said Milly, suddenly hurt. What could Nora possibly want to tell Liza and why couldn't she hear it too? 'Well, don't mind me. I'll be off then.'

As soon as she'd uttered the words – and rather huffily at that – Milly could have kicked herself. It would be something about Liza's brother. Maybe Ned had asked Nora not to write to him after all, or maybe he already had a sweetheart, or . . . Well, there were a thousand and one possibilities. But, if that was the case, wouldn't it be better for Nora to confide in Milly? After all, it would stretch Liza's loyalties to have Nora crying on her shoulder . . .

'Look, I'm very happy to tell *both* of you my news,' said Nora calmly.

'Have you spent another evening with your ear pressed to the library door?' asked Milly with a grin.

'No,' said Nora with a ghost of a smile. 'But you're not far off the mark. After all, can I help it if Daddy and Major Benham choose to take a stroll in the evening air without checking if I'm reading on the window seat directly above them?'

'Ooh. And what did they say?' said Milly. 'Is the Prime Minister coming along to the Christmas party an' all? Clara Butt? The Pope?'

'Shh, Milly,' said Liza crossly. 'Let Nora *speak*.'

Liza was upset, Milly realised. She was upset because of the dig Jack had made at James the day before. Still, there was nothing Milly could do about that – and, anyway, Jack had had a point. James *had* boasted about not signing up for the war effort within earshot of a man who had lost an eye fighting for his country.

'No, it's nothing like that,' Nora was saying. 'This is much more serious.'

'Bad news?' asked Liza, eyes widening. 'About the war?'

'I'm afraid so,' said Nora. She leaned forward and put her fingers to her lips. 'Now, this really is secret and, of course, it might not be true. But I heard Uncle Alf tell Daddy that compulsory conscription is coming in very soon.'

Milly gasped. Oh, there had been rumours. The papers had been full of how it was proving impossible to recruit enough volunteers. So, people had almost expected it. But certainly not so soon!

Of course, it didn't really affect Milly. She didn't have a father, a brother, a sweetheart to be called up. And once more men were away fighting, surely there would be more opportunities for women. When Nan was better, she'd be able to pick and choose where she worked, and that must be a good thing.

But, oh, all those poor men – dragged off to war and an uncertain future against their will. Their lives on hold; their lives at *risk*. It didn't bear thinking about . . .

Liza had sat back abruptly, skin drained of colour, hand to her heart.

'No!' she said, eyes filling with tears. 'When? *Who?*'

Nora sighed. 'I'm really sorry, Liza,' she said. 'Of course, I might be wrong . . .'

'Tell me!' demanded Liza.

'They mentioned January next year. Compulsory military service for single men between eighteen to forty. There are exemptions. Ministers of a religion—'

'So soon,' interrupted Liza, making no effort to stem the solitary tear running down her cheek and into her mouth. It left a pale pink track in the film of beige dust covering all their faces. 'Poor James. Poor all of them.'

Poor James, indeed. He was so opposed to the war, had resolutely refused to sign up and was adamant he would never be put into a position where he had to kill anyone of any nationality. And now it looked like he would have to go after all.

Nora put her hand over Liza's. 'I'm so sorry,' she said. 'It's really not fair.'

Liza shook her head. 'Not your fault,' she said, finally

smearing her cheek with the back of her hand. 'There are many who will say he should go, and a few months ago I would have been one of them. After all, my twin's already out there – and he doesn't want to be, either. But now, I don't know, I feel differently. And partly, of course, it's because it's James – but mainly because we now know just how perfectly beastly this war is. It wasn't over by last Christmas, it won't be over by this one and, who knows, it might not be over by next year, either.'

'Don't think like that,' said Nora. 'We none of us know what will happen.'

'They're still opening up new fronts,' said Liza. 'The one in Salonika, for example, that no one seems to know anything about. And they're always adding yet more extensions to this place. They obviously don't think it's going to finish any time soon.'

'One last push?' suggested Nora. But there was no conviction to her tone.

Nora's head was so close to Liza's – almost touching it – and Milly suddenly felt a stab of jealousy. How she wished she didn't feel edged out all the time. How she wished she could make her friends laugh like she used to.

Well, maybe she could.

'There's one thing for it, then,' she said, clapping her hands lightly together.

The heads parted. Two pairs of blue eyes turned and looked at her.

'What?' they said in unison.

'You'll just have to marry James!'

She held her breath, waited for the peals of laughter; the playful slaps.

Liza's brow furrowed and her eyes became hard as steel. 'That's not funny,' she said coldly. 'How can you joke about something so serious?'

Nora nodded and her hand reached for Liza's again. 'I *knew* I shouldn't have told Milly,' she said. 'I'm so sorry. I should have waited. Told you on your own.'

Her voice wasn't angry. It was disappointed, and somehow that was even worse.

Milly looked from one to the other in bewilderment. All right, maybe her joke hadn't been that funny but surely it hadn't been that bad, either.

Perhaps now wasn't the time to suggest James became a man of the cloth.

Liza and Nora were still staring disapprovingly at her when Miss Parker swept back into the room.

'Oh good, you're still here,' she said, striding purposefully up to Milly and putting a hand on her shoulder. 'Might I have a quick word?'

Liza and Nora gathered up their belongings and were gone in two shakes of a lamb's tail. Milly had the distinct impression they were relieved to take their leave of her.

That hadn't exactly gone to plan.

Wearily, she turned to Miss Parker. 'Of course,' she said.

'I wanted to check you were all right?'

Milly wrinkled her nose in confusion. 'Yes, Miss,' she said. 'Quite all right, Miss.'

Tired, fed up and apparently friendless . . . but otherwise quite marvellous!

'Ah. Good. It was just your new supervisor mentioned you'd had to go to a police station this morning and I wanted to check you weren't in some sort of trouble. Because, if you are, I hope you feel you could come to me . . .'

For goodness' sake!

Miss Parker was the third person since the evening before who'd asked Milly if she'd got herself into some kind of trouble. Why did everyone always have to assume – expect – the worst? Why did it never cross their minds she might be trying to help somebody; that she was trying to do her bit, to do some good in the world?

Why did no one believe in her?

In other circumstances Milly might have chosen to confide in Miss Parker, even to ask for her advice on how best to reach out to Chief Inspector Bell. But not now. Not after what Miss Parker had just said. And especially not now she knew Miss Parker was part of the problem. After all, even if Miss Parker hadn't made the decision to sack Nan herself, she must have signed off the paperwork. She must have known she was sacking a woman who'd just lost her only son. And, as far as Milly was concerned, that changed *everything*.

She smiled blandly at Miss Parker and said, 'Thank you, Miss.'

And then she left the room.

She would keep everything to herself and sort it out on her own. One East-End lady helping another.

And to hell with the rest.

By the time Milly finally left the Home Depot after her extended shift, she was exhausted. What a day she had had! Nothing was going her way – absolutely nothing – and now she'd missed meeting Elsie and Hilda round at Nan's. She wasn't altogether sure what to do about that. She really liked both girls and – even if there was a smidgen of relief about not having to admit her failure at the police station that morning – for the most part, she just felt terrible she hadn't shown up.

Once on the Tube, Milly picked up a discarded copy of *The Day*. She started flicking through it disconsolately, and then stopped with a jolt. As coincidence would have it, there was another opinion piece from Ted Wilmington – the editor and columnist who had written about the reputation of the Home Depot being on borrowed time. And that day's offering was . . . in praise of stopping the separation allowance to women who didn't toe the line! In Mr Wilmington's 'humble' opinion, the job should have remained with the Soldiers' and Sailors' Families Association – but as long as someone kept a firm grip on badly behaved women, that was fine by him.

Milly threw the newspaper to one side with disgust, earning herself a disapproving look from the middle-aged man to her left. Milly ignored him. It was all one more thing to be furious about and she had had her fill of *those* today.

Oh, she couldn't just slink home! She had to try to turn the day around.

She needed to at least make an effort to meet up with Hilda and Elsie, and to explain what had happened. The trouble was, she had no idea where they'd be. Chances were they would already have left Nan's. She thought one of them had mentioned a quick drink afterwards, but whether that was still the plan, she couldn't be sure. And, of course, it was possible they would go round to her house to check where she had got to . . .

By the time the Tube arrived at her stop, Milly had made a decision. She'd go straight to the pub they'd all gone to last time and, if Hilda and Elsie weren't there, she'd walk to Nan's flat in the hope of intercepting them.

Yes, that was exactly what she would do.

The Nag's Head was empty.

To be more precise, it wasn't empty of people – in fact, it was packed to the rafters with men – but it was certainly empty of her friends. Worse still, Hilda and Elsie's uncle wasn't behind the bar and Milly's entrance prompted a great deal of unwelcome male attention. She beat a hasty retreat, accompanied by a chorus of wolf whistles and catcalls.

Damn men. Damn the ruddy lot of them!

Right, now for Nan's.

''Ello, love!'

A soldier was weaving down the street towards Milly. This time, there was absolutely no doubt – it was the soldier who had attacked her. Same gait. Same build. Same – forgotten – slight country burr.

Milly shrank back against the building, heart going nineteen to the dozen.

Stay calm.

You're outside a pub and, even though the street lamps are off, there's plenty of moonlight.

Just stay calm.

The soldier stopped a few yards from Milly and stood there swaying gently from side to side.

'Back for more, love?' he leered. 'Ready to finish off what we started last time?'

Rage jostled with fear in Milly's chest. 'Stay away from me,' she warned. 'If you take one step towards me, I'll scream as loudly as I can and everyone will come running. They'll call the police. You'll see.'

The soldier chuckled. 'The police didn't seem too bothered last time, did they?'

Instinctively Milly knew the soldier was just provoking her – that he didn't have any intention of coming any closer, of trying anything on. Somehow, though, his casual taunts were almost as bad and, for the second time that day, Milly battled the strong desire to throw something – anything – with all her might.

To do something that made her feel more in control.

To make her feel that she *mattered*.

Then, to her exquisite relief, she saw Hilda and Elsie walking down the street towards her.

It was all Milly could do to stop herself running and flinging herself into their arms. But she mustn't. She really mustn't. That would show fear and an awful loss of dignity – and, really, dignity was the only thing she had left. So, she raised a rather shaky hand instead.

'Evening, ladies,' she called cheerily as if she had planned to meet Hilda and Elsie outside the pub all along.

The soldier glanced over his shoulder. Seeing the two women approaching, he touched his hat, echoed Milly's greeting – 'Evening, ladies' – and walked away smartly in the opposite direction. A couple of seconds later, he'd been swallowed up by the shadows.

Hilda and Elsie rushed to Milly's side.

'Was that him?' asked Elsie.

'That were him, weren't it?' said Hilda, before Milly could answer.

Milly nodded mutely. For all her desire to remain calm and dignified, she could feel tears welling up. 'He said . . . he said . . .' she began, and suddenly she couldn't continue because she was crying – huge heaving sobs that bubbled free from deep inside her and set her shoulders shaking.

'Oh, Milly,' said Hilda. 'Come on, let's get in the pub and you can tell us all about it.'

'No,' said Milly vehemently, dashing tears from her eyes. 'They're the same in there. I went in looking for you two and they all whistled and shouted at me. I ain't never going in there again.'

'Oh, Milly,' said Elsie this time. 'Did you go into the public bar?'

Milly nodded. 'I think so,' she said in a small voice. 'I was . . . confused.'

'We'll be right as rain in the saloon,' said Elsie. 'Besides, if our uncle is working tonight, he'll make sure we're not bothered. You'll see.'

Milly hesitated, but then allowed herself to be coaxed and cajoled into the virtually empty saloon bar and settled into a comfy seat by the fire. A brandy was pressed into her hand as Milly told the two girls about her dreadful day. Her decision to go to the Bow Street Police Station in person; her awful second encounter with the duty sergeant; her argument with Liza and Nora; being made to stay late after her shift; and, finally, bumping into the soldier who'd assaulted her.

It did all sound pretty terrible as she said it out loud.

'Oh, Milly, what an awful day,' said Elsie sympathetically. 'Still, there's nothing that can't be turned around. You can still get ELFS' Distress Bureau to campaign for Nan's separation allowance. I'll contact them if you like.'

Milly shook her head. 'No, I'll do it,' she said. 'I said I would.'

'I'm sure you'll make up with your friends at work,' added Hilda. 'And even though you didn't make it round to Nan's, we did and we can still have a nice evening now. Nothing's been lost.'

Milly gave her friends a weak smile. 'I suppose so,' she said. 'How is Nan?'

How dreadful she hadn't asked yet. So preoccupied with her own petty problems . . .

Elsie made a face. 'I think she's all right,' she said. 'She's got food and water and fuel. But her cough ain't getting any better and she seems awful weak. And, of course, she's worried sick about having nothing to live on. In fact, maybe it were better you weren't there today; it might've made her feel worse knowing what that beastly duty sergeant said.'

Milly looked down at her drink.

It was all her fault.

One drink turned into two and, after about an hour, Milly realised she was well on the way to being properly drunk. But, instead of feeling all gentle and swirly in an altogether not unpleasant way, she could feel her rage rising in waves. At first, she managed to keep it in and to answer all Elsie and Hilda's questions about the Home Depot. They looked on the edge of their seats as she told them about the adventures she had had with Nora and Liza. Like the time she'd accidentally returned a letter to Liza's sister before the official telegram telling her her husband had been killed in action had been dispatched. What a traumatic day that had been! Liza had had to rush home in a fearful hurry and had only managed to intercept the letter at the very last moment. Then there was the fire, and how the whole Home Depot had nearly gone up in smoke. Hilda and Elsie had remembered reading about that in the papers. And then – the final *pièce de résistance* – she told them all about the imminent visit from the King and Queen and Princess Mary, and the big party that was being thrown in their honour. It hadn't been made official yet – and she knew Nora had asked her not to say anything – but, really, what harm could it do? And the look on Hilda and Elsie's faces . . .

But her rage didn't go away. It was all too much.

'Oh, how I wish we could actually *do* something,' she burst out finally.

'Do something?' echoed Hilda, looking confused. 'Do something about what? I thought we were talking about the Home Depot.'

'About *men*, of course,' said Milly. 'It don't matter what we were talking about, all I can think about is blinkin' men. Men taking away the separation allowance, men assaulting you in alleyways, men calling you slags, men telling you what you can and can't do . . .'

Elsie swirled the amber liquid in her glass. 'Don't get me started,' she said. 'What's happened to Nan makes my blood boil, but it ain't just her, is it? We've all got our own stories about what men have done to us. Like our ma. She were arrested for soliciting last year; she were innocent but no one believed her and she were sentenced to nine months' hard labour and she died. They said her heart just gave out.'

Milly was shocked. 'I'm so sorry,' she said. 'I had no idea!'

Elsie nodded and drained her glass. 'At Ma's funeral, I promised I would fight to make things better for women,' she said. 'And I really meant it. The trouble is, with everyone's eyes on the war and ELFS putting things on hold, things are getting worse, not better.'

She trailed off, suddenly sounding completely sober.

Hilda sighed deeply. 'I've got my own sorry story,' she said. 'Like you, I were assaulted, Milly. My attack were a year ago but, unlike you, it were by the man who'd been courting me. I thought he loved me an' all. But when I reported it, the police didn't even take my statement. Just called me a slag and sent me on my way. He'd broken my nose, Milly. Broken my nose.'

'Oh goodness. That's terrible,' said Milly.

Somehow it made it even worse when it wasn't a stranger.

'It is terrible,' said Elsie. 'But we ain't nothing special. Every woman's got her own story. You must have your own, Milly.'

Milly paused, remembering her father. Pa, who was lovely and funny and kind, until he'd had a drink . . .

Pa attacking Ma after he'd got back from the pub. The muffled screams which seemed to cut through Milly . . . Running, shouting, into her parents' bedroom . . . The backhander sending her spinning across the floor . . .

The little scenario had played itself out time and time again. Her brother and sisters hadn't got involved; they'd pretended to be asleep, that they couldn't hear. But Milly wouldn't do that. She *couldn't*. And then, Pa had been killed – knocked down by an automobile outside the pub – and, oh, the mix of emotions.

Shock. Grief. Relief.

*Relief.*

But she wasn't ready to share all that. Not now. Maybe never.

'Yes, I've got my own story,' she said, nodding at her new friends. 'We all have. And there must be something we can do about it!'

'I feel the same way, but what on earth can we do?' said Elsie gloomily. 'Everything's stacked against us.'

'There must be *something*. We could . . . write a letter to the newspapers,' said Milly, thinking it through. 'Yes, we could write a letter to Ted Wilmington at *The Day* for starters. He's just written an article in favour of taking the separation allowance away from "badly behaved" women. Why don't we write to him and explain what doing that actually means? Tell him about Nan. How she were only drunk because her son had been killed, and now she hasn't got any money to live on. It might stop the same thing happening to someone else.'

Elsie and Hilda stared back at her, obviously unconvinced.

'The trouble is, even if Elsie and I were capable of writing such a letter, who's going to take any notice of three girls from the East End of London?' said Hilda, gloomily. 'Certainly not Ted Wilmington.'

'Yeah,' added Elsie. 'There's no chance of it being printed. We'd be wasting our money.'

'Isn't it at least worth a try?' asked Milly, feeling a little miffed.

Maybe she would do it anyway.

She could write a letter and maybe if she worded it just so . . .

'The only way Ted Wilmington would take any notice of a letter from us would be if we wrapped it around my half-brick and threw it through the window of his blasted newspaper,' said Elsie.

'Ooh, how I'd love to do that!' said Milly. 'I've been tempted to throw things through people's windows all day! But surely through the front window of his house would be better . . .'

Elsie turned to her. Her eyes were glittering and her cheeks were flushed. 'Now, *that* is a wonderful idea,' she said. '*That* would make him sit up and would be just like the old days, eh?'

Milly hadn't meant it. It had been the drink talking . . . the heat of the moment. But suddenly she could feel something shifting and stirring in the pit of her stomach.

She grinned at Elsie.

Why not?

Hilda was staring from Milly to Elsie, with her brow

furrowed. 'Just a minute,' she said. 'I know where you're coming from and all this might have worked really well before the war. But what about the suffragettes' wartime suspension of hostilities?'

Oh, yes. In the heat of the moment, Milly had quite forgotten about ELFS' new policy. Well, that was that, then.

Milly was surprised by quite how disappointed she felt.

'I bleeding hate that policy,' Elsie was saying vehemently. 'Let's face it, the injustices against women haven't stopped for the war. If anything, they've got worse. So, I really don't see why the fight against them should stop either.'

Milly hesitated. Elsie had a point – a very good point at that. But the fact remained that Miss Pankhurst had expressly forbidden such activity. She would be horrified to hear fully paid-up members of ELFS openly considering such activity. Unless . . .

'Lots of people don't agree with the cessation of hostilities policy,' Elsie was saying.

'Is that because it's possible it's wrong?'

She hadn't meant to say that. The words had escaped, unbidden.

'Milly!' Hilda looked shocked.

'No, hear me out,' said Milly. 'I think Miss Pankhurst is marvellous – of course I do – but that don't mean that she's right about everything. And what Elsie said just now – about the injustices against women going on, even though there's a war on – well, maybe we *should* be doing something about it . . .'

'Believe me, I've thought about it,' said Elsie. 'I'm sure there are others what have done the same. We were all right disappointed when Miss Pankhurst bought in "no militant action" policy.'

'So, what do you reckon?' said Milly, her heart thumping. 'Shall we do it?'

There was a moment's hesitation. 'Yes,' said Elsie emphatically. 'Yes! Let's bleeding do it!'

'I'll write a letter to go around the stone,' said Milly excitedly. 'One that mentions Nan and maybe others who have lost the separation allowance so they can't trace it back to us. Oh, this will make people sit up and take notice, good and proper! I'm so glad I met you girls.'

Hilda was still sitting there quietly.

'You in, sis?' asked Elsie gently, giving her a little nudge.

'We're talking low-level activity,' Hilda clarified. 'Stones through windows, that sort of thing? No one gets hurt?'

'Yes, of course,' said Elsie. 'Just one stone through Ted Wilmington's front window.'

'You're not planning to – I don't know – set fire to Parliament, or something?' Hilda persisted.

Milly and Elsie collapsed into peals of laughter. 'Of course not,' said Elsie. 'The very thought!'

'What do you think we are? Terrorists or something?' added Milly.

'I were just checking,' said Hilda, joining in the giggles.

'So, what's your answer, then?' asked Elsie.

Hilda hesitated for a fraction of a second.

'I'm in,' she said simply.

Milly took a deep breath. These were her people. Where she belonged.

She raised her virtually empty glass. 'To us,' she said. 'To women. To making a difference. And watch out, Ted Wilmington!'

# 12

Milly arrived home all a-dither.

She paused by the gate while she finished her cigarette and then stubbed it out carefully in the flowerbed before making her way to the front door. It swung open before Milly had had a chance to put her key in the lock.

Milly stifled a smile. It would be Ma – Milly knew it would. Ma had eyes in the back of her head and she was coming out to give Milly an earful for smoking in the street. Or rather for smoking at all. Or for coming back so late without getting a message home. Or for coming in the front door when Ma had just cleaned the front step and the passage, rather than through the rear alleyway that ran behind all the houses. Or possibly for all four.

But it was Charlie.

Milly shrugged off a little prickle of unease. Why shouldn't Charlie open the front door to her? Surely it wasn't that unusual. Only . . . it was unheard of. Milly hadn't even got her key into the lock – no tell-tale clink – and Charlie wouldn't have seen her coming unless he was either in Ma's room or Mr Wildermuth's.

Anyway, why wasn't he in bed at this time of night? It was gone 10 o'clock.

All this went through Milly's mind in the time it took Charlie to open his mouth and to blurt out, 'Ma ain't well. She's in bed and Caroline's up with her.'

Milly didn't answer him. She dumped her hat and coat over the banister and bolted up the stairs two at a time. Guilt flooded through her. It was unheard of for Ma to take to her bed before everyone else had retired for the night, and Milly hadn't been there for her.

The gas lamp had been lit in Ma's room, bathing everything in a warm glow. Milly stood in the doorway, holding onto the doorjamb as she took in the little tableau. Ma was already in her nightie and in bed, propped up against the pillows. Caroline was sitting on the far side of the bed, holding her hand and stroking her head. She looked up at Milly with something close to fear in her huge brown eyes. Milly looked at her mother more closely. Ma was flushed and her normally springy salt-and-pepper curls were slicked to her forehead. She was coughing weakly, but the handkerchief she was holding to her lips looked clean enough. Thank goodness there was no trace of any tell-tale spotting – although that didn't necessarily mean anything. There were a hundred and one nasty things it could be . . .

No, Milly. Don't think like that. Everyone gets poorly sometimes.

*But Ma doesn't.*

*Ma doesn't.*

'I'm sorry I wasn't here,' Milly gabbled. 'I met up with a couple of people from ELFS.'

Ma gave her a weak smile. 'You and your suffragettes, you daft ha'porth,' she rasped, not without affection, and then stopped, struck down by a paroxysm of coughing.

Milly watched her with guilt and concern. 'I'll send Charlie for the doctor,' she said decisively. Ma's cough sounded dry and there was no sign it had moved to her chest, but better safe than sorry. And hang the cost!

Ma fluttered a hand. 'No need,' she said. 'Let's see how I go tonight. Alice has gone for some camphor oil and I'm sure that will do the trick. Half the factory has gone down with the same thing and I'm sure I'll be right as rain in the morning.'

Milly sat down on the bed and put her hand on Ma's forehead. It was damp and clammy and hot – definitely hot – but not burning up.

'You'll live,' she said, and Ma gave her a weak smile in return. 'In the meantime, I think you'll be more comfortable without Caroline in bed with you tonight. Caroline, why don't you take Charlie's bed for tonight and Charlie can sleep on the sofa downstairs.'

'I'll sleep on the sofa,' said Caroline quickly.

Milly smiled. Charlie's tiny box room at the back of the house did get very cold – he often had to break ice on the window on a winter's morning. 'Quickly then,' she said. 'Grab yourself some blankets from the chest and send Charlie upstairs, will you?'

Caroline nodded and was gone. Milly turned back to her mother, but she had fallen asleep, chest gently rising and falling, little snores escaping from her open mouth. Hopefully – and Milly crossed her fingers firmly – Ma would be right as rain by the morning, but if she wasn't and she couldn't work, she wouldn't be paid. It was as simple as that. And with one wage down, they would be one step closer to penury.

To the workhouse.

Stop it, Milly! Ma had a cold. That was all. Stop being so . . . dramatic.

Charlie poked a worried head round the door. 'Is everything all right?' he said, and he looked so much like he was trying to be brave that Milly's heart melted.

'Everything's absolutely fine,' she said, hugging him tightly to her chest.

And she fervently hoped that she was right.

\*

Milly couldn't stop tossing and turning that night.

She kept falling into a light sleep and then waking with a start, disjointed dreams slipping out of reach and leaving her with a sense of foreboding.

'Just lie *still*,' said Alice, turning over with a deep sigh. 'Stop coughing and stop stealing all the covers!'

'Sorry,' said Milly, sitting up. The coughing she couldn't help – it was her permanent companion ever since she'd started inhaling the sack dust at the Home Depot – but she had to admit she did have more than her fair share of the covers. She did her best to straighten the counterpane over her sister's recumbent form. 'I've got a lot on my mind,' she added, lying down again.

'What have *you* got to be worried about?' muttered Alice crossly.

'Well, Ma, for a start,' said Milly. 'And what will happen if she can't work.'

'Ma will be fine,' said Alice, shortly. 'She's got a cold, that's all. Everyone's getting ill at the factory, but they're all right as rain after a few days at home. And there's enough of us working that it won't make much difference if she's off for a few days, will it? You earn more than the rest of us put together!'

That wasn't true. While it was fair to say the Home Depot paid well, the munitions factory was just as generous. Why was Alice being so spiteful?

'It ain't a competition,' Milly muttered defensively. 'We're all just doing our bit for the family.'

Alice snorted rudely by way of reply. 'Oh, hush,' she said. 'You've got a plum posting and you know it. *You* don't have to worry about chemicals and explosions and turning yellow like us girls at the factory.'

'No, *you* hush,' said Milly, thoroughly riled. 'It ain't all plain sailing at the Home Depot, either, I'll have you know.'

'Oh, I can only imagine. Does everyone spend all day saying, "This letter's really heavy"? Or "I've broken my nail; I'll have to have a sit down"? Or "Oh dear, the chocolate's leaked all over the parcel; I'd better get my lady's maid to clean up"?'

'It's not like that at all!' said Milly, pulling the covers towards her. 'It's important work. The Home Depot's really important for war morale.'

'Without munitions, there wouldn't be a war,' said Alice, pulling the covers back. 'Now, give it a rest and go to sleep.'

Milly lay there in the darkness, fuming. If only Alice knew the half of it!

For a wild moment, Milly was tempted to confide in her. To tell her everything. From falling out with Liza and Nora, to struggling at work, to meeting Jack – to say nothing of the attack, meeting Hilda, Elsie and Nan, and the decision to throw a stone through Ted Wilmington's front window.

But she didn't. Alice had started snoring and Milly knew she wouldn't take kindly to being woken up. More importantly, Milly didn't feel comfortable admitting her fears and insecurities to her sister – and that made her rather sad. How she wished she enjoyed the same easy familiarity with Alice as Hilda and Elsie did with each other. They always seemed so happy in each other's company, so supportive of each other – a tight little unit. She couldn't imagine Hilda and Elsie having an argument about whose job was better or more important.

She turned onto her side with a little harrumph. How dare Alice pour scorn on her job at the Home Depot like that? How *dare* she? At the end of the day, Milly had been the one with enough spark and brains and wit to get herself out of the East End and to go to work every day in a white pin-tucked shirt – even if it *was* second hand and beige with sack dust. Alice could say what she wanted – but she was the one wearing overalls in Woolwich.

Milly gave another huffy sigh and snuggled back down to sleep, making sure not one inch of skin was touching her sister's. Trust Alice to make this all about her. It was Ma they should be worrying about!

But, tomorrow was another day.

# 13

To Milly's relief, Ma was a little better in the morning.
Not well enough to go back to work – not just yet –
but her forehead felt cooler and she was coughing a little less
often. Alice – who didn't have a shift at the munitions factory
until that evening – would be around to keep an eye on Ma
during the day when everyone else was out, and Milly would
take over in the evening. She would send Charlie around to
the toy factory after school and, with a bit of luck, Maggie
might also come over to help with the younger children.

They were a family and they would all pull together.

Milly couldn't help feeling thrilled when Jack came to find
her at break time. Would she like to take another turn around
the park at lunchtime? Milly thought of demurring, of
pretending she was busy, of employing any of the little ploys
women used to keep men on their toes. But that would be
silly. She liked Jack and she *did* fancy a walk around the park,
and what was the point in denying it? It wasn't as if she
wanted him as her sweetheart or anything . . .

So, as planned, she met Jack at the sentry post on the
perimeter of the Home Depot compound at one o'clock sharp.
Jack was carrying a black box with a strap over his shoulder
– his camera, she presumed with a little thrill of excitement.
Maybe he was planning to take some pictures of her under
the trees or gazing pensively over the water or . . .

She really should have put on a little more rouge.

'Afternoon,' said Milly cheerfully as she drew level with him. 'Shall we head over to the lake?'

Jack shook his head. 'I've got something else in mind,' he said.

Milly stopped walking. Whatever did that mean? Goodness, had she read Jack all wrong? Hopefully he wasn't one of those men who wanted to disappear behind the Home Depot for a bit of a kiss and a cuddle. Hopefully *he* didn't think she was one of those girls who let those men do that sort of thing. She'd had just about enough of soldiers getting the wrong idea . . . or getting ideas of their own . . . Oh, why was everything so difficult?

'I'm not sure that's a good idea . . .' Milly started, preparing herself for a lonely lunch on her own.

Jack laughed. 'The zoo, Milly,' he said. 'I meant the zoo! I thought it would be fun to see the animals. I could take some pictures of them – and of you, too, if you wouldn't mind.'

'Oh!' Milly couldn't help but laugh. 'Well, that would be quite marvellous.'

London Zoo was a mere ten-minute walk across the park from the Home Depot, but Milly had never thought to go there at lunchtime before. In fact, she had never been to a zoo at all. Zoos were expensive. They were for rich children; children with nannies and kites and fathers who wore smart bowler hats and who worked in the City – or at least they had done before they'd gone off to fight for King and Country. But, then again, why not? Nowadays Milly had money of her own and, even though they would only have half an hour to look around before they had to report back on duty, as Jack had said, it might be fun.

And they all needed a little more of *that* nowadays!

'The zoo it is, then,' she said.

It would take her mind off Ma.

And the stone throwing.

And the thousand and one other things she had to worry about.

'I'm happy to pay for mine,' said Milly as Jack went up to the ticket booth.

She was a positively modern woman earning her own money and she should certainly offer to pay her way.

Jack turned around with a smile. 'I appreciate the offer,' he said. 'But as I suggested this outing, I'm very happy to treat you. Besides, it's hardly going to break the bank. We could buy tickets for ten people and still have change from half-a-day's pay.'

'Thank you,' said Milly.

She said it casually enough, but her mind was going nineteen to the dozen, furiously working out the sums. If what Jack had just said was true – rather than some wildly inaccurate throwaway comment – then he earned a great deal more than she did. Oh, she had known men at the Home Depot earned a lot more than the women carrying out the same duties – everyone did – but the difference in scale really was shocking. In fact, it was indefensible. How could the Army Post Office possibly justify paying women that much less?

'We haven't got long,' Jack was saying to the young woman who was checking tickets. 'What would you recommend?'

The young woman was trying very hard – and failing – not to look like she was staring at Jack's eyepatch. 'The penguins are always good fun,' she said. 'And it's nearly feeding time. And there's a new bear called Winnipeg. She's lovely. She's come all the way from Canada and we're looking after her while her owner's fighting in France.'

'Right you are,' said Jack cheerfully. 'Both now top of our list. Ready, Milly?'

'Rather!' said Milly.

She wouldn't mention the money situation. There was no point. After all, it wasn't Jack's fault and it might sour their little trip. Instead, she linked her arm with his and gave what she hoped was a suitably withering look to the woman who was still staring at Jack's eye.

'Don't you mind?' she asked, once they were safely out of earshot.

'Mind?' asked Jack, wrinkling his brow. 'Mind what?'

'People looking at your eye.'

Or, more specifically, the lack of an eye.

Jack grinned. He opened his mouth to reply and then shut it again, the smile fading away. And then he let out a deep sigh.

'Of *course* I bloody mind,' he said. 'I hate it being the first – and often the only – thing people notice about me. It's bad enough getting used to life without the blasted thing, but everyone else's reaction makes it twice as bad. Curiosity I can just about take. But pity? I hate the pity.'

*Oh!* This was the real Jack talking: the one beneath the smiles and the jokes and the boyish good humour. He was confiding in her as he never had before – and the moment felt charged with significance.

What to say, Milly? What on earth to say . . .?

'I'm sorry,' she said simply, giving his arm a squeeze.

It was the truth . . . and she couldn't do better than that.

Jack smiled down at her. 'I know you are,' he said. 'And you never treat me like I'm damaged. "Such a handsome boy . . . such a shame." Gah! Now, where is that bear?'

Winnipeg was tiny.

Barely more than a cub, even when she stood on her hindlegs she barely came up to her keeper's waist. But what she lacked in size, she more than made up for in playfulness, romping around her enclosure, walking logs like tightropes, playing king of the mountain on her pile of rocks. Milly, who had never seen anything like her before, was enchanted. And when Jack took out his camera and started taking some shots, she could have sworn Winnipeg started playing to the gallery.

'Oh, but she's marvellous,' said Milly, clapping her hands together in excitement.

'She is,' agreed Jack. '"Though she be but little, she is fierce."'

'Eh?' said Milly blankly.

Jack laughed. 'Shakespeare,' he said. '*A Midsummer Night's Dream.*'

'Oh,' said Milly. She suddenly felt a little deflated. Jack quoting Shakespeare – *knowing* things like that – seemed to drive a wedge between them, underlining how different they really were. 'Well, I'd say Mr Shakespeare is absolutely right,' she added stoutly. 'Winnipeg, you may be little, but you are fierce.'

Jack smiled at her. 'I'd rather say it applies to you too,' he said softly.

Milly held his eye, breath catching in her throat. She felt . . . She looked away.

'What's the matter?' said Jack. 'Did I say something wrong?'

'No,' said Milly. 'Not at all. It's just I sometimes forget how grand you are.'

Oh, Milly! A lovely moment . . . ruined!

Jack was looking mystified. 'Grand?' he echoed. 'I'm not grand at all!'

'Of course you are,' said Milly. 'You quote Shakespeare and your hobby is *photography*. I don't know anyone else who has a darkroom in their house . . .'

Jack held up a hand. 'Woah!' he said. 'I don't have a darkroom in my house. What the Dickens are you talking about? There isn't room to swing a cat at home, what with my parents and all my sisters and . . .'

Milly was confused. Confused and a little embarrassed at

the turn the conversation was taking – and after such a potentially meaningful moment between the two of them to boot.
But she didn't know how to stop it now. Slightly sulkily, she
waved at Jack's camera. 'Then how do you get your photos
developed then?' she said.

Jack took a step away from her. 'There are loads of cheap
places you can take them nowadays,' he said dismissively.
'Anyway, why does that matter? Look, I'm not sure what's
going on here, but, for your information, my family isn't rich
at all. I went to a grammar school and I was going to go to
university – but then the war came and put paid to all that.
And now I'm here. With you.'

'You could still go to university,' said Milly. 'When the war
finishes.'

'And so could you,' said Jack. 'When the war finishes.'

Milly burst out laughing – and her laughter sounded hollow,
even to her own ears. 'People like me don't go to university,'
she said incredulously. 'I left school at fourteen!'

Jack shrugged. 'People like you don't work for the Army
Post Office either,' he pointed out. 'And, while we're at it,
people like me don't get their eye blasted away in a muddy
hole in a field in France. The world is changing, Milly. It's
already changed.'

'Yes. And then when the war is finished, it will go back to
how it was before,' said Milly flatly.

'Then it's up to people like us to make sure that it doesn't,'
said Jack fervently, reaching out and grabbing Milly's arm.
'Come on, Milly. I thought you were a suffragette. I thought
you *wanted* change.'

'I do,' said Milly. 'But we've got to be realistic . . .'

'No, we *don't*,' said Jack. 'That's the whole point. This
whole war has been so huge, so devastating, that we've got
to make our dreams big. We've got to make sure something
good comes from it all. Something that lasts. So, come on,

Milly. What will you study at university when all this is over?'

'Politics,' said Milly.

The answer had come to her immediately – and quite unbidden.

Politics. She would *love* to study politics.

'That's my girl!' said Jack, slapping her on the back. 'PPE at Oxford for you. That's politics, philosophy and economics,' he added, correctly interpreting Milly's mystified expression.

Milly's stomach had now been joined by butterflies of quite a different kind. They lodged under her breastbone, making her heart pound and her breath catch . . .

Promise. Opportunity. A fresh start.

For her.

For all of them.

'You're mad, you are,' she said, laughing up at him. 'Do you really think it's possible for things to change that much?'

'Of course I do,' said Jack. 'They must! My sisters and my mother are all clever – much cleverer than me – and their time will come. Yours too. It must do!'

Oh, he was lovely.

Behind her, Winnipeg let out a huge roar that belied her size. With a little shriek, Milly ran towards Jack. He caught her with his spare arm, his hand on her waist, his mouth laughing against her hair.

Careful, Milly.

*Careful.*

# 14

The next day, *Liza* asked Milly to go for a walk at lunchtime.

Another day, another walk. This was becoming a habit!

Secretly, though, Milly was thrilled. It felt like a long time
since Liza had invited her to do, well, anything, really, and
Milly had missed her company. Bumping into each other in
the canteen or at a committee meeting really wasn't the same
thing – particularly when it had ended up like the last time.
Maybe now they could make up. They had been so close once
upon a time.

On the other hand, was it really wise to go for a walk with
Liza? After all, with everything that was going on in Milly's
life, she had an awful lot to keep secret from her friend. She
knew exactly how Liza felt about ELFS – how would she
react if she found out Milly was now thick as thieves with
two of its most outspoken members? How, indeed, would
she react if she knew that Milly had agreed to throw a stone
through the front window of one of the country's most pre-
eminent newspaper editors the very next week? Milly
couldn't help but stifle a grin as she imagined Liza's reaction
to that.

In the end, Milly accepted Liza's invitation. As she watched
Liza's back, with her neat old-fashioned plait, disappear
through the Home Depot on her way back to the broken
parcels department, Milly decided that it could only be a good

thing. Perhaps today would be the day that things started to turn around between the two of them.

Maybe Liza was even going to apologise for snapping at her.

How wrong could she be?

Liza was quiet even by her own standards when the two girls met up by the gate at the periphery of the Home Depot site. As they set off across the park, Milly kept up a steady stream of chatter to paper over the gaps in the conversation. About how funny it was that they hadn't thought to walk in the park in the summer months when the weather was sunny and clement, and everything had been at its best. But then again, the canteen had been relatively civilised back then – hadn't it? – and now it was murder trying to get a table at the busiest times. And now, of course, there were all the lovely stalls serving food near the lake, set up precisely to serve the staff at all the temporary army and government buildings, which had sprung up in the Regent's Park. And, of course, the Home Depot hadn't been so darned cold back then. And how was it nearly December? Christmas would be upon them before they knew it . . .

On and on she prattled, with nothing but the occasional nod and murmur from Liza. They had almost reached the lake and Milly had been about to ask what on earth was wrong, when Liza suddenly swung round to face her.

'Are you stepping out with Jack Archer?' she demanded, apropos of nothing.

'I beg your pardon?' Milly was so surprised that she gave a very coy un-Milly-like giggle.

'It's a simple question,' said Liza shortly. 'Are you or are you not stepping out with Jack Archer?'

Well, there was a question. Was she, or wasn't she?

She and Jack had spent a couple of lunchtimes together

modifying the key-list. They'd been walking in the park and they'd had a trip to the zoo.

But did that constitute stepping out?

Probably not – at least nothing had been said to that effect. But she couldn't deny she'd liked the way Jack had held her the day before, his arm around her waist, muscles moving under his skin. And, even though their conversation on the way back to the Home Depot had been nothing more than small talk, there was no doubt that *something* had passed between them.

An acknowledgement. An understanding. Maybe even an unspoken promise.

But then, she didn't want a sweetheart. So where did that leave her?

Liza had stopped walking and was standing silently, waiting for an answer.

'Why?' asked Milly. It seemed the easiest way to answer. 'Why does it matter if I am or I ain't?'

Liza sighed. 'Because,' she said. 'I don't like the way he spoke to James the other day.'

So that was why Liza had asked her for a walk today. Nothing to do with re-establishing their friendship. Nothing to do with building bridges. *Certainly* nothing to do with an apology. And everything to do with the fact that Liza's sweetheart had had his feelings hurt, had probably taken it out on Liza and now Liza wanted to take it out on Milly.

Well, shame on James. And shame on Liza.

Milly had done nothing wrong and, frankly, she wasn't going to put up with it!

'As I recall, Jack didn't say nothing to James the other day,' said Milly carefully.

'Yes, he did,' said Liza hotly. 'He said – very pointedly, I thought – that we all have to do our bit for King and Country.'

'He said that to all of us,' said Milly.

'He meant it for James.'

'I don't know what he meant,' said Milly. 'I haven't asked him and I ain't going to. But I wouldn't blame him if he had meant it for James. After all, he'd just heard James say he was doing all he could to avoid signing up. How do you think that made Jack feel? He lost his *eye* fighting and . . .'

'James hadn't seen *Jack* when he said it!' cried Liza. '*Jack* was still sitting down. He'd never have said it if he'd seen his uniform.'

Liza adopting a silly voice to say Jack's name twice only served to rile Milly further.

'That isn't the point, is it?' she said. 'He still *thought* it.'

Liza put her hands on her hips. 'Milly Woods! What happened to the girl who thought the war was a dreadful thing and should be stopped at all costs,' she demanded. 'A little attention from a man in uniform and it's all gone out of the window. What would your precious Miss Pankhurst have to say about *that*, I wonder?'

That was unfair! So unfair Milly could hardly believe Liza had said it.

Milly put her own hands on her hips. 'You're a fine one to talk,' she said. 'I remember a little girl fresh out of Woodhampstead who thought the war was a fine and patriotic thing because her daddy had told her so. Then she becomes the sweetheart of a man who is too . . . *something* . . . to enrol, and all of a sudden it's fine for a man to do all he can to avoid signing up.'

'How dare you?' snapped Liza. 'You have no idea about James,' she added. 'No idea at all.'

'No idea about what?' said Milly. 'No idea how much of a coward he is?'

Liza lunged forward and Milly put a hand up to defend herself. 'I'm not going to hit you,' said Liza scornfully. 'Where *I* come from, people don't do that sort of thing. But don't you dare ever talk about James like that again. He's not a coward. He was driven right to the edge by what happened to his brother in the war. He nearly . . . that night . . . I thought . . .'

She stopped talking, hand to mouth.

'He nearly did *what* that night, Liza?' said Milly. 'Did something happen the night of the fire you're not letting on?'

It had never added up, Milly realised. Something had niggled in the back of her mind right from the get-go. It had all seemed a bit too convenient that the fire had been blamed on matches in one of the parcels – especially as Liza and James had been in the extension when it started. Would the investigation discover they had had something to do with it?

But Liza was shaking her head emphatically. 'Nothing happened,' she said.

'I don't believe you.'

Where had *that* come from?

The words had popped out of Milly's mouth and now she couldn't put them back again.

Liza looked on the verge of tears. 'I don't want to carry on this walk,' she said, her voice strained and clipped. 'I'm going to go back to the Home Depot.' And without another word, she turned on her heel and started back the way they'd come. She hadn't gone more than a few steps when she turned back to Milly. 'By the way, I would hazard a guess you're not stepping out with Jack Archer but you would very much like to.'

Milly turned and followed Liza's line of sight back towards the Home Depot.

Jack was sauntering up the path towards them, laughing away and arm in arm with . . . *Eloise*!

Milly met Liza's eyes but before she could say anything, Liza had stormed away, brushing past Jack and totally ignoring him as he stopped to doff his cap.

And now Jack and Eloise were heading her way and it was clear Jack had seen her. Milly couldn't bear the thought of . . . well, any of it, really and, without thinking it through, she charged off down a side path.

How *could* he?

How could Jack brazenly step out with another girl the day after he had been out with her? And with Eloise to boot! How could he look at her like that – like she was the most important person in the world? He'd made a point of telling Milly how much Eloise and her old-fashioned views irritated him – and now, here he was, arm in arm with her, the two of them staring deeply into each other's eyes. It seemed a pretty face and a simpering smile made up for anything . . .

Was he taking Eloise to the zoo as well? Or was it to be the slice of pie and a seat by the lake?

Well, either way, she hated him.

She hated her as well.

And she hated herself.

Yes, she hated herself most of all.

How could she have fallen so easily for Jack and his pretty words? How could she have been so naïve? Right at this moment, Jack was probably agreeing with Eloise that the suffragettes were a bunch of unhinged and hysterical women, and he wouldn't let any of them near the vote if it was up to him – and, really, it served Milly right. After all her talk about not wanting a sweetheart, she had fallen hook, line and sinker for the first man to show her any attention.

She was a fool.

Most of all, Milly hated herself for running away rather than facing up to Jack. She should have walked straight past him – past both of them – with a polite smile and her head held high. What she should not have done was bolt away into the shrubbery.

Now Jack knew she minded.

Now Jack knew she cared.

Furiously, Milly pounded the paths of the park until the blood had stopped singing in her ears and she felt ready to face the world again. Slowly, she headed back to the Home Depot. She was ten minutes late reporting back for duty, but hopefully she would get away with it.

Miss Parker was waiting at her station. 'Ah, there you are, Milly,' she said impatiently. 'I wanted to let you know you will be moving departments again. Nothing to worry about but, on Monday, please report for duty in Salonika parcels.'

And that, thought Milly, was the final straw.

# 15

It was a very subdued Milly who arrived home for the weekend.

The good news was that Ma was back on her feet again. After that first awful night, she had gradually begun to get better and stronger, and now she was pottering around the house again, barking out orders, making sure everything was just so and talking about going back to work again on Monday. And thank goodness for that. It could easily have ended up very, very differently.

The bad news was . . . well, just about everything else.

Although she found it difficult to admit, even to herself, Milly was devastated about the turn of events with Jack. She had really liked him. She had enjoyed his company. And, worst of all, she had trusted him. And yet he had let her down. Just like they all did.

And, in a way, she had let herself down too, by letting her guard down. By letting herself get too close.

Never again.

Milly tried hard to throw herself into the gentle family rhythms and routines, and not to be too much of an old misery, but it was hard. Really hard. Even when Ma announced it was mere weeks before Christmas and high time they got started on some Christmas baking, Milly found it difficult to muster any enthusiasm. She usually loved all the measuring and stirring, the enticing smells – to say nothing of the illicit little tastes – but this year it was different. It felt like the fun and joy had been bleached from everything, leaving an empty flatness. It was like looking at her family, her home – her life – through a grimy pane of glass.

She was there and yet she wasn't. Not properly at least.

Like now, for example. It was Saturday afternoon and she, Alice and Charlie were chopping dried fruit at the kitchen table, but Milly's mind was thousands of miles away.

'It's treasure!' said Charlie, spearing a cherry with his knife. 'Don't let the enemy get their hands on it!'

Alice looked up with an indulgent smile. 'Rubies,' she said. 'Particularly rare ones, I'd say. Better keep them safe!'

Charlie leaped to his feet, arms outstretched. 'Diving low,' he shouted, spinning around and hitting Milly on the shoulder.

'Oh, Charlie! Just sit down and stop mucking around,' she said irritably.

Alice put down her knife. 'What's got into *you*?' she demanded. 'Charlie's just having a bit of fun. You've been like a bear with a sore head all weekend.'

'Don't talk to *me* about bears,' muttered Milly. It was unlike Alice to be the cheerful one with Milly taking on the role of the old grump – but Milly couldn't help it!

Suddenly there was a commotion out in the backyard. A dog whining. Raised voices. Ma's.

Caroline's.

As one, Milly, Alice and Charlie scuttled out of the kitchen, through the scullery and into the backyard to find out what was going on. Caroline was standing by the gate to the alleyway that ran along the back of the houses holding a tan-and-white terrier by the scruff of its neck. The fur on the dog's ears and most of its face was burned away, the flesh below raw and weeping. The whining grew exponentially in volume.

'And what's this?' Ma was saying wearily.

'He's not a "what",' said Caroline, indignantly. 'He's a "who". He's one of God's creatures just like you and me.'

Ma sighed. '*Who* is this creature of God, then?'

'He's Mr Arnold's dog,' said Caroline. 'Or at least he was. Mr Arnold don't want him no more.'

'I'm not surprised,' muttered Ma and, next to Milly, Alice snorted loudly with laughter.

Caroline gave Alice a vicious look. 'Mr Arnold's thrown him out!' she cried, turning her attention back to Ma. 'He's living on the streets.'

'What on earth's happened to his face?' asked Ma, bending down to the dog. 'Poor little thing.'

'Jane at number twenty-two said he had the canker,' said Caroline. 'Mr Arnold tried olive oil but it didn't work, so he poured paraffin into his ears and lit it. Jane said there were a huge fire and then Mr Arnold threw a pail of water over him and threw him out the house. She saw it all from her window.'

'Ouch!' said Ma, putting her hands to her own ears. 'What an awful thing to do!'

She bent down to the little dog. He flinched away from her hand but didn't flee or fight. He stood there silently, looking up at her.

'I thought we could adopt him,' said Caroline, sensing weakness.

Ma stood up. 'He can't stay here, Caroline,' she said tiredly. 'I can't be having you bringing in every waif and stray in Bow.'

'But I don't bring in every waif and stray,' said Caroline indignantly. 'Apart from Cat, who else have I brought in? And Cat's *useful*. You know she is. All those mice.'

'She'd be a lot more useful if she had a tail,' muttered Ma. 'But at least she pays her way and doesn't need feeding. Whereas this thing . . . sorry, *God's creature* . . . well, it would be far kinder to put it out of its misery. That vicar is doing sterling work on all the strays with his gas chamber.'

'No!' Milly ran out into the yard and placed herself between Ma and the dog as if Ma was about to dispatch the animal there and then. 'No! I understand killing an animal if it's really suffering but you can't destroy something because it doesn't look perfect. You can't. It's what's inside that matters!'

Where had that come from? She hadn't planned to say any of it, and now her family were all gawping at her in amazement.

'Well, who would've thought it?' said Ma, hands on hips. 'Our Milly going all sentimental on us. Whatever's got into you? You've never been one to stick your neck out for lame ducks!'

'Yes,' said Alice with a sneer. 'When Mabel used to come to school with her clothes like rags, I don't remember you telling *her* it was what was inside that matters.'

Milly flushed.

'Please, Ma,' persisted Caroline, obviously keen to capitalise on Milly's outburst – and thus saving Milly the need to answer. 'I'll pay for his food out of my babysitting money. I'll be able to afford it if I get it from the dog barrow and only get the bits with knobs on. And I'll even volunteer to help the vicar deal with the strays what are ill and in pain.'

'Please, Ma,' echoed Charlie. 'Please can we keep him?'

'He ain't neither use nor ornament,' said Alice dismissively.

'Neither are you,' shot back Caroline, making a face at her sister.

Alice gave her a little shove in return.

'Girls,' said Ma mildly. 'Well, he ain't no ornament, that's for sure. But he might have a use. Can the wretched creature still hear?' She clapped her hands smartly together and the dog turned to the sound. 'Hmm,' she muttered. 'That's something, at least.'

Caroline sensed her chance. 'Can he stay? Please, Ma.'

'Please, Ma,' echoed Milly. She found she was crossing her fingers behind her back.

'Well, he ain't coming in the house,' said Ma. 'But a guard dog would be useful. Folks are getting ever so bold nowadays, sneaking into backyards at all hours of the day and night. Someone even came into Mrs Adams's yard the other day and pinched her bloomers off the line.'

The children burst into laughter.

'Who would want Mrs Adams's bloomers,' said Charlie with a delighted chuckle.

'Oh, I don't know, you could make a couple of shirts out of one pair,' said Caroline.

'Shirts?' added Alice with a giggle. 'You could make a whole sail from them.'

'Girls!' said Ma. 'What were we saying about it being the inside that matters?' But she was smiling. 'And bloomers is one thing. But if someone pinches our coal, we're going to be in a right pickle and no mistaking! So, yes, he can stay. We're going to need something he can sleep in at night. And some cream for his face. Once the plum pudding is done and dusted, we'll get onto that . . .'

'Oh, thank you, Ma,' cried Caroline, flinging her arms around her mother.

'What's his name?' asked Ma, gently extracting herself.

'Boniface.' Caroline replied, without a shred of irony.


Milly resumed her Christmas fruit chopping, deep in thought.

There was no doubt she'd responded to Boniface as she had because of Jack.

If nothing else, Jack had taught her that how a person looked really didn't matter. To be honest, Milly had long stopped seeing his patch – she just saw the laughing, golden boy who was wearing it – and it was only when someone else, like the girl at the zoo, made some comment or looked at him a certain way that Milly even remembered he was disfigured.

So, Milly was glad they had rescued Boniface from an uncertain life on the streets or from the local well-meaning priest, who had made it his business to rid the streets of disease-spreading strays. Boniface would be safe here – loved, even – and he deserved a second chance. He had done nothing wrong.

But with Jack it was different. Milly might have stopped noticing he only had one eye, but she could not forgive him for stepping out so blatantly with Eloise – and the day after he had taken her to the zoo, to boot. Of course, Eloise was probably a more suitable choice for Jack – she was, after all, more in his class – but still! You couldn't help what you were like on the outside, but you *could* do something about what you were like as a person inside and, here, Jack had shown himself to be wanting.

Milly returned to her chopping, hacking away at the dried fruits with a vengeance.

She would put Jack from her mind. She would concentrate on Hilda and Elsie and the plans she had hatched with them. Throwing the brick might be frightening and it might be difficult but, at least, they were fighting to make things better.

At least their hearts were in the right place

And that was a lot more than she could say for Jack.

## 16

Throwing the first brick was frightening.

*Really* frightening.

Milly and Elsie carried out the 'mission' together. Elsie had said Hilda was needed at home and couldn't be spared but, the way she was talking, Milly surmised there might also have been a touch of cold feet involved. No matter . . . it would, no doubt, be easier for two girls to slip away from the scene of the crime than three . . .

Oh goodness. Were they really going to go ahead with this?

Mr Wilmington lived at the end of a row of huge terraced houses in a grand London square. Even better, his house was situated right next to a quiet side street. And the side street led, conveniently, to busy, anonymous Knightsbridge. It was dark and cold and raining heavily. Virtually no one was out and about. With her heart in her mouth, Milly followed Elsie down the side street. Elsie pulled the half-brick – with Milly's letter tied to it – from her bag, and lobbed it with all her might through the dark front window. Then, with the crash still reverberating in their ears, they slipped into the shadows and walked calmly back down the side street.

But what was that? Footsteps?

Was someone rounding the corner behind them? Was that someone closing in on them?

Any moment, there would be a heavy hand upon Milly's

shoulder, the police would be summoned and all would be lost.

Resisting the temptation to run, Milly risked a panicked look over her shoulder.

Nothing. Just darkness and shadows.

They'd got away with it.

Five minutes later, Milly and Elsie were on the Tube, hurtling back towards the East End. Fizzing with adrenaline and swinging from the ceiling straps, they found they couldn't stop laughing.

They'd done it!

That had been for Nan.

Nan and Hilda and Elsie and Ma and Maggie and . . . all of them, really. Every East-End woman who had suffered because of decisions taken by men.

They'd done it and now it felt great.

And, to be honest, Milly couldn't wait to do it again.

It was in all the papers.

Milly devoured them all. It transpired Mr Wilmington had not been at home at the time of the attack. He and his wife had been visiting their sons at boarding school in the north of England, and the damage had been made good before they'd returned. Milly couldn't help being disappointed Mr Wilmington hadn't been frightened out of his wits but, on balance, it was probably a good thing. Had Mr Wilmington been around, the whole affair might have been hushed up. As it was, one of his servants had clearly leaked the entire contents of the letter to the press.

Her letter was 'out there' for all the world to see!

The newspapers, of course, were scathing. They condemned the person or people who had carried out such pointless vandalism – and in the middle of a war to boot. Such an action, they said, would do nothing but delay women's suffrage by years. It was entirely counter intuitive and counterproductive.

Milly didn't care.

She didn't care at all.

Of course, the newspapers would write those sorts of things. That much was entirely predictable. But *people* were talking about it – and that was what mattered. The day afterwards, Milly overheard a woman in the canteen saying she hadn't known the police could take the separation allowance from someone who was legally entitled to it – and praising the stone-thrower for drawing women's attention to it. And then a very la-di-da girl in Milly's new department casually said she would quite cheerfully have chucked a stone through a window herself as the new rules were quite ridiculous, and of course the police shouldn't be allowed to take money from anyone. This had been met by horrified giggles from the rest of the team, to which Miss La-Di-Da had replied, 'Well, sometimes you've got to take the law into your own hands, haven't you?' Milly had almost laughed out loud at this – the most Miss La-Di-Da would probably ever 'take the law into her own hands' would be to add milk before sugar to her tea!

And then Ma – *Ma* – had said, 'I'd like to shake the hand of whoever showed everyone what women think about that new policy.' And it had been on the tip of Milly's tongue to own up when Ma added, 'Of course, if any of you try anything like that, I'll have your guts for garters.'

Milly had held her tongue.

The icing on the cake had come in the papers a couple of days later. Arthur Henderson – a politician, no less – wrote an article in *The Times* opposing police powers. He didn't exactly condone the stone throwing, of course, but he did state that he believed the cause to be worthy and just.

Milly was thrilled. *Thrilled*. The small, deliberate act of sabotage had given her a real boost. She felt more in control, more confident – part of something bigger than herself.

It was all strangely addictive; a real cat and mouse game – just like the heyday of the suffragettes. It was really quite marvellous.

And, a few days later, she and Elsie did it all over again.

This time, it was the home of a prominent MP who had been vocal in support of the new police powers. Another note tied to another half-brick through another window – this time in Notting Hill and this time thrown by Milly. Emboldened by their earlier success, they risked carrying out their mission in daylight on a Sunday morning. After all, didn't they want as much publicity as possible? They plotted their escape route carefully in advance – a small alleyway that led directly to Holland Park where they could lose themselves in the prom-enading crowds – and their plan worked perfectly. This time there *were* shouts and there *were* running feet – lots of them – but the would-be pursuers headed off in the wrong direction.

Milly and Elsie took a quick turn around the park and were back on the Tube in no time at all.

Oh, this might be frightening, but it was also almost fun!

By now, Milly had got her confidence and the bit between her teeth, and she couldn't wait to go it alone.

'Oh, it was *wonderful*,' she said, once she was safely back in the Nag's Head after her solo mission. She flopped back in her seat, glass of brandy in hand, and let out a sigh of pure satisfaction.

'Do tell,' said Hilda, pulling up her chair and propping her chin in her hands.

'Well,' said Milly, savouring the moment. 'I chucked the brick as we'd agreed and started walking away – as quick as I could, mind. Then I heard footsteps behind me. *Running* footsteps.'

'No!' Elsie's eyes widened. 'What on earth did you do?'

'I *wanted* to run,' said Milly. 'Course I did. But I knew, if I did, the game were up and that he – and I just knew it were a he – would be able to run faster than me. So, I made myself stop walking and I turned round, all polite like.'

'Oh, Lordy! What happened next?' Hilda had her fingers over her mouth.

She and Elsie really were the most appreciative audience.

'Well, the gentleman were bright red in the face,' Milly continued. 'I wasn't sure whether it were because he were angry or because he'd been running. He were quite thick set – didn't look like he often had much cause to run—'

'Yes, but what did you *do*?' interrupted Hilda impatiently. 'What did you say?'

Milly paused for dramatic effect. 'I said, "He went that way, sir. Gave me ever such a fright, he did, sir." And then I pointed down a nearby alleyway. I even gave him a little curtsey for good measure . . .'

Hilda and Elsie dissolved into peals of laughter.

'Oh, you are a one, Milly,' said Hilda, wiping her eyes. 'What happened next?'

'Well, the gentleman touched his hat and said, "I'm very obliged to you, Miss."' Milly giggled at the memory. 'Then he waddled off down the alleyway and I carried on my way. I made myself carry on walking at a sedate pace – very calm and composed like – although I were dying to dance a jig, or punch the air, or laugh until I wet my drawers.'

As the three laughed together, Milly thought again how much *fun* this all was. How glad she was that she had met Hilda and Elsie, and was 'doing her bit' in a way she couldn't have imagined only a few weeks ago.

Jack was free to step out with as many silly girls as he wanted.

She, Milly Woods, had more important things on her mind.

# 17

All this stone throwing might be great fun but it was doing nothing to help Nan.

At least, Milly reflected, it would do nothing in the short term and, even if their militant activity eventually bore fruit, it might take months.

Milly had, of course, written to Chief Inspector Bell after her failed visit to Bow Street Police Station. She had heard nothing back. At first, she assumed that once Chief Inspector Bell had finished his investigations, he would make contact with Nan rather than reply to Milly. But Hilda and Elsie told her that nothing had arrived. In the meantime, Nan was apparently getting sicker and weaker and, even worse, she seemed to be losing hope that things were ever going to get better for her. Time was clearly of the essence.

She'd write again, Milly told herself on the train into work the next day.

She would write to Chief Inspector Bell in altogether stronger terms and, if push came to shove, she might well follow it up with a strategically placed stone through his front window. Well, maybe not yet. She didn't want to give herself away as the master stone-thrower wreaking havoc around London. But, further down the line, it was definitely an option.

And so, that lunchtime, Milly skipped a meeting of the Christmas party planning committee. This was far more important than making decorations. Christmas was still several weeks away and, anyway, there were dozens of girls who could cut out bunting or twist paperchains. Only she could write this particular letter. She secreted herself in a mercifully quiet corner of the canteen (it was a crisp day and many people had gone into the park) and took out the paper, pen and ink she'd taken to keeping in her bag. After meeting Elsie and Hilda, she was far more organised – she even had scissors and glue in her bag nowadays. Maybe, when she'd finished the letter, she'd make a modified key-list for the new department she was working in.

And maybe not.

If the Home Depot couldn't pay her the same as they paid a man – if they could sack you when you were grieving – well, why should she spend even a moment of her spare time helping herself to work more efficiently.

'Afternoon.' A male voice interrupted her thoughts.

Milly looked up in irritation. She'd hardly got beyond the salutation in her letter and she didn't want to be interrupted. She certainly didn't want to share her table with a soldier who would either make a half-hearted attempt to flirt with her or would hold forth on how a woman's place was in the home. Or both.

It was Jack.

'Hello,' replied Milly shortly.

She wasn't really sure how to respond to him. Oh, she knew he hadn't exactly done anything wrong. He had made her no promises and they weren't stepping out together, so he was perfectly entitled to go strolling with whoever he chose. But she still hadn't forgiven him.

She hadn't forgiven him at all.

Maybe if she turned back to her letter, he would take the hint and go away.

No such luck. Jack had swung out a chair and was sitting down with an easy grace. Now he was ordering sausages and suet pudding! There would be no space on the table – or in her mind – for letter writing.

'What are you doing?' asked Jack, looking at her paraphernalia.

'Never you mind,' said Milly tartly.

There was no reason she shouldn't tell him what she was doing; taking up Nan's case was hardly a secret after all. Besides, Jack might be able to help her strike the right tone between authoritative and strident . . .

But no.

She wasn't inclined to give Jack any windows into her world at the moment.

'Look. About the other day,' said Jack. 'When we saw each other in the park . . .'

Milly held up a hand. 'Stop,' she said. 'It really doesn't matter.'

Jack's one eye blinked slowly in surprise. 'I wanted to explain . . .'

'There's nothing to explain,' said Milly. 'You are perfectly entitled to go walking in the park with Eloise. You're perfectly entitled to go walking in the park with whoever you like. In fact, you can go walking in the park with a different girl every day of the week, for all I care. I just ain't going to be Tuesdays, if you understand what I mean. I hope that's clear?'

Jack didn't react for a moment. Then he got to his feet. 'Abundantly clear, Miss Woods,' he said stiffly. 'Perhaps it would be best if I left you to your lunch and your letter writing.'

'Perhaps it would, Private Archer,' replied Milly.

It was best. It really was. Why, then, did she feel like crying?

Jack sketched a bow. Milly watched out of the corner of her eye as he walked across the canteen and sat down with a group of soldiers. There was a shout of laughter and Milly felt a flush come to her cheeks. Were they talking about her?

She bent back over her letter. She had sworn off men and she wanted nothing more to do with Jack. She had more important things to think about.

The day didn't improve.

Nora bumped into her and took her to task for missing the Christmas party planning committee meeting. There was no point in signing up for something if you weren't going to commit to it, she said, and there were miles of Christmas bunting to make . . .

And then a parcel containing something very red and very sticky exploded over her clean white shirt, and Liza totally blanked her in the lavvies when she went to try and clean it off.

Milly was relieved when the day was finally over. Exhausted, she dragged herself home from work. Even the carol singers lustily – if tunelessly – barking out 'Silent Night' in aid of the Soldiers' Fund at the Tube station couldn't raise her spirits. This working lark really wasn't for the fainthearted.

She froze as she reached the house. Who was that shadowy figure lurking by her front gate? Now the gas lamps were being dimmed at night, it was hard to make out who was who.

Milly's heart started to pound uncomfortably. Maybe it was *him* – he'd found out where she lived and was lying in wait for her.

Oh, Milly. Don't be daft!

It could be anyone. A neighbour. A friend of Ma's. A tradesman running late . . .

In fact, now Milly was a little closer, she could see there were two 'anyones'. Two young women, about the same height . . .

Hilda and Elsie.

They rounded on Milly as soon as she drew level, talking frantically over each other.

'We came as soon as we heard.'

'We knocked on the door. Your sister answered.'

'She's dead, Milly,' said Hilda, her eyes wide with shock.

# 18

Milly looked from Elsie to Hilda with mounting horror. What on earth were they talking about?

For a horrible moment, Milly thought they meant Ma. Hilda and Elsie had come round to see her, had knocked on the door and someone had told them Ma was dead. The illness she'd been suffering from a week or two ago – the one Milly thought she'd recovered from – had come back with a vengeance and carried her away.

Then she realised that didn't make any sense at all.

'Who?' she cried. 'Who's dead?'

There was a brief pause.

'Nan, of course,' said Elsie.

'Nan's *dead*,' added Hilda.

Milly turned from one to the other. 'You'd better come in,' she said.

We failed. *We failed.*

Those words rang again and again through Milly's head as she unlocked the front door and shepherded her friends down the front passage and into the kitchen.

*We said we would do something and we failed.*

Milly introduced Hilda and Elsie to (a very much alive) Ma who was serving up supper to a full house of siblings. Her sisters and brother didn't take any notice of her friends: they were hungry and it was just two boring grown-ups. But what to do now? The little kitchen was already full and, while

Nan's death was hardly a secret, neither was it something she particularly wanted to talk about in front of her family. The scullery was too small, the passage likewise, the yard too dark and already Boniface's domain.

'Let's go upstairs,' she said to Hilda and Elsie.

Ma raised her eyebrows at this unorthodox way of receiving visitors, but there must have been something in Milly's expression that prevented her speaking out.

'I'll bring you up some tea,' was all she said.

Milly, Hilda and Elsie headed back down the passageway towards the stairs. It was already a squash and a squeeze, but then the front door swung open and Mr Wildermuth swept in.

'My apologies,' he said, jumping onto the bottom step.

'It's not your fault, Mr Wildermuth,' said Milly. 'But my friends and I are actually going upstairs, so if you would be so kind . . .'

'Oh. I see.'

There was more squashing and squeezing – and a bit of nervous giggling – and then Elsie said, 'Hello,' in a surprised sort of voice.

Milly turned in surprise. Did Elsie know Mr Wildermuth? There was no reason she shouldn't, of course; after all, people were always saying the East End was nothing more than a series of villages. But Mr Wildermuth, head on one side, was looking at Elsie in confusion. Any connection obviously wasn't clear to him.

'Do I know you from somewhere, Miss?' he asked politely.

'Yes, a little,' said Elsie. 'You work at the bakery on Brick Lane, don't you? Clarkson's.'

Mr Wildermuth's brow cleared. 'Ah, yes,' he said. 'And you are maybe a customer?'

Elsie laughed. 'I wish I could afford your cakes,' she said. 'No – my chap has a connection there. Harry Watson? He does your deliveries and I've accompanied him at the week-ends. I do love to drive in a motor!'

'Indeed,' said Mr Wildermuth. 'I've met Mr Watson a couple of times. But he is not one of our regular drivers?'

'No.' Elsie looked a little crestfallen. 'Ever since his company lost its contract at the Home Depot, he's had to get driving work as and where he can.'

'Times are hard for us all,' said Mr Wildermuth diplomat-ically. He gave another little bow. 'Delighted to make your acquaintance, ladies,' he added, and disappeared into his room.

Milly led Hilda and Elsie upstairs and into her own bedroom. Luckily, it was reasonably tidy: the counterpane was straight on the bed – even if not meticulously smoothed – the chamber pot was under the bed and all the clothes had been returned to the wardrobe. Had she and Alice left it like this or had Ma popped in and worked her magic?

Hilda sat down on the bed and tucked a stray strand of straight blonde hair behind her ear. 'Mr *Wildermuth*, did you say, Milly?' she said, pursing her lips. 'I daresay he's awfully handsome, but a *German*? Living in your house?'

'My Harry never said there was no German working at Clarkson's,' added Elsie. 'That man has definitely helped load the van and I'm sure his name weren't Wildermuth.'

Milly swallowed a sigh. This was all so unimportant and, frankly, irrelevant. Particularly when Hilda and Elsie had come bearing such bad news.

'Mr Wildermuth sometimes goes by the name of Wildsmith,' she said patiently. 'Particularly after the Zeppelin riots. But it's no secret he's German – Clarkson's will know – and he's been here for years.'

'But a German. Living right here in your house,' said Elsie doubtfully. 'I know there have always been Germans in the East End, but things are different now there's a war on. Everything's different. You've got to be careful.'

Milly laughed. 'I *am* careful,' she said. 'Not that there's any need.'

Hilda frowned. 'But all the things you've told us. About how the King and Queen are coming to visit the Home Depot. And how everything works. You must never, ever, tell Mr Wildermuth anything like that. You do know that, don't you?'

Milly paused, a little shiver of unease passing down her spine. Mr Wildermuth *had* seemed awfully keen to find out about life at the Home Depot, and she *had* probably told him more than she should have done when he had joined them for dinner the other week. She couldn't specifically remember exactly what she'd told him, but surely there wasn't any harm in it?

Then again, maybe she would be more careful in future. Maybe she would even warn Maggie off.

She gave herself a little shake. This was Mr Wildermuth they were talking about!

'Tell me about Nan,' she said.

There had been no drama, no emergency. Nan had just slipped away.

Her neighbour had checked in on her as she had promised and, that morning, had found Nan's lifeless body curled up on the sofa.

'She were already cold,' said Elsie, eyes brimming with tears. 'She hadn't taken her medicine and she hadn't heated the broth the neighbour had left her the day before. It were like she'd given up.'

Milly felt her own eyes fill up. 'But that's awful,' she said. 'I can hardly believe it. I mean, I knew she were poorly. Really poorly, even. But I thought we'd got to her in time. I thought she would be saved.'

Hilda sighed. 'It ain't anyone's fault,' she said. 'We all did our best . . .'

'The trouble is that sometimes our best ain't good enough,' Elsie finished for her.

Milly hung her head, deep in thought. *Had* she done her best? Oh, she'd written a couple of letters on Nan's behalf and thrown a few stones through a few windows but that was all . . .

Ma bustled in with a tray of tea. Milly, belatedly, introduced Hilda and Elsie, but didn't share the reason why they'd called round. She was reminded of the thought she'd had when she'd visited Nan – what had happened to Nan could happen to anyone. They were all just a few steps away from the work-house – or worse – and Ma didn't need any reminders of *that*.

'I'll tell you who's fault it is,' said Elsie, as soon as Ma had gone. 'Men's! The powers-that-be!'

'Too right,' added Hilda. 'Nan and her family did everything right. Her husband and son went off to fight and her son made the ultimate bloody sacrifice. And then what happens? The Home Depot sack her – sorry, Milly – and the police take away her only source of income. It's a scandal, that's what it is. A bloody scandal.'

'These men go away to fight assuming their women will be looked after,' said Elsie. 'They contribute to the separation allowance! Thank goodness my Harry ain't got no intention of signing up.'

'I think he might find that he has to.'

The words were out before Milly could stop them. Damn her and her big mouth!

Hilda and Elsie turned to her with shocked faces.

'Why?' demanded Elsie, rattling her cup back into her saucer with a shaking hand. 'There's no "has to" about it? No one can make our men do nothing.'

Oh goodness. Milly realised she was in danger of getting into very deep water.

She'd been so shocked about Nan she'd blurted out the first thing to come into her head. She really shouldn't have done! It was one thing telling her friends something fun and frivolous like the King and Queen visiting the Home Depot; it was quite another blabbing about something like compulsory conscription.

Meanwhile, Elsie and Hilda were staring at her.

'It were just something someone at work said in passing,' said Milly, trying her hardest to sound light and carefree. 'This person is known for saying silly things. Don't give it another thought.'

Hilda frowned. 'It's a funny thing to make a joke about, though,' she said.

'It is,' added Elsie. 'Spill the beans, Milly.'

'I'm sure it were nothing . . .'

'Milly!' cried Elsie and Hilda together.

Both looked furious – Elsie looked positively menacing – and Milly was too tired, too overwrought to carry on concocting a web of half-truths. So, with a deep sigh, she told them what Nora had overheard. About how it looked almost definite that compulsory conscription was going to be introduced in mere weeks.

There was a silence when she had finished speaking. Neither Hilda nor Elsie said anything for at least ten seconds, and then there was a rap at the door. Alice poked her head around and said that Ma had suggested they come downstairs to the kitchen because the younger children were going to bed. And then Charlie poked his head below Alice's and pretended to shoot them all.

'Scram!' said Milly, getting up and slamming the door on her siblings.

Could there have been a more inopportune time for Charlie to remind them of the horrors of war?

'I'm so sorry,' she said.

Elsie flapped her hand in a 'don't mention it' sort of way.

'There's just one thing for it,' she said, slapping her knee. 'We're going to have to up our game.'

But, for Milly, everything had changed.

Elsie started talking about more and bigger bricks, more strident letters, maybe even an incendiary device to boot – although, as Hilda pointed out, wouldn't that merely set fire to the letter? – but Milly sat there quietly, deep in thought.

Nan had *died*.

And even though Milly had only met Nan once, to a certain extent, she had died on Milly's watch. On *their* watch. And while it wasn't actually their fault, it was true that they had become focussed on their stone throwing almost to the exclusion of everything else.

Milly hadn't been back to visit Nan. She hadn't even sent a note. As for the blanket she'd pledged to knit – well, she'd only managed a couple of decidedly uneven squares. She hadn't consulted the ELFS' Distress Bureau, she hadn't tried to go back into the police station to see Chief Inspector Bell and she had only written two letters.

It was a sorry state of affairs.

And, true, maybe those things wouldn't have saved Nan, but why on earth had they thought all that stone throwing might?

Milly suddenly saw it for what it was: a distraction. A childish, petty and vindictive distraction conceived while tired and overwrought and under the influence of alcohol. Nan had deserved better.

And, by the same token, Milly was better than that.

It had been partly her idea – she couldn't blame anyone else – and now she felt thoroughly ashamed of herself.

'No more stone throwing!' she blurted out, holding up a hand and interrupting Elsie, who was outlining an elaborate scheme to throw stones through the windows of the Houses of Parliament.

Elsie – and even Hilda – turned to her in surprise.

'Surely we should be throwing *more* stones, not less,' said Elsie. 'After all, they've got blood on their hands now! Surely we should be upping our game!'

'It won't help,' said Milly. 'It really won't. And it certainly won't bring Nan back.'

'That weren't what you were saying the other day,' said Elsie. She was close to tears and almost shouting, and Milly was very aware of her family waiting to go to bed and possibly overhearing every word they were saying.

'Shh,' she said. 'Listen, I'm as angry as you are, but I really don't think it would help. People are going to be looking out for it now, and the last thing we want to do is get caught. I suggest I write a letter to that MP who came out in support of us and tell him Nan has died. He's in a much better place to make a stink about it than we are . . .'

'But . . .' started Elsie.

'Please, Elsie,' said Milly wearily. 'Please, let's hold off for a few days. We're all tired and sad and angry and . . . my family needs to go to bed.'

For the first time, Milly really felt she might be at odds with Elsie. How she wished Nora and Liza were here to comfort her instead. They would offer genuine sympathy about what had happened to Nan rather than just making more and more radical political suggestions.

'We won't do anything,' said Hilda, to Milly's relief. And then, on seeing her sister's mutinous face, she added, 'At least not for a while. Let's meet after the ELFS meeting next Monday and talk about what we'll do then.'

Milly turned to Hilda gratefully. 'That's a good idea,' she said. 'That gives us all time to cool off and to mourn Nan. There's no need to decide on any action now.'

Elsie stuck out her bottom lip. 'All right,' she said reluctantly. 'We'll wait. But then we'll bite back stronger.'

# 19

As she'd promised, Milly wrote a letter to Mr Henderson. She was amazed to receive a letter back from the politician, almost by return of post. Mr Henderson expressed his condolences on Nan's death and the sad circumstances surrounding it, and promised to do all he could to make sure such a thing never happened again. And then an article about Nan's death appeared in the newspapers, accompanied by a quote from Mr Henderson reiterating his pledge to fight for the withdrawal of police powers over the separation allowance.

Milly could hardly believe it. Suddenly, it seemed, things might be happening.

The very changes they wanted were being considered . . . not because of civil disobedience, but because she was now working from the inside. She should have done this first of all. She should never have resorted to throwing stones.

At work, Milly kept her head down, trying to get used to her new section. She was almost used to moving sections on a regular basis now, and had given up trying to second-guess what was going on. All she could assume was that either she wasn't sorting fast enough or her colleagues objected to working with her. And, suddenly, it seemed of the utmost importance that she didn't lose her job, that she didn't deprive her family of an income . . . that she didn't steer them all one step closer to the workhouse. She worked as hard as she could, creating a new key-list for every new department and trying to get her head wrapped around each new combination of numbers and initials. She might still be angry at the Home Depot, but doing her job poorly was not the way to effect the change she so desperately wanted.

Maybe she would set up a pressure group campaigning for fairer wages for women within the Army Post Office.

Or maybe she should go the whole hog and set up a Home Depot suffragette group.

It was certainly something to think about.

In the meantime, though, the work was relentless and Milly found herself getting caught up in the pre-Christmas mania. There were just so many letters and – particularly – so many parcels, and it was absolutely imperative that every single one got to its destination intact and on time. The soldiers were ordinary men and boys who'd found themselves in a hellish situation a long way from home, and it was crucial every single man got his post in time for Christmas. Milly imagined some lad sitting empty-handed on Christmas Day while his comrades opened their gifts all around him – and her heart broke silently for him. It wouldn't matter if his parcels arrived a day, a week or a month later. The fact was, Christmas would have been missed . . . and that was what counted.

That was why they were all working so hard.

That was why they were sorting until their fingers were crisscrossed with paper cuts and they started to see double in the dim light of the Home Depot.

A couple of days after Nan's death, Milly was wheeling a basket over to the extension to get her next load of sacks.

She'd sort five more sacks before break time and then she'd treat herself to a jammy bun.

'I hear your friend's sweetheart admitted to it all,' came a voice as she passed Mediterranean.

Milly swung round with a start. It was Belle from Team

Incomparable, also pushing a basket and falling into step with her.

Milly stared at her blankly. Whatever could she mean?

For a moment, Milly assumed it must be something to do with Eloise and Jack – although what she couldn't immediately fathom. Maybe the two were engaged. No – that didn't make any sense at all. Getting engaged wasn't something you 'admitted' to, like stealing a loaf of bread or robbing a bank. Or 'forgetting' that you'd promised to knit a blanket for someone.

Belle had stopped pushing and was staring at Milly, waiting for an answer.

Milly shook her head. 'I'm sorry, Belle,' she said. 'I'm sure I don't know what you're talking about.'

Belle looked puzzled. 'The investigation into the extension fire, of course,' she said. 'Apparently James Blackford admitted it was his fault. He was having a ciggie and he dropped the stub and the sack dust just whooshed into flames . . .'

Milly took a deep breath, her thoughts a-whirr.

She had, of course, known the internal investigation into the fire was imminent – although there hadn't been a huge fanfare about it – but she hadn't realised that it was *today*.

Why hadn't she been told? Why hadn't Liza confided in her?

In fact, why hadn't she been *involved*? After all, once Liza had raised the alarm, Milly had been one of the very first people on the scene. She should have been consulted. Surely she might have something useful to contribute. And yet, here she was, finding out about it from *Belle* of all people. How on earth had Belle, who barely knew any of the people involved, heard the outcome of the investigation before she had?

It was almost unfathomable.

But now was neither the time, nor the place, to dwell on such things.

Milly gave Belle a stiff smile and said the first thing that came into her head.

'Those people ain't my friends.'

And then she stalked away.

'Your basket,' Belle shouted after her.

Milly didn't turn around. Hitching up her skirts, she fairly ran to Nora's office in the returned letters department. Nora wasn't there, one of the other girls told her briskly. She was out 'on business' and wasn't expected back until the next day. It was the same story in the broken parcels department. Liza was out for the day and wouldn't be back on duty. Milly was too proud to ask anything else and slunk back to her own station. She listened out for any chatter that might give her a clue as to what had happened, but there wasn't any.

It wasn't until Milly had left the Home Depot for the evening that she found out what was going on. Grabbing the evening newspaper, she ran down to the platform and plonked herself on one of the benches, frantically rifling through the pages.

And, yes, there it was. On the third page, no less.

A huge, black headline: 'Army Postal Worker Pleads Guilty to Starting Home Depot Fire!'

With her heart hammering against her chest and her mouth suddenly dry, Milly skim-read the article. *James Blackford, a civilian supervisor in the honour letter department . . . admitted smoking a cigarette and carelessly tossing the stub in a newly built extension to the Home Depot on the Regent's Park . . . a flagrant breach of army rules . . . the fire partially destroyed the newly built extension along with an estimated one hundred sacks of letters and parcels destined for men at the front . . . the flames could be seen as far away as Finchley . . . Mr Blackford has been dismissed from his position . . .*

Milly swallowed hard. Why hadn't anyone told her? Why was she having to find out like this?

'Are you all right, Miss?'

Milly looked up in irritation. A besuited gentleman with a very luxuriant moustache was looking down at her with concern.

'I'm perfectly all right, thank you,' said Milly.

'It's just three trains have gone past and you haven't got into any of them,' the man persisted. 'And you're as white as a sheet. Are you quite well?'

'I'm perfectly well, thank you.'

She wasn't, of course.

She was obviously totally useless and dispensable. And now she had irrefutable proof Nora and Liza weren't really her friends at all. There was no point in trying to pretend otherwise.

# 20

'**O**h, do be *quiet*!'

Milly sat up and tapped Alice sharply on the shoulder. Her sister had been coughing non-stop ever since they'd got into bed, and there was no way Milly was going to sleep with that going on. It was Sunday night and she needed her beauty sleep. Worse still, it was the third night running Alice had kept her awake. At first, it had been gentle snorts and snuffles – nothing especially loud, but very, *very* annoying nonetheless. The night before, Alice had progressed to the odd cough and, every time Milly finally dropped off, she was startled awake again. And now, when Milly was genuinely exhausted and in need of sleep – *this*! A near-continuous hacking cough that cut through Milly and set her nerves on edge. And it wasn't as if Alice was coughing much during the day. In fact, she had barely coughed at all that evening. It was almost as if she was doing it deliberately to antagonise Milly . . .

Alice sat up beside Milly. 'You're a fine one to talk,' she rasped. 'You cough all the time. You cough so much you don't even know you're doing it. You're always clearing your throat and you're always sniffing, and it drives us all *mad*.'

Milly blinked into the darkness. The Home Depot echoed with coughing morning, noon and night (but it wasn't right in her ear, and it wasn't when she was trying to get to sleep) but she hadn't realised she was *that* persistent an offender at home. Anyway, it was hardly her fault . . .

'It's the sack dust,' she said defensively. 'Hazard of the job.'

'Going yellow is a hazard of my job, but at least that doesn't annoy everyone,' said Alice, lying down again with a huff.

It was typical that asking Alice to be quiet had been somehow twisted so that she was once again the one at fault! Why couldn't Alice just apologise for once? And now the darned girl had started coughing again and . . .

Oh, it was all hopeless! She might just as well get up.

She'd go downstairs and have a ciggie. After all, Alice was clearly sickening for something and a cigarette would kill any germs she had breathed in.

Maybe she would have two, to be on the safe side . . .

Milly wriggled her toes into her slippers, wrapped her shawl around her and crept downstairs by the light of the moon streaming through the glass panel above the front door. The kitchen was still warm and it was tempting to cuddle up on the sofa and light up there – but Ma had a nose like a bloodhound and there was no way Milly would get away with it. Sighing, she walked through the chilly scullery and unlocked the door into the backyard.

She was greeted by a volley of ferocious barking. Boniface had proved himself a most diligent guard dog, but he didn't differentiate between strangers coming through the gate from the alleyway or family members coming out of the back door.

'Be quiet, you silly dog,' said Milly, sitting down on the back step and trying to ignore the cold seeping through her nightdress. At least it was a dry night.

She lit a cigarette and took a deep draught. Boniface settled down beside her and rested his head on her knee.

'Oh, Miss Amelia! It's you.'

Startled, Milly scrambled to her feet and swung around. Mr Wildermuth was standing in the scullery, dressing gown untidily fastened, face creased with concern.

'Yes. Sorry. I just . . .'

Milly debated whether to hastily stub out her cigarette and try to hide the evidence, but decided against it. It was too late and, anyway, Mr Wildermuth was hardly her father.

'Are you alone?' said Mr Wildermuth.

Whatever Milly had imagined Mr Wildermuth might say, it certainly wasn't *that*. His insinuation was clear and she blushed into the darkness. How dare he assume she was that type of girl! Smuggling a boy into her backyard for a bit of how's-your-father . . .

'Of course I'm alone,' Milly replied with great dignity.

'Oh,' said Mr Wildermuth, looking discomfited. 'I didn't mean . . . *that*. I meant maybe your friends from the other night . . .'

Now Milly really was confused. Why on earth should Hilda and Elsie be here?

'It's just me,' she said, with a little shrug.

Mr Wildermuth ran a hand through his hair. 'Forgive me,' he said. 'The dog was barking and I wanted to check all was in order. I didn't mean to pry.'

Milly exhaled. 'It's all right,' she said. 'I thought you might be Ma and I'd be in trouble.' She waved her cigarette at Mr Wildermuth with a rueful little shrug. 'I couldn't sleep,' she added.

Mr Wildermuth nodded and gave her a sympathetic smile. 'Problems at work?' he asked.

'Partly,' admitted Milly.

'Would you like to tell me about them?' asked Mr Wildermuth. 'After all, don't they say a problem shared is a problem halved?'

It was tempting.

'It's nothing really . . .'

'The visit from the King and Queen is causing you headaches perhaps . . .'

Milly stiffened, alarm bells ringing in her mind. What was it Elsie and Hilda had said? Things were different now and Germans – any German – couldn't be trusted. Something like that. Why was Mr Wildermuth asking her about the royal visit? She barely recalled mentioning it to him – had *certainly* only referred to it in passing. And, yet, not only had Mr Wildermuth remembered, but he was pressing for more details.

She gave a tinkly laugh as she stubbed the cigarette out against the wall.

'It's got nothing to do with that,' she said lightly. 'In fact, I've never heard it mentioned again – it must have just been a rumour. Now, if you'll excuse me, I really should get back to bed, or I'll be dead on my feet tomorrow.'

Milly pushed past Mr Wildermuth and headed upstairs, deep in thought.

The little exchange had unsettled her. Should she tell someone – Miss Parker, perhaps – that a German had asked about the royal visit? But, how could she? It would mean betraying Nora's confidence – and, despite everything that had happened between them, Milly still blanched at the thought of being disloyal to her friend.

No. She wouldn't say anything. Not for the time being, at least.

But if her suspicions were aroused – in any way at all – then she would have no choice than to take matters further.

# 21

Monday night and the next ELFS meeting came around all too quickly.

Milly had wondered if she should miss it – after all, she had no wish to have an argument with Elsie. But that was the coward's way out. She needed to make it clear to both girls she wanted to remain friends, but that she was going to try and effect change from the inside from now on.

Milly arrived late after another long and frustrating shift at the Home Depot, and the upstairs room at the Mother's Arms was already packed to the rafters. Hilda and Elsie were sitting together in the middle of the assembled throng, surrounded by chattering women. They waved and made regretful faces that there weren't any free spaces next to them and Milly, unconcerned, slid into a seat at the back.

There would be plenty of time to talk afterwards.

To Milly's consternation, the first part of the meeting was all about Nan! Miss Pankhurst informed the meeting of Nan's death – although the muted response suggested everybody already knew. She went on to lay out the circumstances: Nan losing her son and her job, the grief-induced lewdness, the loss of her separation allowance and her subsequent mental and physical deterioration. It was a familiar but very sad story, said Miss Pankhurst, made even sadder by the fact that Nan was part of the ELFS family. And yet ELFS had been unable to save her. From this day forwards, it was incumbent on each and every member to bring cases like this to the federation's – indeed to Miss Pankhurst's – attention. ELFS had built up a great deal of experience in contesting instances when the separation allowance had been unfairly removed. If only they had known . . .

Miss Pankhurst didn't single anyone out by name; neither did she so much as glance at Milly. Nonetheless, Milly felt herself squirming in her seat. Even though she wasn't being publicly hauled over the coals – even though people weren't pointing and staring – it still *felt* like both a personal and a public rebuke. Of course, there was a possibility Miss Pankhurst didn't know Milly had tried and failed to get Nan's separation allowance reinstated on her own. But, somehow, Milly doubted it. Miss Pankhurst had a tendency to know *everything*. Maybe she couldn't see Milly sitting by herself at the back of the room, or maybe she was just adept at not looking at the person she was reprimanding, but Milly was sure she knew. Was that, she suddenly wondered, the reason Elsie and Hilda hadn't saved her a space? Twenty minutes ago, she hadn't given it another thought – as she wasn't naturally given to being over-sensitive – but now she wasn't sure. Could her friends possibly be distancing themselves from her because of what she'd done (or, rather, what she *hadn't* done)? Had they, in fact, told Miss Pankhurst what had happened . . .?

Milly stayed sitting quietly at the back of the room. Even when Miss Pankhurst moved on to another topic, she remained deep in thought and didn't contribute. Before the meeting, she'd begun to tell herself that Nan would probably have died even if her separation allowance had been reinstated. She'd been so poorly and the infection had got so strong a hold on her chest there was probably nothing anyone could have done . . .

But Miss Pankhurst had turned all that on its head by

suggesting that, if ELFS had got involved, there might have been a very different outcome.

Maybe it was true.

After the meeting, Milly sought out Elsie and Hilda.

'Drink?' she asked brightly. 'My treat.'

Was she imagining the glance between Elsie and Hilda? The glance that told her she was now a liability, a *persona non grata* – a *failure*. She braced herself for one or the other of the girls to tell her they were tired or they had a headache, or they were needed at home . . .

Sure enough, Elsie was clearing her throat. 'We're going straight home, tonight,' she said. 'We've got to mind Rachel so Da can go out.'

'All right.' Resigned, a disappointed Milly turned to leave.

But then Elsie touched her arm. 'Why don't you pop round?' she said. 'We said we'd chat this evening, didn't we? And there's certainly lots to talk about.'

'There certainly is,' said Milly. 'Wait until I tell you about that MP.'

Elsie and Hilda lived in a tenement building not far from Nan's. Milly wasn't sure why, but she had been expecting something different. That said, this apartment had nothing in common with Nan's. Oh, the exterior and the courtyard were much the same – and by the time they reached the communal staircase, the hem of Milly's skirt was splattered with the animal excrement they all politely called 'mud'. But, inside, it was very different. It was nothing grand – the well-worn furnishings were the sort of thing you could pick up from the market – but it was warm and cosy, and spotlessly tidy, and there were so many delicate coverings on the tables and so many antimacassars on the chair arms and backs that Milly stifled a smile. That would be Hilda's work . . .

A middle-aged man was clearly waiting for them; his narrow face, worried expression and thin, sandy hair immediately marked him out as the girls' father. The slight stoop was all his own.

'You're back,' he said, blinking furiously behind his spectacles.

'We are, Da,' said Elsie. 'Came back as soon as the meeting finished.'

Da nodded. 'Your sister's asleep, but keep an ear out for her. She were very unsettled earlier on.'

'It's fine, Da,' said Elsie, placing her hand against the teapot. 'Don't you worry about her. Have a good night.'

Da smiled, put on his hat and coat, and was gone, shutting the door quietly behind him.

'Da works at the docks,' explained Hilda, busying herself with the kettle and teapot.

Milly nodded. 'How old's your sister?' she asked curiously. Elsie and Hilda must be in their early twenties so it was unlikely their sister was a babe in arms. Why couldn't she be left on her own of an evening? After all, Charlie was barely twelve but he was left alone and sent out to do chores on his own all the time.

'Rachel's nearly twenty but she . . . ain't well,' said Elsie.

'I'm sorry,' said Milly politely. Hopefully it wasn't something catching. 'I do hope she feels better soon.'

Elsie laughed. 'No, I mean she's always "not well",' she said. 'She's mentally deficient and blind, an' all. We love her and we want her here with us, but she don't half take a lot of looking after.'

'Our ma would never hear of her being taken away and we feel the same,' added Hilda staunchly. 'That's why we all work shifts. There's always someone here to look after her.'

Milly looked at Elsie and Hilda through new eyes. What a lot they had to cope with, and how gracefully they accepted their lot. Suddenly, she found she had tears in her eyes and, to cover her self-consciousness, she picked up one of the antimacassars and studied it. Antimacassars were so old fashioned – Ma wouldn't have them in the house – but the workmanship was exquisite. Hilda really was very talented.

'This is beautiful,' she said.

Hilda smiled. 'Thank you. I like making them,' she said. 'Even though the light in here is so terrible in winter, I worry I'll end up as blind as Rachel.'

Elsie shrugged. 'We're lucky here in many ways,' she said. 'We're high up so there ain't no damp and we're surrounded by so many other apartments that we never get too cold.'

Milly thought about it. She tended to look down on the tenements, but Ma's bedroom did have a big damp patch in it and Charlie's bedroom was literally freezing in winter – so maybe Elsie had a point.

Hilda put a couple more pieces of coal into the range and settled back against the sofa. 'About that meeting—' she started.

'Oh, Lordy,' interrupted Milly with an exaggerated shudder. 'I'm sure Miss P were telling me off. I thought any minute I'd be sent to the corner and then out would come the cane!'

Elsie and Hilda smiled but didn't otherwise comment, and Milly felt a flush of shame.

'I know I should've asked ELFS to help,' she said, staring into her teacup. 'I'm so sorry, really I am.'

'It's *all* our faults,' said Elsie briskly, patting Milly's hand. 'We could *all* have done more.'

'But I have news,' said Milly. 'I wrote to that MP, Mr Henderson . . .'

Elsie sat forward. 'That's good,' she said distractedly. 'But we have news too. An idea for something we might do. And we wouldn't be able to do it without you.'

Milly's heart sank. More stone throwing, she presumed.

Even though any fool could chuck a stone through a window, she would be needed to write the letter. It seemed Elsie was still hell-bent on the public mischief route . . .

'Let me tell you about Mr Henderson first,' said Milly. 'Because I really don't think we need to do that sort of thing anymore.'

'Oh, but this is different,' said Elsie, with a little glance at Hilda. Milly noticed Hilda didn't quite meet her sister's eyes.

Milly swallowed a sigh. 'What do you have in mind?' she asked.

Elsie took a deep breath. 'We want to bomb the Home Depot,' she said.

## 22

For a moment, there was silence.

Then Milly burst out laughing. 'Course we do,' she said, clapping her hands together. 'Tell you what – why don't we do it when the King and Queen are visiting, an' all?'

But as the silence lengthened, Milly's laughter evaporated into thin air.

'Come on,' she said, looking from one to the other. 'This ain't no time for jokes. We've got Mr Henderson starting to fight our corner.'

Still, no one laughed and, this time, the silence persisted until it became uncomfortable. There was a muscle going like the clappers in Elsie's cheek, and Milly felt the first ripple of unease.

'Come on, girls,' she repeated with a nervous giggle. 'Be serious.'

'We're deadly serious, Milly,' said Elsie quietly. 'We want to explode a bomb in the Home Depot when the King and Queen are visiting.'

Milly's ripple of unease turned into a jolt of icy fear, which propelled her to her feet.

'You want to murder the King and Queen?' she fairly shouted, voice squeaking and cracking.

'Shhh! No. No,' hissed Hilda, flapping her hand at Milly. 'Of course we don't.'

'We don't want to kill *anyone*,' added Elsie coolly. 'Stop

shouting, will you? You'll wake Rachel and we'll have a devil of a job getting her to sleep again.'

Milly sat down, her heart rate returning to normal. 'That weren't funny,' she said crossly. 'You scared me something proper.' She exhaled noisily, puffing out her cheeks.

Elsie leaned forward, elbows on knees, pale blue eyes boring into Milly's. 'We *are* thinking about planting a bomb in the Home Depot when the King and Queen visit,' she said. 'Not to hurt them. Not to hurt anyone, for that matter. Just to cause damage and a lot of bother.' She paused and took a deep breath. 'Think about it,' she added, eyes sparkling in a way Milly had never seen before. 'It would get into every paper in London – in England; in the *Empire* for that matter. Then, the very same evening, we'll write an anonymous letter to *The Day* taking responsibility for it and bringing everyone's attention to what's happening with the separation allowance and to women's rights in general. It can't go wrong . . .'

Milly was about to interject and say that, of course, it could go wrong – and in a most spectacular fashion – when Elsie carried on.

'It's no more than Nan deserves,' she said with a sideways little look at Milly. 'You yourself said the whole world deserves to hear what happened to her and now here's our chance. You've got to admit it's perfect.'

Milly's heart was pumping and she felt slightly sick. There was no doubt what Elsie was proposing would cause a massive stir. The movement for women's rights would be ingrained into everyone's hearts and minds in way it hadn't since Emily Davison had been killed by the King's horse at the Epsom Derby two years before.

On the other hand . . .

'You're mad,' said Milly baldly. 'It's a ridiculous idea and you'd never get away with it. Even if we overlooked all the letters and parcels that would be destroyed, there are too many things outside our control. How would we ensure the bomb didn't go off in front of the King and Queen? How would we make sure no one else got hurt, for goodness' sake? And what would Nan think about all this?' she added. 'You say you'd be doing it in her name, but surely she'd be shocked – *horrified!* – to hear you talking like this. It's *terrorism!*'

To Milly's amazement, both Hilda and Elsie burst out laughing.

'Whatever you or I might think about the plan, I'm afraid Nan would've loved it,' said Hilda.

'She would absolutely have loved it,' added Elsie. 'She were one of us, you see!'

Milly wrinkled her brow in confusion. 'You mean . . . she were an activist?' she said.

'Too right she was,' said Elsie. 'In her heyday, she were one of the best. That's what our ma always said, anyways.'

Milly took a deep, steadying breath, trying to take it all in.

'Nan weren't out drowning her sorrows the night she were stopped,' said Hilda. 'In fact, she weren't drowning her sorrows at all. No, she were out to set fire to Lord Emmett's London flat.'

'No, she were not!' spluttered Milly, hand to heart.

'She were,' said Hilda. 'When she got stopped by the law, she pretended to be drunk and out on the game. Good at thinking on her feet, Nan were. Just like you, Milly.'

'No!' said Milly, burying her head in her hands. She'd had Nan down as a mild, middle-aged lady – not a fast-acting, quick-talking activist. 'So, the story about her son dying at the front – was that made up, an' all?'

'No!' Elsie looked shocked. 'That bit were absolutely true. Her Sammy were the apple of her eye. Signed up as soon as he were able and broke her bloody heart. Thought the war would be one big adventure and needed saving from himself, she always said, just like all men. Nan were convinced if women had had the vote, the war would never have started. Women would've seen sense, she used to say. They wouldn't have blindly followed the rich into signing up for this hell on earth.'

Milly sagged back against the sofa, head reeling. 'Where would you get a bomb from, anyway?' she asked. 'They hardly grow on trees.'

Was she really having this conversation?

'That's what we wanted to tell you,' said Elsie. 'It was all there, under Nan's bed. We found it when we were helping to clear out her things. It was almost as if it's meant to be.'

'Nan had a bomb in her bedroom?' echoed Milly weakly.

'Not a live bomb, silly,' said Elsie. 'But enough stuff to make one up. Just one. Nan were really active with the suffragette bombing campaign before the war. She told us all about what they did at the Bank of England and St Paul's Cathedral, didn't she, Hilda? It must be left over from that.'

Milly was tempted to pinch herself to see if she was dreaming. There was a tiny part of her still wondering if it was all an elaborate ruse; if Elsie and Hilda were suddenly going to poke her in the ribs with loud guffaws of laughter and go on to discuss throwing a stone through the window of a local paper or something.

But, in her heart of hearts, she knew they were deadly serious and, suddenly, she was scared.

*Very* scared.

Because now she'd been told of this ridiculous plan, surely she was dangerous to them?

For a moment, Milly considered running – maybe slinging a couple of antimacassars in her wake – but what was the point? Hilda and Elsie knew where she lived – they'd made sure of *that* . . .

She would have to get the whole family to up sticks and move in with their relatives in East Ham. No, that wasn't nearly far enough away. They'd have to go further afield; throw herself on the mercy of Nora or Liza.

Except her friends weren't talking to her. She really was all alone.

Hilda leaned over and touched Milly on the knee, and Milly flinched involuntarily.

'You all right, Milly?' she asked.

Milly stared back. 'Yes, no . . . I don't know. I'll have to think about all this. I can see where you're coming from but it's all . . . a bit much.'

To her exquisite relief, both Elsie and Hilda smiled at her.

'Of course,' said Hilda. 'It's a bit of a step up from Mr Wilmington's window, ain't it?'

'Takes a while to get your mind wrapped around it, eh?' added Elsie.

Milly nodded. That was an understatement.

'It's just an idea,' Hilda was saying. 'It might not work and we certainly wouldn't do nothing you wasn't comfortable with.'

'Course,' said Milly, taking a rather shaky gulp of air. She hadn't, until that moment, realised she'd been holding her breath. 'I want to do something for Nan as much as you do, but . . .'

'Just promise us you'll think about it?' said Elsie.

'I will,' said Milly. 'And now, it's getting late. Ma will be wondering where I am.'

'Of course,' said Hilda easily. 'We'll see you soon.'

# 23

Milly walked home in a state of shock.

Had that really just happened? Had her friends really said they wanted her help to *blow up the Home Depot*?

They can't have done. Or if they had done, they can't have been being serious. Could they?

Had it been daylight, Milly might have pounded the streets for hours, trying to make sense of it all. But it was dark – and ever since the attack, Milly hadn't felt totally comfortable being out by herself after dusk. So, she didn't linger or change her route – and she *certainly* kept more than half an eye on her surroundings – but that didn't stop her mind from going nineteen to the dozen trying to think it all through.

Because, as well as being confused, Milly was also conflicted.

She was as furious as Hilda and Elsie about what had happened to Nan, and she felt just as much of a burning need for justice and change. And there was no doubt bombing the Home Depot would cause a stir – heavens, it would make the front page of newspapers around the world, especially with the King and Queen in attendance and especially coming so hot on the heels of the fire. Two huge incidences in a matter of months would mean the reputation of the Home Depot would hit rock bottom, unlikely ever to recover – and that, in turn, would hit the morale of both the public and the troops. As well as getting publicity for women's rights, might a bomb change the whole course of the war? Might it end the war?

And, if all that could be achieved without shedding a single drop of blood – well, surely only a fool would dismiss it totally out of hand?

But on the other hand . . . no! Wasn't Hilda and Elsie's plan more about revenge than justice? The powers-that-be were hardly likely to give women the vote because they'd managed to smuggle a bomb into the Home Depot. And, wasn't it all a little . . . crude? To say nothing of potentially disastrous. At 'best', hundreds of sack-loads of parcels and letters would be destroyed and, at worst . . . well, it simply didn't bear thinking about. Worst of all, if she went ahead and got involved, wouldn't she become the person Liza and Nora had feared she was. Wouldn't she be confirming their worst fears?

Milly's thoughts were going round and round in circles. She had the mother of all headaches brewing and she was no closer to reaching a decision as she pushed open the gate.

Ma.

She would talk to Ma.

Even if it meant admitting she'd spent a goodly part of the last few weeks slipping around London under cover of darkness and throwing stones through windows of some of the capital's most pre-eminent residents, she would tell Ma. Milly cringed inwardly at how angry – how disappointed – her mother would be, but she had to tell her.

But there was no opportunity to talk to Ma that night.

Ma's attention was entirely taken up with Alice.

Far from getting better, Alice's cough had worsened and she was now running a fever. Nothing to be unduly worried about, Ma said. Alice had been moved in with Ma, and Caroline was to share Milly's bed that night. And no – they couldn't see Alice; it was best she wasn't disturbed. Just for the night. Just until she felt better.

'Do you think she's really poorly?' whispered Caroline,

as they lay in the bed listening to the racking coughs next door.

'Of course not,' said Milly quickly. Too quickly. Because how could she possibly know?

'It's just that game at Hallowe'en,' said Caroline, her breath catching. 'When Alice picked the clay. That might have been a sign.'

Milly had forgotten all about that.

'That's just superstition,' she said briskly. 'It said you were going to take holy orders, for goodness' sake.'

'But I am helping the vicar with the strays, aren't I?' said Caroline earnestly.

'That's not the same,' said Milly firmly. 'Charlie hasn't travelled anywhere, and I'm not in love.'

She pushed away the thought that compulsory conscription might force Charlie to travel whether Ma liked it or not. And as for the suggestion she was in love . . .

The fact was, though, there might be a beastly war on, but that didn't stop other terrible things happening. People got ill all the time. Nan had died – even though everyone had said she would get better. And now Alice was lying there next to Ma in a room that had a nasty damp patch in it and that stupid Hallowe'en game had predicted something awful would happen . . .

Alice might be prickly and straight-talking, and positively maddening at times, but Milly couldn't bear the thought she might die.

# 24

Alice was no better in the morning.

Ma insisted Milly should go to work as usual. There was no point in everyone moping around at home.

Milly sat on the train feeling totally discombobulated. She hated Alice being ill. Really hated it. In fact, she hadn't realised how much she loved her sister, even though she never seemed to agree with anything Milly said or did. She and Alice fought like cat and dog – had done so for as long as Milly could remember. By contrast, Milly had always envied Hilda and Elsie their closeness. But, last night, Milly had noticed a very different dynamic between the two. Elsie had been the one pushing for bombing the Home Depot and Hilda had been quiet. Very quiet. In fact, come to think of it, Elsie always seemed to be the driving force behind most of the ideas . . . with Hilda coming along for the ride . . .

Was that really better than two sisters arguing? Particularly if they were arguing as equals?

And, as for the conversation about bombing the Home Depot – well, *that* seemed almost laughable in the cold light of day. It was a ridiculous notion and she was having nothing whatsoever to do with it. Not even if it meant Hilda and Elsie thinking less of her. She might agree to doing a little more stone throwing but that was that. And even more stone throwing might be a bad idea now Alice was ill. The family really could not afford Milly losing her job . . .

With a lighter heart, Milly threw herself into her duties that morning and – for once – found herself really enjoying it. She immersed herself in the gentle rhythms of the work, her fingers flicking swiftly through the piles of letters, each flying – as if by magic – to the right basket. Without slowing her pace, she managed to join in with the lusty singing of 'It's A Long Way to Tipperary', which sprang up from somewhere over Salonika way, and then discussed the latest flicks with the girl standing next to her.

'Wow, you're quick,' said the new girl on the other side of her, and Milly felt a glow of satisfaction.

It had seemed impossible to begin with, but she had got there in the end.

'Good morning, Milly.'

Looking up, Milly saw Miss Parker standing to one side of them. Because Milly's eyes barely left the circuit from bag to letter to open sacks, she hadn't glanced up for ages. Thank goodness she'd been behaving herself. Well, in the Home Depot at least – and Miss Parker couldn't possibly know about anything else.

'Good morning, Miss Parker,' replied Milly, trying to keep a question mark out of her voice.

'Milly, would you come with me please?'

Carefully avoiding everyone's eyes, Milly rose to her feet and followed Miss Parker through the narrow 'corridors' that separated the various sections of the sorting floor. Miss Parker didn't offer any conversation – the corridors were too narrow and the clanking of trolleys and baskets too noisy to make chatting practical – so Milly was left with her rather panicked thoughts. What could Miss Parker possibly want with her this time?

Another reallocation? Milly prodded the thought of starting again as one might a rotten tooth, and found she would be quite disappointed if that was the case. She was as fast – faster

– than just about everyone else and she finally liked being at
the sharp end of the Home Depot. After all, as Jack had once
said, it was what the whole place was all about.

Milly followed Miss Parker into her office and then started
in surprise. The man himself was sitting in one of the chairs
facing Miss Parker's desk. Milly was totally thrown. What on
earth was *Jack* doing there? More specifically, had she told
him anything – anything at all – which he might use against
her? She racked her brains but drew a blank.

Milly was even more thrown by the feeling – the *sensation*
– that caught behind her breastbone and made her catch her
breath. It wasn't conscious – and it certainly wasn't welcome
– but it made Milly's cheeks flush and her stomach swoop as
if she had gone too high on one of the swings in Victoria Park
and wasn't certain of her landing. Jack had stood up as the
women entered the room and was looking down at Milly, his
face inscrutable. His hair, copper and gold among the brown,
the peak to his eyebrows, the firm set to his jaw, the little
mole in front of his ear. He was familiar and dear, a cad, a
stranger . . .

Oh, Lordy, Milly . . .

'Sit down, both of you,' said Miss Parker briskly, waving
her hand at the chairs.

Milly sat, studiously avoiding Jack's eye and hoping it wasn't
obvious her heart was going like the clappers. Every muscle,
every fibre was painfully aware of Jack's proximity, and she
had to keep her hands folded primly in her lap to resist the
temptation to reach out and let her fingers brush casually
against the fabric of his jacket.

'Now then, Miss Woods,' said Miss Parker, walking around
her desk and sitting down opposite them. 'Private Archer has
been telling me all about what you've been up to on the
sorting-room floor!'

Milly's eyes flew to Jack in alarm. What the devil had he

been telling Miss Parker? Deliberately mis-sorting mail? Heated arguments about Edith Cavell? Inciting insurrection when she'd agreed violence was sometimes justified?

'Not at all, Miss Parker,' Milly gabbled, looking wildly around the room. 'I'm sure Private Archer's made some sort of mistake . . .' She trailed off miserably. What on earth could she say? All she could do was sit there, steeling herself against the crushing disappointment she felt towards Jack for ratting on her – how *could* he? – and against whatever was coming to her from Miss Parker. Because one thing was for sure – it wasn't going to be good.

And then she noticed Miss Parker was smiling.

'Oh, come now, Milly,' she said, with something approaching laughter. 'It's most unlike you to be so modest!'

Milly wrinkled her nose in confusion. 'I'm sorry, Miss Parker,' she said. 'I really don't know what you're talking about?'

Miss Parker raised her eyebrows in mock-frustration. 'Very well,' she said. 'Private Archer, perhaps you would remind Miss Woods about the scheme she's come up with for improving the efficiency of the sorting-room floor.'

'By all means, Miss Parker,' said Jack.

Without even the hint of a grin, he started describing how Milly had cut up her key-list and fashioned a new one, featuring only the regiments and brigades that related to her section of the sorting-room floor. Milly's stress and misery grew in waves. Of all the things to be getting in trouble for, this really took the biscuit. Oh, no doubt the key-list was army property and strictly speaking she had no business vandalising it – but she had only done it to help herself work as quickly and as accurately as she could.

It was all so unfair.

'I didn't know I shouldn't have done it, honest I didn't, Miss,' Milly blurted out, cutting across Jack. 'If I'd have known it were against army rules . . .'

Miss Parker held up a hand. 'Shh, Milly,' she said. 'I believe Private Archer has more to say.'

With great effort, Milly stopped talking. Jutting out her jaw, she slumped back and tried to control her breathing. Jack – the *traitor* – was now describing in frankly unnecessary detail how she had fashioned little signs with the most common abbreviations for the units in her sections and pinned them to the sacks. Honestly, never mind the golden highlights in his hair or the shape of his eyebrows – the man was an absolute pig. One moment he was encouraging her to take a degree in politics and the next . . . this. And to think she'd let him take her photograph and put an arm around her waist . . .

You just couldn't trust men. In the end, they all let you down. Every. Single. Bloody. One.

Milly was so lost in her misery, she hadn't noticed Jack had stopped talking and that he and Miss Parker had turned to look at her.

'I'm so sorry, Miss,' said Milly forlornly. 'I were just trying to . . .'

'Oh, Milly, stop it,' said Miss Parker, slapping her hand down on the table. 'You must know, I think it's absolutely marvellous. All of it!'

'You do?'

'Of course I do,' said Miss Parker. 'And I'm very grateful to Private Archer for bringing it to my attention.'

'Oh!'

Milly's eyes flickered to Jack and she saw he was smiling at her, the dimple dancing in his cheek. Maybe he wasn't such a cad after all. There was the small matter of Eloise, of course, but . . .

'In fact,' Miss Parker was saying. 'We think it's such a good idea we're planning to introduce your modified key-lists throughout the Home Depot. It's all been approved by Sergeant Major Cunningham. You're quite right, Milly – the current system is far too unwieldy. There are literally thousands of army units now, and it's taking new recruits far too long to get up to speed. It's also putting us off rotating staff when we really need to.'

Milly exhaled in one big noisy breath and beamed around her, all animosity forgotten.

'Oh, that's marvellous. I'm right grateful, really I am,' she said.

'We're very grateful to you,' said Miss Parker. 'Now, before we let Private Archer go, there's one more thing I want to discuss with you both.'

Milly and Jack exchanged a brief glance. It seemed neither of them had any idea what Miss Parker was about to say.

'As you both know, the Home Depot Christmas party will be on us before we know it and, Milly, I know you are part of the organising committee.'

Milly nodded, her heart beginning to thump uncomfortably against her rib cage. Surely Miss Parker hadn't got wind of what had been discussed the night before.

*Surely.*

'We have a number of . . . distinguished guests coming along that afternoon,' continued Miss Parker. 'After consultation with Sergeant Major Cunningham, we've decided we'd like you two to make a presentation of two large envelopes featuring postmarks that have been specially created for the occasion.'

Jack's expression didn't change. 'That would be an honour, Miss Parker,' he said politely. 'Thank you very much.'

Milly had to remind herself Jack didn't know who the 'special guests' actually were.

She also had to remind herself not to jump on her chair and to shout loudly, 'I've been invited to meet the bloody King and Queen of England.' Because, even though she might distrust the powers-that-be, this was still the biggest thing that had ever happened to her. Wait until they heard about it at home!

In the meantime, of course, she wasn't supposed to have an inkling as to who the dignitaries were, so she did her best to mimic Jack's polite but casual words.

'Thank you very much, Miss Parker. I should like that very much, and shall try ever so hard not to drop the envelope.'

Miss Parker and Jack both laughed easily, and Milly felt a giggle welling up inside her.

Oh, this was all quite marvellous. Nora and Liza would be furious Milly had been chosen over them and as for Team Incomparable – oh, she would love to see the look on their faces.

And then Jack was leaving the room with a little bow and a smile. Miss Parker indicated Milly should stay seated, and got up to show him out. After a few moments, Milly could hear her chatting to someone in the corridor outside her office and Milly's eye started to wander around the little office. Not that there was much to see. The hat-and-coat stand would be useful on the sorting-room floor – she and the others had to hang their hats and coats on hooks attached to the wooden pillars, and they got so crowded the coats were always tumbling to the floor and getting trampled underfoot. But, apart from that, it was all very sparse.

Not much to see, at all.

Then Milly's eye landed on a bulky blue book on Miss Parker's desk. Squinting at the upside-down label, she could just about work out the words on the front: *Record of Women Employed as Temporary Sorters in the Army Post Office*. Oh, how she would love to look inside and see what was written about herself. About them all! Would it detail her lost admission cards and the fact she had cheeked the poor woman who had tried to train her in sorting the post? Would it detail the fact Liza had been in the extension building when it had caught fire? And would it mention that Nora was Major Benham's niece?

More seriously, what would it be able to tell her about Nan? It still rankled that the Home Depot had fired poor Nan when she had been so grief-stricken. Of course, no one could have foreseen what would happen next but, nonetheless, it seemed to Milly that Nan's firing was a stain on both the Army Post Office's judgement *and* its reputation. She wondered how that was explained away in the book.

With her head partially turned and her ears cocked for Miss Parker's return, Milly reached out and put an index finger on the bulky book. She hesitated a moment and then slowly, slowly she dragged the book towards her, simultaneously swivelling it around. Then, when she was past the point of no return, she leaned forward, opened the book and started feverishly slicking through the pages. Each employee had at least one page dedicated to her; as well as her name, age and address, the book also detailed each woman's pay together with notes on her conduct and any accidents or injuries she had sustained while at work.

Quick, Milly.

*Quick.*

Nan Reid.

R.

Milly flicked through the book as quickly as she could, heart in mouth. She could still hear Miss Parker talking in the corridor, but the conversation could end at any time and it would only take seconds for Miss Parker to walk back in . . .

N . . . O . . . P . . .

Ah, here was R.

And . . . here was Nan Reid.

Milly scanned the page. Yes, it was the right Nan. Nan Reid, aged forty-one, lived at the address in Bow that Milly recognised. She had been employed since August in the parcels for prisoners of war department.

Milly scanned further down the page and then started in shock.

Nan had been cautioned for stealing supplies and then dismissed two weeks later for repeating the same offence.

Milly closed her eyes for a moment, trying to take it all in. There must be some mistake – everyone had been very clear Nan had been 'let go'. In fact, Milly had been led to believe the death of Nan's son had meant she'd arrived late on two days and not at all on a third. But, when Milly opened her eyes and looked again, there it was in Miss Parker's perfectly legible – if loopy – handwriting. Nan had been cautioned for stealing cigarettes and then, two weeks later, had been summarily dismissed for repeating the offence.

Surely that changed *everything*?

But there was no time to think about it further, because Milly could hear Miss Parker saying goodbye to whoever she was talking to in the corridor. There was just time for Milly to quietly shut the book and swivel it back into place before Miss Parker strode back into the room.

'I'm so sorry to keep you,' said Miss Parker pleasantly, walking around the table and sitting down. 'There's one last thing,' she added. 'And this is actually the most important – for you, at least.'

She stopped and took a sip of water from a glass on the table, and Milly found she was holding her breath.

What else could Miss Parker possibly want to tell her on top of all the surprises the morning had already held? And what could be better than what she had already been told about the royal visit and about the key-lists?

Miss Parker put the glass down leisurely. 'I won't beat around the bush, Milly,' she said. 'You're to be promoted. From the new year, I will be putting you in charge of thirty women in Salonika.'

Oh. *Oh!*

Milly sat there opening and shutting her mouth like a fool.

Promoted? A team of women? Things like that simply didn't happen to women like her.

'Oh, Miss,' she said eventually. 'I don't know what to say.'

'It can't have come as a huge surprise to you.'

'Oh, but it has, Miss. A total surprise.'

How could she possibly have known? Or even guessed?

'But all that moving from section to section?' said Miss Parker. 'No sooner had you got your feet under one table, we were stationing you somewhere else. Surely that rather gave the game away?'

'Not at all, Miss,' said Milly. 'I were worried you thought I weren't up to the job and were giving me a chance some-where else!'

'Oh, dear,' said Miss Parker. 'I'll admit you didn't get off to the best start by cheeking Miss Rich, but after that you were flying. We wanted to try you out in different roles before we increased your responsibilities.'

'I can hardly believe it, Miss,' said Milly. 'My own little department!'

'Yes,' said Miss Parker. 'They will mostly be new recruits specifically brought in to replace some of the temporary staff who have joined us for the run-up to Christmas. You will need to get them up to speed as quickly as possible. You've been here long enough to know that if any department isn't working properly, the whole machine is in danger of grinding to a halt.'

'I won't let you down, Miss,' said Milly fervently.

'I know you won't,' said Miss Parker warmly. 'And a word of advice, if I may?'

'Of course, Miss.'

Miss Parker's hand strayed absent-mindedly to the cameo locket she always wore on a tight ribbon around her neck – almost like a choker. She started rubbing it, eyes fixed on a point in the corner of the ceiling, searching for words.

'I know you're a member of ELFS, Milly,' she said. 'I've heard you holding forth very eloquently on the subject of women's rights and the injustices that are meted out to our sex, and I must say I agree with you.'

'Oh, Miss. You're a suffragette,' cried Milly.

She had had her suspicions.

'I am,' said Miss Parker. 'Or, at least, I was. And I know Sylvia Pankhurst is doing some marvellous work over in the East End with her social initiatives, and I have every respect for that. But it's my fervent belief that women will create the changes we want – we *deserve* – by doing so quietly, from the inside. From doing work formerly thought to be the preserve of men and by doing it so well no one can possibly doubt we are in every way their equal. *That's* how I believe we'll bring about the changes we want. Not by the public mischief the suffragettes indulged in before the war. I have no time for those who throw stones or who set fire to letterboxes, or who throw themselves under horses for that matter. Don't those things just underline the notion that we're weak, hysterical creatures without the means to pull together a cohesive thought or put forward a rational argument?'

Milly suddenly found herself unable to meet her supervisor's eye. She sat mutely, staring at her lap, feeling a flush spreading up her neck. It all seemed too close to home . . . too personal. Almost as if Miss Parker knew exactly what Milly had got herself into.

But Miss Parker couldn't know. She couldn't possibly. She was talking generally, recognising Milly as a fellow suffragist, sharing a confidence. And she certainly had a point. Of course, doing men's work better than men themselves was an excellent way to promote women's rights. It might take more time – it was certainly less spectacular and showy – but surely slow and steady would one day win the race. But, did that mean there wasn't a role for direct action at all? Milly wasn't sure she agreed wholeheartedly with Miss Parker on that. Certainly, her protests to date had been disorganised and ineffective – and a bomb was definitely a step too far – but . . . doing nothing at all? That could take *years!*

Milly liked the Home Depot. It had given her opportunities beyond her wildest dreams – and she had no wish to do it harm. She didn't want to blow up the extension and destroy hundreds of sacks of mail, she didn't want to spoil the Christmas party and she didn't want the reputation of the Home Depot to be in ruins. And, if what was in the blue book was correct, then it painted everything in a different light. The Army Post Office hadn't been unfair or unsympathetic to Nan. In fact, the Army Post Office hadn't been at fault at all.

But, there was still a battle to be fought and won.

'Do you mind if I ask something?' said Milly.

'Not at all,' said Miss Parker.

'Well, I think the Home Depot is marvellous in many ways,' said Milly. 'But everyone knows women are paid less than men for doing the same job, and that ain't marvellous at all, is it? In fact, it's really unfair. Why should we do the job as well as – *better* than – men, and not receive the same wages?'

Milly held her breath. Had she gone too far?

But Miss Parker just gave a deep sigh. 'Of course it isn't fair, Milly,' she said. 'It isn't fair at all, but we have a long way to go on that front, I'm afraid. It's something I constantly remind my male superiors of to no avail, and it's tricky during a war when we can't realistically go on strike.'

'I see that,' said Milly. 'But I don't see why we should sit back and do nothing. And . . . I've been thinking of setting up a group within the Home Depot to represent the rights and interests of the women working here . . .' She trailed off and looked expectantly at Miss Parker, fully expecting to be slapped down. Indeed, Miss Parker was frowning.

'Sergeant Major Cunningham will not like that at all,' she said.

'I know,' said Milly, with a rueful smile. 'But that's . . .'

'That's not any reason not to go ahead,' Miss Parker finished for her, slamming a hand down onto her desk. 'I absolutely agree with you, Milly, and – as your supervisor – you have my blessing to go ahead and to hold your meetings on Army Post Office premises. Nothing militant, nothing illegal . . .'

'Of course not,' said Milly, heart soaring. 'Oh, thank you, Miss Parker. Thank you. Just one more question?'

'Of course.'

'I hope you don't think this is rude, but I've often wondered about your cameo. It's ever so beautiful and unusual.'

As soon as the words were out of her mouth, Milly cursed herself for having gone too far. She sat there, shoulders hunched, fully expecting Miss Parker to tick her off for her impertinence or even to turf her unceremoniously out of the office. And, indeed, Miss Parker did take her time in answering. But then, to Milly's surprise, she reached behind her neck and unclipped the velvet band. She put it on the desk in front of Milly and started fiddling with the tiny clasp until it opened.

On one side of the locket was a photograph of a middle-aged woman, with an uncompromisingly direct stare, a firm chin and dark hair cut daringly short into the new-fangled 'bob'. On the other side was a lock of – presumably – the same dark hair. Milly looked at Miss Parker in surprise. Whatever she had been expecting, it hadn't been . . . *this*!

Miss Parker was staring down at the photo. 'This is a picture of my very good . . . friend, Prudence,' she said softly.

Milly wasn't sure how to respond.

'Is she . . . still with us . . .?' she asked hesitantly. It seemed a little insensitive to come right out and ask if Prudence had died, but why else would Miss Parker have a picture of her around her neck? After all, Milly was very fond of her own friends – although she seemed to be at sixes and sevens with them all at the moment – but she wouldn't think to wear their likeness around her neck.

Miss Parker barked with laughter. 'No, Pru is very much alive,' she said. 'In fact, in some ways she is the most "alive" person I know. In some ways she reminds me of you, Milly. Always tackling life straight on, not letting anything get in the way of what she thinks is right.'

Goodness. Was that really how Miss Parker saw her?

Milly wasn't sure she saw herself like that at all.

'Where is Prudence now, Miss?' she asked.

'She's in France,' said Miss Parker. 'She's driving an ambulance with the medical corps and she's putting herself in harm's way every single day.'

'Gosh,' said Milly. 'How brave. I didn't know women did that sort of thing.'

'They didn't,' said Miss Parker. 'At least, not until Pru came along. She was one of the first. That was what she wanted to do, so she upped and offed and did it – laughing at all the obstacles in her way. And I decided to stay in Blighty, keeping the home fires burning and making sure the post gets through.'

For a moment, there was silence. Milly had a thousand and one questions but, for once, she didn't know quite what to say. Then Miss Parker clapped her hands together.

'And on that note, I'd say we both need to get back to work, wouldn't you?'

And the moment was gone.

Milly left the office, mind full to bursting. It was only half an hour until they were dismissed from lunch; maybe she could disappear early into the park, have a ciggie and think everything through. Yes, that was exactly what she would do. She might even attempt a circuit of the lake before the masses packed out the park with their noise and their chatter . . .

Jack was waiting for her.

He was lounging against a pile of sacks by the edge of the sorting-room floor and grinned at her as she approached.

'How about all that, then?' he said, pushing himself upright so that he towered over her.

Milly allowed herself the ghost of a grin. 'It was not at all what I expected,' she said.

She still hadn't forgiven Jack for stepping out with Eloise . . . but it *had* been jolly decent of him to tell Miss Parker about her ideas. Many men – women too – would have claimed them as their own. And now, because of Jack, all those other lovely things had happened. At least, she assumed that was why they had. Would she have been invited centre stage at the party and promoted if Jack hadn't told Miss Parker about her various schemes? She had no way of knowing . . .

'About this party,' said Jack. 'Who do you think these dignitaries are, then?'

A matter of months – no, a matter of *days* – ago, Milly would likely have spilled the beans, unable to keep the secret of the royal visit and not really seeing why she should. But something had changed. It wasn't just she had had her fingers burned by Elsie and Hilda trying to exploit her indiscretions. It was also because Miss Parker had given her a different way of looking at how to promote rights for women; that instead of just shouting about them, she should instead be trying to paint women in a good light in everything she said and everything she did. So, she wouldn't break Nora's confidence and she wouldn't tittle-tattle – even though she was dying to tell Jack.

'I don't know,' she said demurely. 'Who would you guess?'

'Major Benham if we're very lucky,' said Jack with a little grin.

'It's more likely to be Sergeant Major Cunningham,' said Milly, with a little snort of laughter. 'Ooh, I can hardly contain myself.'

The two laughed easily together and Milly thought, again,

how much fun he was and how much she enjoyed his company. It was such a pity about all the . . . complications.

'I wonder why they choose us?' she asked.

Jack regarded her with his head on one side. 'Oh, that bit's easy,' he said.

'Is it?'

'Of course it is,' said Jack. 'Go on. Think about it. The brave war hero who lost an eye at Marne . . .'

Milly thought about it. 'And the plucky girl from the East End who stepped in to help out,' she finished for him.

This time their laughter was louder and longer. 'There you go,' said Jack. 'I knew you wouldn't let me down.'

'Never,' said Milly. Oh, goodness – whatever had made her say that? Then she added, 'Thank you.'

'*Thank* you?' echoed Jack, looking surprised. 'Whatever for?'

'Oh, you know,' said Milly, pleating the side of her skirt between awkward fingers. 'For telling Miss Parker about my scheme. For not claiming it as your own.'

'Why on earth would I claim it as my own?' Jack looked aghast. 'That would be an exceedingly rum thing to do. Honestly, Milly, what sort of man do you think I am?'

Milly wasn't sure how to answer that and wasn't sure whether to be relieved or disappointed when Miss Parker came bustling out of the office towards them.

'You two still here malingering?' she said, shooing them away with her hands. 'Go on, both of you, back to your stations. There's a war on, don't you know?'

# 25

Milly decided not to go for a stroll in the park, after all. But she was also far too wound up to head straight back to her station. Instead, with a quick look over her shoulder to make sure Miss Parker wasn't watching her, she found herself heading off across the Home Depot in search of the parcels for prisoners of war department – the section that Nan had worked in. The Home Depot was still growing week on week, month on month: hundreds – no, thousands – of people all busy packaging, sorting, wheeling, unloading, shouting. It was a veritable village – even a small town – and Milly didn't know the half of it; heavens, most of it hadn't even been built when she'd started in the early summer! She kept asking directions, kept walking through narrow passages bordered by trolleys and baskets and too many piles of sacks to count, and, eventually, on the other side of an area that seemed to be being used as storage, she saw the handwritten sign – *POWs* – on a wooden partition.

Milly took a deep breath, threw her shoulders back and walked through the gap in the partition. She had to know the truth. Had Nan really stolen from parcels destined for prisoners of war or – as she claimed – had she been heartlessly dismissed for poor timekeeping after her son had died?

Behind the partition was a hive of activity. The department seemed to be staffed almost entirely by stout middle-aged women bustling about officiously as they packaged up industrial quantities of cigarettes, tea, biscuits and tins of various description. Most of the ladies hadn't taken off their hats, and Milly wondered why. Maybe they didn't think of the Home Depot as 'inside' – after all, it could be considered a glorified garden shed – or maybe they simply wanted to keep their heads warm in the frigid air. Before the war, these would have been the women who had bossed everyone around at the village fete. But, then, before the war, she had been the sort of girl who'd scuttled between stairs, her hands rubbed raw from washing and scrubbing. And now look at her! Like a giant kaleidoscope, the war had scattered everything apart and rearranged it into a wholly different pattern.

'Can I help you?' asked one of the women sharply, and Milly sprang to attention. The woman – the stoutest and most officious-looking of the lot – was peering at her suspiciously, and it wouldn't do to be chucked out before she had even worked out how to phrase what she wanted to ask.

'Yes, please,' she said politely. 'I'm Milly Woods, one of the supervisors from Salonika, and I'm here to make enquiries about a lady called Nan Reid. She worked in this department, I believe?'

The stout woman narrowed her eyes at Milly. 'There are a lot of women who pass through this department,' she said shortly.

'Of course,' said Milly. 'But I'm sure you remember Mrs Reid. She's sadly since died – she's been in the papers, an' all – and I want to know why she were dismissed.'

'And what has this to do with you?' asked the stout lady, sucking in her lips until they were surrounded by disapproving little lines.

Milly paused. How could she possibly explain she had travelled around London throwing stones through windows partly because she'd believed Nan had suffered a huge miscarriage of justice at the hands of the Home Depot? That she couldn't quite believe what she'd read in Miss Parker's ledger earlier that morning? And that she wanted to know if there was a possibility someone had lied? Not Miss Parker, of course – Milly could never believe that of *her* – but someone else who had wanted Nan gone?

Had they bent the truth in the ledger? Or had Milly herself been misled?

'I knew her,' said Milly, with a confidence she didn't feel. 'I'm a member—'

'Listen, young lady,' interrupted Stout-Lady. 'Information about staff members is strictly confidential so unless you have a letter from someone in authority giving you clearance, I suggest you leave before I personally escort you out of my department.'

'But—'

'No ifs. No buts,' hissed Stout-Lady, hands on hips. 'Scram!'

Milly felt her resolve sag. The stout lady looked so like her old mistress at the big house in Hornsey, and Milly was suddenly back to being a maid of all work, without rights, without a voice. Without another word, she turned and slunk away.

Stout-Lady hadn't given her chance to explain, hadn't even let her say her piece. And it mattered. It really mattered.

'Oi!'

Milly spun around. A slip of a girl who had been packing tins of dripping in the parcels for prisoners of war department was hurrying to catch up with her. 'I've said I'm popping to the lavvy, so I ain't got much time.'

'Ain't got much time for what?' Milly was thoroughly confused.

'I heard how Mrs Bradley spoke to you,' said the girl. 'I hate it when ladies like her start throwing their weight around when we're all just doing our bit. Now, what did you want to know?'

Milly took a deep breath. She had a second chance and she mustn't mess it up.

'I knew Nan Reid at ELFS,' she said. 'And I wanted to find out what happened to her.'

The girl wrinkled her nose. 'If you knew her, you probably already know what happened,' she said. 'And if you don't . . .' She trailed off doubtfully, fingers nervously pleating the cuffs of her shirt. It was, Milly noticed, much too big for her – a hand-me-down.

Milly took another deep breath. 'I were told she were sacked because she were late for work and maybe missed a day or two – and I thought it were really unfair when her son had just been killed. But then . . . someone else said she'd been sacked for stealing and I were really confused. I didn't know her well myself, so you won't be upsetting me. I just need to know.'

The girl hesitated and looked around her. 'Look, don't tell any of them I told you, but Nan were caught nicking stuff,' she said. 'She were caught red-handed trying to smuggle ciggies out of the depot. I heard she'd even hidden some down her drawers – but that might have been people talking. She wasn't popular here. She could be right sharp.'

Milly exhaled a long breath. Who had lied, then? Nan herself? Or Hilda and Elsie – to make Nan's cause more cut and dried.

'She were given a warning that time,' the girl continued. 'But then, blow me, if she didn't try the same thing a couple of weeks later. They couldn't do anything but sack her that time. Without a reference an' all.'

'It must have been the grief,' said Milly, not yet prepared to believe the worst about Nan. 'She must have been that heartbroken she weren't thinking straight.'

'Nan's son hadn't died by the time she left here,' said the girl. 'Or, if he had, she didn't know about it then. I were talking to her that very day and she were telling me about the letter she'd received from him, thanking her for the parcel she'd sent. It probably contained some of the ciggies she'd pinched.'

'Oh!' Milly was stunned to near silence.

'I'd better go,' said the girl. 'They'll be sending a search party out for me!'

She gave Milly a gap-toothed smile, spun daintily on her heel and was gone, while Milly could only stare after her in bewilderment.

It was a good thing Milly was able to do her duties without thinking too much about them nowadays, because her mind certainly wasn't on the job that afternoon. There was just so much to consider. The Home Depot adopting her revised key-list idea; her promotion; being asked to make a presentation to the royal party; being given permission to set up a women's group . . . any one of those would have made today a red-letter day. The fact all three had happened in one twenty-minute meeting was almost too much to comprehend.

And that was only the tip of the iceberg. There was Jack's role in it, of course, and Milly's conflicted feelings towards him. There was little point in thinking about *that*, though. Jack wanted to be able to step out with a different girl every day of the week, and that was fine. Absolutely fine. Because she, Milly Woods, neither needed nor wanted a sweetheart.

So, she wouldn't think about Jack. Not for the moment, anyway. No, what she really needed to think about was how could she have got it all so wrong?

How could she have fallen in with Elsie and Hilda so easily? How had she been so taken in by everything they'd told her? Oh, maybe they hadn't known the truth about Nan either; maybe they'd really believed Nan had been unfairly dismissed from the Home Depot. And, of course, it wasn't right what had happened to Nan's separation allowance – no woman should be left without an income for being (apparently) drunk and disorderly on one occasion. But, even so, how had she been so easily persuaded throwing stones through windows was the right thing to do? How could she possibly have thought creating public mischief would have helped Nan in any way?

So, that was that! No more stone throwing. *Certainly* no bombing.

Should she talk to Hilda and Elsie? Tell them what she had discovered about Nan and make it absolutely clear she wanted nothing more to do with their little schemes.

She decided against it. If Nan had lied to Hilda and Elsie about why she'd been fired, it would be kinder for Milly to hold her tongue. And as for bombing the Home Depot – well, that was just preposterous and the best thing to do would be not to dignify the suggestion with a response.

Least said soonest mended.

But could Hilda and Elsie blackmail her?

Milly stopped short with a sharp little inclination of breath.

'You all right, Milly?' asked the girl next to her sympathetically. 'Cut yourself?'

Milly nodded and sucked on her finger for good measure. As she started sorting again, she weighed up the possibilities in her mind. If Elsie and Hilda did decide to get nasty, what did they have on her? They could, of course, threaten to expose her role in throwing stones though the windows of three pre-eminent addresses across London. That, obviously, would be far from ideal! She would be arrested and fined – if not imprisoned – and she would certainly lose her job. Her reputation would be in tatters, she would be left without a reference and just imagining the look of sadness and disappointment on Ma's face (and the scorn on Alice's) sent her heart plummeting to her boots.

Then again, what exactly did Elsie and Hilda have on her? She hadn't been caught. There was no evidence; there were no witnesses; there had been no tell-tale flash of a camera. At the end of the day, it would be her word against her friends' – and, surely, Hilda and Elsie would end up implicating themselves along with her. Surely, they wouldn't think it worth the risk of going down with her?

There were other things Elsie and Hilda could threaten, of course. Strictly speaking, Milly knew it was Elsie who would do any threatening – she was definitely the ringleader – and Milly had told her all sorts of things about her life at the Home Depot she really should have kept to herself. The imminent royal visit was the obvious contender – why, oh, why couldn't she have kept her big mouth shut about that? – although surely it was only a matter of days before that became common knowledge and she was in the clear. But she'd also told them about accidentally returning the letter Liza's sister had written to her fallen husband before the official telegram announcing his death had been dispatched. She would hate for that to get out . . . but would it really be the end of the world if it did?

Worth bombing the Home Depot to avoid? No. Of course not.

Whatever Elsie might have on her, Milly wouldn't bow to pressure.

'Are you sure you're all right?' the girl next to her asked again. 'You look awfully pale.'

Milly stopped her sorting. She did, it had to be said, have the mother of all headaches brewing. It had crept up on her and was beginning to pound away in ominous fashion. Worse, her vison was starting to blur, the letters jumping around on the envelopes. Milly had only had a headache like this once before in her life – the night Pa had died – and she had ended up bedbound for a couple of days. She had no wish to repeat the experience.

Milly turned to her neighbour. 'I do have a terrible headache,' she admitted. 'Maybe I should go to the surgery.'

# 26

Half an hour later, Milly had been dismissed from duty for the day.

The nice red-headed nurse who'd bandaged her thumb up several weeks before hadn't hesitated in signing Milly off for the afternoon.

'It's so relentless in here at the moment,' she said. 'People can't keep up this workload indefinitely. Go home, have a nice cup of tea, put your feet up and hopefully you'll be right as rain in the morning.'

Milly didn't need telling twice. Five minutes later, she had grabbed her hat and coat, and had set off down Broad Walk on her way to the Tube station. It was a clear and crisp day with high, scudding clouds and not much colder out of the Home Depot than in. Milly strode out briskly, taking in deep gulps of air, and gradually began to feel better. The tension in her shoulders and neck started to disappear, her headache dissipated to a dull ache and her mind started to clear.

By the time she got to the other side of the park, Milly was feeling much better. There was nothing, she decided, more liberating than having danced with danger and come out unscathed on the other side. Despite the war and the dull December day, life suddenly seemed to be full of optimism and possibility. Suddenly, Milly didn't want to go straight home. Straight home to the ironing and the mending and Boniface's barking and Alice's being ill and Ma being worried.

Ma could spare her for an hour or two – in fact, she wouldn't be expecting her for hours – and, for once, Milly would do something just for herself. Something to celebrate her promotion and everything else that had happened that day. To say nothing of the fact she'd peered over the precipice and stepped back just in time.

She would go Christmas shopping.

In Selfridges, no less.

So, instead of getting on the Tube, Milly kept walking. She wasn't a great one for department stores – not unless one counted throwing stones through their windows! But, to actually go in, to shop there; that was a different thing entirely. Milly had always considered department stores too grand for the likes of her, had always assumed she wouldn't get past the superior-looking men in uniform who guarded the doors. But Selfridges was different. Mr Selfridge was always in the papers making it clear women from all social classes were welcome in his stores. And, of course, he supported the suffragists – publishing advertisements in their newspaper and flying their flag above his shop. As Miss Pankhurst said, Mr Selfridge was a good egg and that was probably the reason Selfridges had never been attacked by the suffragettes.

Anyway, things were different now, weren't they? Milly was a supervisor at the Army Post Office, about to have a team of women reporting to her. She was earning good money. No one would dare deny her entry now.

Would they?

Even so, Milly found her heart beating a little faster as she approached the store. It was so big. So *grand*. Almost like a palace with all those huge stone columns. And the windows! Selfridges was famous for its window displays and at the moment they were decked out in all their Christmas finery. Of course, with all the wartime rules, they were much more subdued than they would usually be but, even so, there was such a crowd in front of them, Milly couldn't actually see what they contained! The only one that wasn't being mobbed was the 'War Window' and Milly gave it a wide berth too; she'd had enough of bulletins and maps at work, thank you very much. Instead, she took a deep breath and marched up to the nearest entrance. The doorman touched his hat, opened the door and elaborately ushered her inside.

What a day!

And what a store!

As soon as Milly stepped into the beauty department, she could tell this was like no other store she had ever dreamed of – let alone frequented. Instead of being hidden behind counters, all the wares were enticingly laid out on tables and customers were free – nay, encouraged – to pick them up. Everywhere Milly looked, elegantly dressed ladies were spraying themselves with scent and the air was so exotically fragranced that Milly had barely taken ten steps inside before the stench of horse dung from the street outside had totally disappeared.

For a while, Milly wandered around taking in the festive decorations. Christmas trees, their boughs heavily laden with red and gold decorations, competed with matching streamers and paperchains strung high overhead. If only they could put on such a display at the Home Depot! There was even a large banner over by the stairs, proclaiming *18 days to Christmas*. Well, that was a call to action if ever there was one! Suddenly, Milly was determined everyone in her household was going to get a gift from Selfridges. It didn't matter if it was only a trinket – a mere bauble – everyone was going to get a little something they would love but absolutely, definitely didn't *need*.

For the next hour, Milly skipped around the ground floor, a smile playing on her lips as she carefully chose her treasures. Ma was easy – it had to be scent and Milly spent a happy ten minutes sniffing away before settling on Guerlain's L'Heure Bleue with its expensive yet comforting smell of luxury candles and almond cake. Ma would love that. She couldn't fail to. For Alice, she chose some fancy violet bath salts and Morny June Roses talcum powder; Alice was always carping she never felt clean after a long shift in the factory. Besides, as they all shared the same bathwater, Milly would also get to enjoy the bath salts – although Charlie probably wouldn't be too thrilled about going to school reeking of violets. Milly swallowed a snort of laughter and ignored a couple of curious glances from ladies browsing nearby. This was fun! For Maggie, she chose some Bourjois rouge – her lovely sister had been looking very peaky recently and no amount of pinching her cheeks seemed to bring colour into them. Maggie would never dream of spending money on fripperies for herself, not when she had Arthur to worry about, but surely if she knew she looked better, she would start to feel better about herself too?

Now for the younger children.

For Caroline, she selected a very smart collar and lead. Well, strictly speaking, that was for Boniface – although Lord knew her sister needed them sometimes soon! – but she knew Caroline would love them and Boniface was very much hers. Then it was upstairs to the toy department for a toy motor car for Charlie and a colourful ball for Arthur.

Easy!

Milly was about to head back downstairs when she saw it.

A doorway. An enticing sign. Elegant women sweeping out.

And suddenly Milly had an idea.

Here was her chance to do something that told herself and everyone else she meant business. A woman who knew herself, knew what she stood for and, most importantly, wasn't going to let anything or anyone stand in her way.

Should she do it?

If she did, there was no going back for a very long time.

It was now or never . . .

★

A few hours later, Milly walked into the kitchen as casually as she could. Chance were her family wouldn't even notice. After all, they didn't notice when she had a pimple the size of a toffee on her cheek or cabbage in her teeth. Maybe this, too, would pass without comment.

Ma, Caroline and Charlie turned as one, slack-jawed.

'Lordy,' breathed Ma, hand to heart. 'Whatever possessed you?'

'Oh, no! You're going to grow a moustache now!' said Caroline cheerfully. 'Either that or go bald.'

'I won't do either of those things,' Milly fired back. 'Is that the sort of nonsense they teach you at school nowadays?'

'No. But it's *true*,' said Caroline. 'Everyone knows cutting your hair short weakens the scalp muscles.'

'I'm assuming you haven't just had it cut at the front and rolled it up at the back like some of the girls are doing?' asked Ma wearily.

'No,' said Milly, giving a little twirl. 'I've gone the whole hog and had a bob!'

'Dearie me,' said Ma, not without affection. 'Still, any half measures wouldn't be our Milly, would they? And it will grow back. It will grow back!' she added, almost to herself.

Charlie didn't say anything. He just collapsed on the sofa, cackling with loud, delighted laughter, only stopping occasionally to point weakly at Milly before his laughter started up again.

Milly stuck her tongue out at them and went back outside into the passage. She had left her parcels stacked neatly at the bottom of the stairs while she went in to say hello to her family, and now she needed to hide them in her bedroom before her siblings started asking questions. But she couldn't resist a quick look in the mirror by the front door before she did so. Her hair, indeed her whole reflection, looked so different! And it had been a shock when she had first seen her new look – so much so the hairdresser had offered her a bottle of smelling salts in case she fainted! (Milly had waved them away impatiently – she wasn't the sort of girl who fainted!) But now she loved it! Oh, it wasn't as if she had disliked her long, naturally curly, dark hair before – indeed she had always been rather proud of her crowning glory and more than a little smug she didn't have to spend hours ragging or coaxing it into kiss-curls like Alice did. And it would certainly take a bit of getting used to – her head felt so light, her neck so exposed and vulnerable. But she loved the way it made her *look*. Her violet eyes suddenly looked even larger, her cheekbones sharp, her jaw firm and defined. And, even more than her physical appearance, she loved the way it made her *feel*.

She looked like the sort of woman who could efficiently manage a team of sorters at the Army Post Office and set up a group to represent women's interests there.

She looked like the sort of woman who would state her case for women's emancipation clearly and rationally.

She looked like the sort of woman who might decide to study politics at university when the war was over.

And, dare she even admit it, she looked like the sort of woman a man might fall in love with.

Once Milly had stashed her Christmas shopping carefully under the bed, she went next door to Ma's room. Alice was asleep in bed. She was damp with sweat, tendrils of dark hair clinging to her forehead and her chest seemed to be rising and falling very quickly. For the first time, Milly felt the stirrings of real fear along with a good dollop of guilt. Even though she wasn't late, she should have come straight home when she was given the afternoon off work. She shouldn't have gone gallivanting around London and getting her hair cut.

She should have been here. Helping Ma.

Milly reached out and touched Alice's hand.

Hot.

Too hot.

'Hello,' she said, determinedly cheerful.

She willed her sister to open her eyes but Alice didn't stir.

Blinking back tears, Milly went back downstairs to join the family.

Milly couldn't sleep that night.

She tossed and turned, and when Caroline started gently snoring beside her, she couldn't bear it any longer. She pushed back the bedclothes and padded barefoot round to Ma's room. There was a low candle burning and Ma was sitting on the side of the bed, stroking Alice's forehead. The fact Ma also wasn't in bed chilled Milly to the bone.

'Will she be all right?' asked Milly, sitting on the other side of the bed.

Ma smiled at Milly. 'I'm sure she will,' she said, but her pinched expression and the hollows under her eyes told a different story.

Milly swallowed the sudden lump in her throat. 'I couldn't bear it if anything happened to her,' she rasped. And suddenly she was crying, tears spilling down her cheeks, sobs bubbling up inside her.

Ma reached across and patted her hand. 'Oh, sweetheart,' she said. 'You and Alice really are the salt in each other's boiled eggs, aren't you?'

'Are we?' Milly gave a shaky smile and wiped her eyes.

'Of course you are. You're very alike.'

'But I'm not nearly so grumpy,' protested Milly.

Ma laughed. 'Oh, believe me, you were the same when you were sixteen! And you're both so stubborn and strong-willed. No danger of one of you leading the other astray. And both so competitive. You both competed for your father's attention since you were knee high to grasshoppers.'

A silence.

'Do you miss Pa?' asked Milly softly.

Ma sighed. 'In some ways,' she said. 'He wasn't a saint. But then, people aren't all good or all bad. And, in some ways, he was a good person. And he loved you children. Loved you all to bits, he did. Now, off to bed. You need your beauty sleep for that fancy job of yours.'

Milly nodded. She walked around the bed and kissed her mother on the head. Then she hesitated a moment and, bending over, she kissed Alice on the cheek.

Alice opened her eyes. 'What the bleeding heck have you done to your hair?' she asked.

# 27

As she might have anticipated, Milly found herself very much the centre of attention the next day at work. Women with short hair were few and far between at the Home Depot, and there were certainly none near where Milly was stationed. And so, the moment she took her hat off and hung it on her usual hook on the wooden pillar, there was a short sharp silence. Milly ignored it and made her way to her post with her head held high. She was a thoroughly modern woman, doing things her own way and no one was going to be allowed to ruffle her composure.

'Goodness, you're more daring than me!' said the girl next to her. 'My mam would have my guts for garters if I came home like that.'

Milly smiled at her. 'My ma were a bit shocked as well,' she said. 'But we can't always do what our mothers want, can we? We'd still be stuck in the Dark Ages if so.'

The girl muttered, 'I suppose so,' and turned back to her work, without another word.

'Never had *you* down as a blue-stocking, love,' sneered a man as he took away some of their sorted letters.

Milly knew she didn't look like a blue-stocking. She had applied just the right amount of powder and rouge that morning to make sure that, while she didn't look fast, she still looked like she took pride in her appearance.

Confident in that knowledge, Milly had shot back, quick

as a flash, 'Well, if you're the alternative . . .' with a demure smile. The whole section had erupted with laughter and the look on the soldier's face had been a picture.

But the *pièce de résistance* was when another man came up to their section. He was about to say something to Milly but, when he caught sight of her hair, he turned tail and fled.

Oh, it was wonderful! Why hadn't she cut her hair before?

At lunchtime, Milly went in search of Liza.

It was time to patch up their stupid argument or, at least, to talk things through. Now Milly had cut herself loose from Hilda and Elsie – if only in her mind – she could see things a little more clearly. Only now could she admit to herself that perhaps she'd helped to both create and perpetuate the rift with her erstwhile friends. She might not have done it consciously – in fact she was almost sure she hadn't – but maybe she had done so all the same. And supposing Liza became ill, like Alice had done. Supposing . . .

Yes, she would talk to Liza.

So, Milly went over to the broken parcels department in search of her. Hopefully they would have the same lunch hour. And yes, there was Liza, her pretty face in repose as she bent over her clipboard. She started in surprise when she looked up, and Milly's heart dropped. Unless it was her hair that had made Liza react like that . . .

'Lordy me,' said a tall, middle-aged woman who was sitting at one of the tables and attempting to repackage a badly oozing parcel. 'What is it with all you young gals cutting your hair off? The men will be taking liberties with you, young lady, don't you know?'

And now, thank goodness, Liza's lips were twitching.

'Hush, Mrs B,' she rebuked the older lady mildly. 'I think it looks absolutely marvellous, Milly. I'd do the same if I had the courage.'

She smiled warmly at Milly, and Milly felt any residual resentment melt away. How lovely Liza was. And how funny too. There was nothing less likely she could imagine than Liza having her hair cut into a bob. Why, half the time she wore her hair in a simple plait down her back – and even today when she'd made an effort to pin it up, she'd followed the natural silhouette of her head shape with no attempt to exaggerate either the height or the width. No, Liza was hardly a follower of fashion, let alone a trendsetter.

'Are you busy this lunchtime?' asked Milly, still unsure of what the reaction might be.

Liza looked back at her levelly. 'No,' she said. 'No plans.'

'Would you like to spend it with me?'

Liza's smile broadened. 'I would!' she said. 'I wasn't due to go off duty for an hour, but I can give myself an early pass. Shall we go to the canteen?'

Milly laughed. It was the sheer relief. 'Not the canteen,' she said fervently. 'There'll be a thousand and one people all staring at my hair. Shall we go for a stroll in the park? That way, I can pull my hat right down and . . .'

'The park it is,' said Liza. She was laughing, too. 'Just give me a moment and I'll be all yours.'

'No good will come of trying to look like one of the boys,' muttered Mrs B. 'No one will marry you now!'

'Good!' said Milly. 'I have no wish to get married.'

She and Liza exchanged a glance and then, arm in arm and snuffling with supressed giggles, they left the broken parcels department together.

It was all going to be all right.

Despite the smiles and giggles, Milly couldn't help but feel awkward once she and Liza were out in the park. After all, the last time the two girls had properly talked, they had both rather vehemently accused the other of abandoning their principles for a man. In fact, if Milly remembered correctly, she had accused Liza of never having had any principles at all!

Milly took a deep breath and stopped walking. 'I wanted to apologise . . .' she began.

Liza put a hand on Milly's arm. 'No, *I'm* sorry,' she said urgently. 'I feel terrible about what I said that day. It was . . . unforgiveable.'

Milly shook her head. 'It weren't any worse than what I said to you,' she said. 'And, in fact, I've been much worse than you because I wasn't there for you during the investigation. I didn't even know about it. I'm so sorry!'

Milly meant it. Despite her anger at the time, her bitterness and resentment that Liza hadn't kept her up to date with what was going on, she could see now much of that – as with everything else in this whole sorry mess – was her own fault. She could have – should have – taken the initiative and made it her business to find out what was happening with Liza. She should have offered Liza her support, rather than hanging back waiting to be approached. She could see now she had been so bound up with her own pride, so captivated by new friends and her new causes, she had lost sight of what was going on – of what mattered – closer to home.

Liza sat down on a bench and Milly perched beside her. 'It wasn't your fault,' said Liza. 'The whole thing was so awful I didn't want to talk about it to anyone. Nora came along as a witness because she was with me for a lot of the time that night . . . but I should have told you and I should have asked you too. I'm sorry.'

'Not at all,' said Milly. 'I spent most of that night trying to rescue the bloody cat so I probably wouldn't have been much use anyway.'

She thought it politic not to add that she understood why Liza had really chosen Nora to be a witness. After all, who *wouldn't* choose the niece of the man who ran the Home Depot over a nobody from Bow? Milly would have done the same if the situation had been reversed.

'Thank you,' murmured Liza.

'So how *is* James?' asked Milly, lighting a cigarette. 'I was so sorry to hear what happened.'

She had grown very fond of James during their early weeks at the Home Depot. Like her, James had a healthy cynicism and a burning desire to right injustices – to say nothing of not being able to cope without his ciggies.

Suddenly, Liza's eyes flooded with tears. She pulled out a handkerchief – which looked like it had already been used for the same purpose – and blotted them away.

'Oh, it's all too awful,' she said. 'He's off to Egypt.'

'No.' Milly was, it had to be said, shocked to the core. 'Surely there's another way?'

Liza gave her a look that was almost fierce. 'What other way?' she demanded. 'He's been dismissed without a reference, so what else can he do? Besides, you and I both know that come the new year, he and countless other young men would be off to the various fronts anyway. He's just getting in early.'

'But I can't believe James is voluntarily enlisting,' said Milly. 'He doesn't believe in the war! He's always said he would never fight, would never kill anyone. It doesn't make sense.'

'Oh, he hasn't joined the army,' said Liza with a little bark of laughter. 'Even if they would have him, Hell would freeze over before he agreed to do *that*! But he still wants to do his bit, especially after . . . what's happened. So, he's got a job with the Red Cross.'

'Well, that makes more sense,' said Milly. 'But, still . . . *Egypt*. What's he going to be doing there?'

'I'm not entirely sure,' said Liza. 'He said something about interviewing wounded soldiers in hospitals to try and get information about other soldiers reported missing. It sounds like a good role. An important one. But, oh, how I shall miss him! We've only been courting for a matter of months. I had hoped for a little longer.'

Her voice cracked and Milly took her hand. 'Of course you'll miss him,' she said. 'But it's a great opportunity for him. And the best thing is, he should be safe.'

'Oh, I hope so,' said Liza, squeezing Milly's hand and then letting go to blow her nose. 'Anyway, none of this excuses how I behaved towards you. I'm so sorry, Milly.'

Out of nowhere, Milly had an overwhelming urge to tell Liza what she had done and what she had been asked to do. She suddenly realised how tired she was of keeping things to herself, of having so many secrets. It would be a huge burden off her chest if she could get Liza's perspective on it all. After all, wasn't that what friends were for? Sharing things with each other? And wouldn't it be the best way to get her friendship with Liza back on track?

'There's something I should tell you,' she said slowly. 'Promise you won't tell anyone?'

Liza turned to her with wide eyes. 'Of course I do,' she said. 'Oh, Milly, I knew there was something. I could just tell. Nora and I have been so worried about you.'

And then it all came out.

Her attack; meeting Hilda and Elsie; trying and failing to help Nan with her lost separation allowance; Nan's death; and Milly's increasing anger at and disillusionment with such an outdated and patriarchal society. She finished off by hesitantly telling Liza about throwing the stone through Ted Wilmington's front window and the other attacks. And, all the while, Liza's mouth grew rounder and rounder until she put both gloved hands in front of it and just sat there, staring at Milly.

'Go on. *Say* something,' said Milly, when she had finished speaking. But Liza carried on staring at her with unblinking, saucer-shaped blue eyes.

Milly ploughed on. 'I regret it now,' she said. 'I were promoted yesterday and Miss Parker gave me a speech about women being best able to create change from the inside and by doing a man's job better than he can. So, I ain't going to do anything like that again. I ain't going to break the law. But you're my friend and I wanted you to know . . .'

'I had a feeling it might be you,' burst out Liza, suddenly finding her voice. 'I saw the article about the stone through Ted Wilmington's window and I just wondered . . .'

'I hate him. The things he writes . . .'

'I do, too. He's an odious man. But violence won't solve anything . . .'

'I know! I just wish the men who started the war knew that too.'

'Oh, me too, Milly. Me too!'

'You don't hate me then?' ventured Milly.

'Of course, I don't,' said Liza. 'In many ways, I admire you. But, Milly, you were really playing with fire.'

Milly grinned. 'Not as much as literally *setting fire* to the Home Depot,' she said with a giggle.

Liza joined in with the giggles, hand to mouth, and Milly felt herself relax. Maybe she should tell Liza about Hilda and Elsie's suggestion to bomb the Home Depot and cause havoc during the royal visit. It would be so good to hear herself say that out loud as well. To hear how it sounded . . .

'You girls meeting without me?'

Milly spun around. It was Nora, peeling off from the little gaggle of young women she was with and coming over to join them. Suddenly Milly felt the tiniest bit uncomfortable. It was one thing confiding in Liza, but Milly couldn't quite shake the fact that Nora was Major Benham's niece. She gave herself a little shake. This was Nora, the very first person she had met at the Home Depot! And hadn't Nora included Milly in her confidences about both royal visit and compulsory conscription? Yes, surely she had nothing to fear from Nora?

So, Milly accepted Nora's kiss of congratulations on her promotion. Then – cringing slightly – she told Nora about her involvement in the stone throwing and reiterated she had henceforth sworn off any form of militancy. And Nora hugged her again and said, in her view, it had been (very nearly) justified.

In the end, Milly kept quiet about the plan to bomb part of the Home Depot and, after a while, the conversation moved on to the Christmas party.

'I've been asked to present a new postmark to one of the esteemed guests,' said Milly, with a little wink and unable to stop herself beaming.

The others girls fell on her with cries of delight.

'Milly Woods meeting the King and Queen,' squealed Nora. 'That's so exciting. I've been chosen too,' she added. 'I'm presenting a bouquet to the Queen. What's the betting I drop the darn thing?'

Of course Nora had been chosen too! After all, there was no way they would have totally overlooked the major's niece. Some things never changed . . . and probably never would.

'My team have got to demonstrate repacking some broken parcels,' said Liza with a grimace. 'That'll be exciting for them! I'd better make sure they don't get eggs or chocolate all over the Queen's ermine stole.'

'She won't be wearing an ermine stole, silly,' said Nora, with an air of great knowledge.

'What will she be wearing?' asked Milly. 'After all, you should know.'

'Well, the King will be wearing some sort of army uniform,' said Nora, suddenly sounding less sure.

'And what about the Queen?' asked Liza. 'If she's got to leave the stole at the palace.'

Nora shrugged elaborately. 'Probably just a nice dress under her coat,' she said vaguely.

'In other words, you have no idea,' said Milly.

'None at all,' admitted Nora cheerfully.

'Maybe we could offer her some advice,' said Milly with a laugh. 'Sturdy shoes so she doesn't trip on the uneven floors.'

'An extra woolly to hand – or she'll get jolly parky!' Nora giggled.

'But not a dark-coloured one – or the tidemarks will show up something rotten.'

'A pinny would be useful so she can help with the washing-up afterwards,' said Milly.

All three girls, snuffling with giggles, fell back against each other in their mirth.

Oh, it was good to be among her friends again.

## 28

Slowly, slowly, Alice began to get better.

By the weekend, she was still bedbound in Ma's room – but she was sitting up and beginning to find fault with all and sundry in her own inimitable manner. Milly knew she must be on the mend.

'Take Charlie and Caroline to the park, would you?' Ma asked Milly on Saturday morning. 'I need to tend to Alice and they're under my feet the whole time. And as for that blasted dog . . .'

'Of course, Ma.'

It was a lovely day and Milly quite fancied a stroll around Victoria Park, herself.

'And check in on Maggie on the way, would you?' added Ma. 'I half expected her to pop in this week, especially with Alice being so poorly, but I haven't seen hide nor hair of her.'

Milly rather suspected Maggie simply wanted to avoid her and Arthur picking up Alice's germs.

'Of course, Ma,' she repeated.

Half an hour later, the ragged little party wound its way up the streets towards Victoria Park. Progress was slow because Boniface – now usually shortened to Boni – on a rope lead, was constantly distracted by all manner of enticing smells and stopped to enthusiastically greet every passer-by. Milly couldn't help but notice how often people recoiled in horror at his poor burned face, and children thought nothing of pointing and laughing. Milly, fuming, wanted to bash their heads together! Was that what Jack had to put up with every day? Well, if compulsory conscription did go ahead, there would be an awful lot more men who came home injured and disfigured, so everyone had better get used to it . . .

Maggie lived conveniently close to both the ELFS toy factory where she worked and the Mother's Arms, and she was only a ten-minute walk to the park. From the outside, her house looked very similar to the family home – a neat Victorian house in a terrace of identical homes – but, inside, the property had been divided into two. Maggie and Arthur lived upstairs in two main rooms and a tiny box room and, like Mr Wildermuth, she had set times when she might use the kitchen and the scullery.

As Milly and her siblings rounded the corner, they could see Maggie in the front garden, wrestling Arthur into his perambulator. The perambulator always made Milly smile: a hand-me-down from Ma – Milly could distinctly remember Charlie in it – it was now rusty and a million miles away from the sleek and shiny affairs that populated the Regent's Park. How lucky it was that they had arrived when they had; a couple of minutes more and Maggie would be gone.

'Yoo-hoo,' called Milly. 'Wait for us!'

Maggie straightened and spun around as they approached, and Milly could immediately see her face was pink and blotchy from crying.

'Whatever's the matter?' asked Milly, as they drew level.

'Nothing,' said Maggie, dashing tears from her eyes and bending back over the pram.

Milly gave a short bark of laughter. 'Yes, I can see that it's nothing!' she said. 'Come on, you can tell me. Although, if it's Alice, she is very much better and Ma said you're not to worry.'

'No. It's not Alice. Although, of course I was worried.'

'What, then?'

Maggie glanced up. 'Not here,' she muttered.

Caroline and Charlie had picked up Boniface and were holding him in front of a chuckling Arthur. Both seemed blissfully unaware of their eldest sister's tears.

'Where are you off to?' Milly asked, sotto voce.

'Just the mother-and-baby clinic at the Mother's Arms,' replied Maggie.

'So, you can delay half an hour?'

'I can,' said Maggie. 'Except I've just wrestled the pram through the house and I really can't bear the thought of . . .'

'Oh, for goodness' sake,' said Milly. Sometimes Maggie seemed to *look* for problems. 'No one would pinch that rust bucket if you left it outside for a fortnight! Let's pop back inside and you can tell me what's upset you. Then we can go to the Mother's Arms together and meet Charlie and Caroline at the park later.'

Maggie nodded mutely, and Milly turned to her younger brother and sister. 'Right, off you go,' she said, clapping her hands. 'No paddling, Charlie,' she added severely. 'And no adopting any more animals, Caro – I don't care how few legs they've got! I'll meet you by the lake in an hour and if you've behaved yourselves, I'll buy you each a toffee apple.'

Caroline and Charlie scampered off and Maggie scooped Arthur out of the pram.

'Oh, listen to you,' she said, grinning at Milly as she unlocked the front door. 'A bleeding supervisor already!'

Milly laughed. 'A first-class chump, if you ask me,' she said. 'I'll have had no idea if they've behaved themselves or not, and now I've got to shell out for two toffee apples!'

She was rewarded with the ghost of a smile from Maggie. The two girls made their way upstairs and into Maggie's spotless little parlour at the front of the house. Maggie deposited Arthur unceremoniously onto the hearthrug and then, just as unceremoniously, burst into tears.

'Oh, what's the matter?' cried Milly, wrapping her sister into a bear hug. 'What's happened?'

Without saying a word, Maggie gently extracted herself from Milly's clutches. Then she walked over to the mantelpiece and picked up a buff-coloured piece of paper.

A telegram.

'Read it,' said Maggie, thrusting it into Milly's hands.

Heart racing, Milly scanned the few lines. 'Deeply regret to inform you . . . Private L. Byrd . . . died of wounds . . .'

Milly, feeling physically winded, sank onto the sofa, telegram hanging from limp fingers.

Private L. Byrd – Leonard Byrd, Maggie's erstwhile husband – was *dead*. Milly glanced at the telegram. He had died over three weeks ago out in the Dardanelles – as had countless other young men. A life brutally snuffed out much too early.

Oh, when would this dreadful, *dreadful* war be over?

'I didn't know Leo had joined the army,' said Milly softly. It was the first thing that came into her mind and out of her mouth.

'Neither did I!' burst out Maggie, semi-hysterically. 'I'm his wife and I didn't know either! I've never heard a thing from him ever since he left me.'

'Oh, Leo,' said Milly.

Handsome Leo with his jet-black hair and his glittering green eyes and his endearing lop-sided grin. A footman at the big house where Maggie had been a housemaid – what chance had poor, naïve Maggie had when he'd turned the full force of his charm onto her? Before long, she had been in the family way and, when it had become obvious, both had lost their jobs. Pa had insisted on a quick wedding and found Leo employment at the docks. Milly could remember the damp, drizzly wedding day like it was yesterday: the bride's big bump; the groom's rictus grin; the determined jollity on all sides. And that might have been the end of the story had Pa not died. But die he did – and Leo had upped and offed and abandoned Maggie and Arthur with almost indecent haste. No one seemed to know for sure where he had gone. There were rumours there had been another sweetheart all along – a lady's maid from the big house – and the assumption was that Leo had eloped with her. But, with the war and with Pa gone, it was hard to find anything out, and Maggie hadn't known where to start. Leo's mother – his father had already died – had claimed ignorance of the whole affair and there were no other leads to follow. Maggie had been left in limbo with a young son, still married, unable to move on.

And now Leo had been killed on a battlefield thousands of miles away from them all, and Milly found she had so many conflicting thoughts she had to shake her head from side to side in an attempt to quieten them all down.

Maggie was pacing up and down the little room. 'He was the last person I thought would ever enlist,' she said. 'I assumed he were still in London somewhere, but all this time he were in the Dardanelles doing his bit for King and Country.'

Milly didn't say anything. She rather suspected Leo had signed up because he had run out of options at home, or because he sensed adventure elsewhere. It was unlikely to have been for any particular patriotic fervour. But now wasn't the time or place to say that out loud and, besides, Milly couldn't know for sure. The sobering thing was that they would *never* know now.

'The telegram came to me, so he must have put me down as his next of kin when he enlisted,' Maggie was saying. 'He still regarded me as his wife, Milly. That's something at least.'

Of course he did, thought Milly. Law dictated he did so. It was probably nothing to do with sentiment. Again, though, there was no point in saying anything.

Maggie turned to Milly and her face was etched with grief. 'I loved him, Milly,' she said. 'I really did. He were so handsome and funny and kind. And, even though it were wicked of him to leave me like that, there were a little bit of me never gave up hoping he would come back to me and claim Arthur for his own. And now that will never, ever happen.'

She was crying properly now – huge tearing sobs that racked her slight frame. Milly stood up and wrapped her arms around her big sister.

'I know you did,' she said. 'Oh, Maggie, I'm sorry. It's just awful.'

'It is,' said Maggie. She pulled away from Milly and wiped her eyes. 'But the worst thing about it is that I'm also happy. Happy. Because – don't you see? – this changes *everything*.'

Milly thought about it. And she did see.

In one fell swoop, Maggie had thrown off her shackles. She had lost the shame and stigma of being an abandoned wife and had become a war widow – the most respectable of women. Now she no longer had any need to hide away, her life could start again. She could even remarry if she so chose.

Milly reached out and hugged her sister again. It wasn't the kind of news that warranted dancing around the parlour – not at all – but Milly could see it had changed things for Maggie. In some ways, it changed things for them *all* because Milly was mature enough to know that Maggie's disgrace had been in danger of tainting the whole family – and that was partly the reason Maggie hadn't been invited back into the family home after Leo had left.

But now . . . everything was different. And to think Milly had been putting all that at risk with her ridiculous stone throwing.

What a fool she had been.

'How long have you known?' Milly asked.

'A few days,' replied Maggie. 'I'm sorry I didn't come round and tell you straight away, but you were all worried about

Alice and I needed a few days to get used to it myself. I've written to Leo's mother and I think I've spent the past few days crying. Thinking. And now I suppose we'd better get going. I don't want to miss the clinic.'

The ELFS mother-and-baby clinic was held weekly in the Mother's Arms. As well as the opportunity to get a baby or toddler weighed and checked over by a nurse, the clinic also provided free eggs, Virol and barley. With the Germans now sinking supply ships, and the food shortages and price rises getting worse, it was invariably well attended.

Milly helped Maggie manhandle Arthur's perambulator up the stairs into the old pub. Was she imagining it, or was Maggie's back straighter, her head held a little higher? The clinic was drawing to a close, the last of the women chatting cheerfully as they gathered up babies and rations and baskets. Milly stood to one side while Maggie queued up, letting the conversation and the air of busy enterprise wash over her. This was such a wonderful example of women helping each other and, once again, she reminded herself that if there were more places called the Mother's Arms and fewer called the Gunmaker's Arms (as the pub had been called before the war), the world would be a much better place . . .

'Hello, there!' There was a tap on her arm and Milly spun round in surprise. Elsie, Hilda and a nurse Milly vaguely recognised were carrying boxes and cartons into a side room behind her. Milly cursed herself for not having anticipated she might bump into Hilda and Elsie that morning. They were both such stalwart members of ELFS that it should have been no surprise to find they volunteered at its clinic.

'Hello,' replied Milly with an enthusiasm she didn't feel. She was about to make up some excuse about having to go and join Maggie when she stopped herself. That was the coward's way out. She should really take the opportunity to make it clear to Hilda and Elsie that she had no intention of taking part in any more activism – let alone bombing the Home Depot.

'Could I have a word?' she added quickly before she could change her mind.

'Of course,' said Elsie. 'Sarah, could you excuse us for a moment?'

The nurse nodded and disappeared, and Elsie beckoned Milly into the side room. Little more than a glorified store room, it was quite a crush with the three of them inside.

'I'm glad we've bumped into you,' said Elsie. 'We was going to wait until the next ELFS meeting, but now you're here . . .'

Milly took a deep breath. 'I've been thinking about our conversation the other night,' she said firmly. 'I'm not sure how serious you was being, but I wanted to let you know I'm not going to get involved—'

'Good!' interrupted Hilda emphatically.

Milly turned to her in surprise. Whatever she had been expecting, it hadn't been . . . that.

'It's too dangerous . . .' Milly continued.

'Remember, the intention is that no one gets hurt,' said Elsie. 'Ideally, the Home Depot is evacuated into the park; there's lots of excellent publicity with no chance of any injuries. That's why hoax bombs can be so effective.'

'Oh!' Milly was a little taken aback. That wasn't how she had remembered the plan at all. 'So, you weren't planning for it to be a real bomb?'

Did that make a difference? If it was just disruption, inconvenience, embarrassment . . .?

'It has to be a real bomb, this time,' said Elsie. 'The first time has to be real or no one would believe us the next.'

'Right.'

'Come on, Milly,' Elsie continued. 'You told us about how people sometimes smuggle alcohol inside cakes, and about how sometimes sorters at the Home Depot let it through if they believe it helps the better cause. Isn't this the same thing?'

'No!' spluttered Milly. 'It isn't the same at all. And I don't want nothing to do with your plan. All right?'

'But you've already helped us more than you know.' A wheedling note had now entered Elsie's tone. 'You told us the King and Queen were visiting. You've given us the idea and all the inside information we need. Now we're just asking you to help us execute it. For Nan's sake, if not for ours.'

Milly looked from Elsie to Hilda, eyes round with horror. Hilda quickly dropped her gaze but Elsie stared straight back at her, defiantly. Oh goodness – was this where the blackmail started? Because, no matter what she did next, she was already implicated in the whole thing. Why, oh, why couldn't she have kept quiet?

But she couldn't back down now. 'I'm sorry, Elsie,' she said firmly. 'No matter what you say – what you *threaten* – I ain't going to change my mind. I'm only going to effect change from the inside from now. No more breaking the law.'

Milly braced herself for what was coming next. The withering look; the scorn; the turning of the screw . . .

But, to her surprise, Elsie just gave a little sigh.

'You're right,' she said. 'It were a mad idea. I don't know what I were thinking.'

*Oh!* Thank goodness for that.

'Hallelujah,' said Hilda, before Milly could answer. 'I thought you were losing your bleeding mind, Elsie.'

Elsie sighed. 'I'm just so angry about Nan,' she said. 'And then I found the bomb – and with you working at the Home Depot, Milly, and the King and Queen visiting an' all – it seemed too good to be true.'

Milly gave her a sympathetic smile. 'It's too dangerous, Elsie,' she said. 'People might get hurt. *Worse*. And that would set back women's suffrage by years . . .'

'Yes, I see that now,' said Elsie. 'So, that's that, then. Thank goodness for you – and for Hilda, to be fair.'

'You need to give the bomb to the police,' said Milly, pressing home her advantage.

'Steady on,' said Elsie with a shaky laugh. 'I'm not sure I'm ready to involve the police. But we will get rid of it all, I promise. To be perfectly honest, I'm not altogether sure how to make a bomb anyway. Or even if the powder is dry.'

Milly allowed herself a sigh of relief. 'Oh, I'm so glad to hear you say that,' she said. She paused a minute and then added, 'Friends?'

'Of course,' said Hilda earnestly.

'Friends,' replied Elsie. 'And thank you, Milly. For being nice about it and making me see when I was going too far.'

Milly smiled and left the storeroom feeling lighter than she had done for weeks. She hadn't realised how worried she had been about confronting Hilda and Elsie, but it had all gone much more smoothly than she'd anticipated. She had spoken honestly and effected change from the inside.

Miss Parker would be proud of her.

'There you are,' said Maggie, coming over to join her. 'I've been looking all over for you. I thought you must have left without me.'

'Sorry,' said Milly. 'I had a little ELFS business to sort out. Now, shall we go and join the others in the park?'

For no reason – for *every* reason – she leaned over and gave Maggie a kiss on the cheek.

What a strange day this was turning out to be.

'Why don't you move back home?' asked Milly as the two girls crossed the canal that bordered the southern edge of Victoria Park. 'It would be lovely to have you and Arthur back.'

Maggie negotiated Arthur's perambulator past a pile of

rubbish on the street. 'You mean, now I'm a respectable woman?' she said with a wry smile. 'The answer is, much as I love you all, I have no wish to share a bed with you and Alice. Besides, Arthur snores something rotten . . .'

Milly laughed. 'No, silly,' she said. 'You could have Mr Wildermuth's room. It would be perfect. The whole family back under one roof again.'

'Evict Mr Wildermuth?' Maggie looked shocked. 'I couldn't do that.'

'Yes, you could,' said Milly, as they entered the park. 'It's our house and we have every right. Happens all the time.'

'But Mr Wildermuth is German,' said Maggie. 'He'd never find anywhere else. Not while the war is going on, anyway. Besides . . .' She trailed off, cheeks flushing pink.

Milly could see exactly where her sister's thoughts were going.

'Oh, no,' said Milly. 'Don't you go getting designs on Mr Wildermuth.'

'I haven't.'

'That's all right, then.'

Maggie stopped walking. 'But, speaking theoretically, why shouldn't I "have designs" on him?' she asked. 'He's kind. He's handsome. He has a job.'

'He's German.'

'He's Mr *Wildermuth*, Milly. What's got into you?'

Milly took a deep breath. 'He's been asking all sorts of questions about the Home Depot and about the royal visit,' she said. 'To be honest, I'm a bit worried he's up to no good.'

'Milly! He's just showing an interest. And he'd be really hurt to hear you talking like that.'

'I think we need to be cautious,' said Milly coolly. 'And not get too involved.'

'Who said anything about getting involved?' said Maggie. 'Oh, look. There are the others – over by the lake, like they said they would be. You owe them a toffee apple apiece.'

The first thing Milly noticed was Boniface shaking himself vigorously.

The damn dog had obviously been for a dip in the lake and the whole house would smell of damp fur for days.

The second thing was that Caroline and Charlie seemed to be acting very strangely. They were standing stiffly beside each other in a most unnatural manner. They were also trying to get Boniface to sit in front of them, but no sooner had they pushed his rump down, than he would spring up again.

Milly stifled a smile.

Whatever was going on?

'They're trying to persuade that fellow to take their photograph,' said Maggie, pointing off to one side. 'Poor chap. He doesn't stand a chance against the two of them.'

With a pulse of excitement, Milly followed her sister's line of sight.

Was it?

Could it possibly be?

'Fellow's got a patch over one eye,' said Maggie, whose long-distance eyesight was obviously significantly better than Milly's. 'I do hope he's not up to no good.'

Outrage crackled through Milly. 'Maggie,' she exploded. 'That's a *terrible* thing to say. Why on earth does the fact he's wearing a patch mean he's up to no good?'

'I said he "might be" up to no good.'

'Because he's wearing an eyepatch!'

How quick they all were to jump to conclusions, she thought. She had warned Maggie off Mr Wildermuth because he was German and Maggie was suspicious of Jack because he wore an eyepatch.

'What's got into you?' said Maggie. 'Why are you being so prickly?'

'Because I know him,' said Milly simply. Now she was a bit closer, she could see that it was indeed Jack and, she surmised, the reason her heart was beating a tiny bit faster. 'He works with me at the Home Depot. He lost an eye in France and he's the last person I know who might be up to "no good".'

Maggie shot Milly a curious look. 'Ah!' she said. 'I must say he's awfully handsome despite . . .'

Milly nudged her sister in the ribs with more force than was strictly necessary. 'He's awfully handsome, full stop,' she said firmly.

And then they were nearing the little party. Boniface was at last behaving himself and sitting still, and Charlie and Caroline were posing formally – faces grave – just like the little groups you saw in the newspapers. Caroline even had her hand resting lightly on her brother's shoulder, for goodness' sake.

Jack, focussed, was snapping away, occasionally asking Caroline and Charlie to move this or that way, raise their chins, put their shoulders down. Milly watched, mesmerised. Jack did indeed look very handsome with his slight frown and his hair lightly ruffled, and out of his soldier's uniform he also looked younger – more boyish.

Milly couldn't help a slight pang for what might have been.

And then Jack had stopped shooting and Milly and Maggie were stepping forward, and, for a moment, chaos reigned. Milly flattered herself she saw Jack's face light up in delighted surprise when he saw her and then crease up in confusion when he realised she knew his photography subjects. Caroline and Charlie started jumping around and squealing with the excitement of it all, Arthur started bawling and Boniface chose that moment to dance back into the lake – shortly followed by Charlie.

'Aren't you going to introduce me?' asked Jack cheerfully when calm had finally prevailed.

'Oh, of course,' said Milly. This was all too strange for words. 'This is my sister Caroline and my brother, Charlie.

And this is my elder sister, Maggie, and her son, Arthur. Oh, and Boniface the dog.'

Jack turned towards Caroline and Charlie. 'Well, why didn't you just say?' he said with a grin.

'Because we didn't *know*,' replied Charlie, dissolving into loud, delighted laughter.

Maggie stepped forward. 'I'm sorry to break up the party,' she said. 'But I'm afraid we'd better get this young man home before he catches his death of cold. What did we say about not going in the lake, Charlie?'

Right on cue, Charlie sneezed and started stomping around, water oozing from his sodden shoes.

'Oh dear. Come on, Charlie,' said Milly briskly.

It wouldn't do for another member of the family to get sick just before Christmas. They would have to go straight home.

It was a shame though . . .

'I'll walk with you as far as the gate,' said Jack, falling into step with Milly.

Caroline, Charlie and Boniface ran on ahead, Maggie and Arthur dropped behind, and the little party started retracing their steps.

For a moment or two, Jack and Milly walked in silence. Then Jack cleared his throat.

'Not that it was any of your damn business,' he said. 'But I'd like to explain about that lunchtime you saw me in the park with Eloise.'

'There's no need,' said Milly, a little stiffly. 'You have every right to step out with whoever you like.'

'Eloise is the sweetheart of an old schoolfriend of mine,' continued Jack as if Milly hadn't spoken. 'He's away in the army and she was frantic she hadn't heard from him for a week or so. The letter finally came through. I'm guessing there was a hold-up in the honour letter section . . .'

Happiness surged through Milly like a bright spring day.

'I'm pleased for Eloise,' she said. 'And I'm sorry, I had no right to be grumpy with you.'

'She's pleased too,' said Jack. 'Her sweetheart had requested an honour envelope because he wanted to propose to her. So, there are smiles all around now. And I wanted to explain . . .'

'No need,' said Milly. 'As you said, it's none of my damn business.'

Jack gave her a level look. Milly noticed that his jaw was set into an almost grim line and his hand was clenched into a light fist by his side. 'I said it *wasn't* any of your damn business,' he clarified. 'And,' he added softly. 'I would very much like to make it your business.'

A flash of pure joy shot through Milly and everything she had ever thought about not wanting a sweetheart melted away.

Jack wanted to step out with her. He wanted her!

And she realised – had known for weeks – she wanted him too.

But, before she answered, she had to be honest with him. She had to tell him what she'd done. What she'd been asked to do. There were to be no secrets between the two of them.

Not now.

Not ever.

'There's something I need to tell you,' she said.

As Jack's eyes narrowed, she took a deep breath. Out it all came in one big rush. She told him about meeting Elsie and Hilda, and through them, Nan; about Nan losing her separation allowance and how that had prompted Milly to go on her – now regretted – stone-throwing spree. She didn't dare look at Jack while she said it – stayed staring determinedly at the path ahead – but when she had finished talking, she risked a little glance at him.

What would he say? What would he *do*?

Jack's face wasn't giving anything away. 'Does your sister know?' he asked neutrally.

Milly shook her head. 'No.'

'Then we'd better keep walking, eh?' said Jack. 'Look, I understand – even admire – your passion and your commitment,' he continued. 'And I will never tell you what to do. That's not how things will be between us. Not now. Not ever. But I'm very glad you've decided not to continue down that path.'

'I really have,' said Milly. 'I'd just about worked it out for myself, but then Miss Parker made me realise it's better to try to change things in a different way, even if it might take a bit longer.'

'And are your "friends" all right with you stepping away?' asked Jack.

Milly nodded. 'They are,' she said. Oh, how lovely it was that Jack was just talking to her sensibly about it all, rather than storming off or trying to lecture her. 'They've actually got themselves into a bit of a pickle because they asked me to get involved in bombing the Home Depot before realising that *that* really wasn't a good idea.'

Jack stopped walking so abruptly Arthur's perambulator nearly crashed into him from behind.

'Sorry, sorry,' he said to Maggie. 'You go in front.'

And Maggie, giving the pair a curious glance, wheeled the pram ahead of them.

Jack turned to Milly. 'They did *what*?' he said. There was a muscle going like the clappers in his cheek.

'Not to hurt anyone,' said Milly hurriedly. 'Just to cause a lot of disruption when the King and Queen come to visit . . .'

'The King and Queen,' echoed Jack incredulously. 'What on earth are you talking about?'

'Oh, Lordy,' said Milly, her hand going to her mouth. 'I wasn't meant to say. But.' She took a deep breath. 'The distinguished guests at the Christmas party are actually the King and Queen. Nora told me. She overheard her uncle, Major Benham, talking about it.'

Jack let out a low whistle. 'You don't say!' he said. 'I thought there was an awful lot of fuss over the Army Post Office's Christmas party. All that talk about huge Christmas cakes and specially created postmarks . . . it all falls into place now. But, Milly, bombing the Home Depot! That's a whole different kettle of fish to chucking a few stones through a few windows. This is serious! Have you told the police?'

'No. Because . . .'

'I think we'd better do so . . .'

*We.* Milly liked the way Jack said that. It made her feel safe. That she belonged.

That she *mattered*.

Jack was staring at her, waiting for an answer. They still hadn't started walking and, although Boniface was leading Caroline a merry dance and progress ahead was slow, they were now a long way behind the others.

'It's all right,' she said. 'I've said no and they know it ain't going to happen. And, to be fair, they backed off pretty quickly. I think they were actually a bit relieved.'

'Maybe you should have said yes,' said Jack.

Milly stared at him, open-mouthed. 'What?' she spluttered. 'You think it's a good idea to bomb the Home Depot?'

'No, of course I don't. But, that way, at least you would know where the bomb was and you could take it somewhere safe and call the police,' said Jack. 'This way, they might take it somewhere else and if they take it somewhere like a munitions factory – well, we'd all know about that.'

Milly shuddered. 'There's no need,' she said. 'One of the girls always knew it was a ridiculous idea and the other realises it now. They found the stuff in Nan's apartment and Elsie said she wasn't even sure the powder was dry and she didn't really know what to do with it anyway. They said they would destroy it all. It will be all right, I'm sure.'

'You're sure,' said Jack. 'They were just being hot-headed?'

'Yes,' said Milly. 'They were.'

Jack took a deep breath and ran his hands through his hair. 'All right, then,' he said. 'Well, that was all a bit of a shock.'

'Sorry,' said Milly. 'I just thought you should know.'

'Thank you. So, on another matter entirely, when all the Christmas rush is over, would you like a trip out with me? A bite to eat? Perhaps lunch?'

Milly smiled at him. 'Yes,' she said simply. 'I would like that very much.'

Jack grinned in relief. 'Marvellous,' he said. 'We're all working such ridiculous shifts at the moment, but before Christmas?'

'Marvellous,' echoed Milly, her heart singing.

'And just one more thing,' said Jack.

'What's that?'

'Fabulous hair. Very avant-garde. You can't really see it under the hat, but I noticed it at work.'

Milly gave him a little twirl. 'Very like the sort of girl who might one day go to university to study politics?' she asked pertly.

'Exactly that,' said Jack.

'Hurry up,' called Maggie from ahead of them.

Milly and Jack smiled at each other and hurried to catch the others up.

## 29

The last week before the Christmas party sped by.

The mounds of post showed no sign of abating – were growing, if anything, and everyone was encouraged to do double shifts. Everywhere Milly looked, there were dull eyes and haggard faces, cut fingers, aching backs and eyes that could hardly focus. But spirits remained high. They were working for King and Country and, whenever someone felt they couldn't go on, there was always someone else to gently – or otherwise – remind them that the boys at the front had it a thousand times worse. And, besides, for those on shift at the right time, there was the official Christmas party and the visit from the King and Queen to look forward to.

Yes, the royal visit had finally been announced and the excitement around the Home Depot was palpable. Milly and the rest of the Christmas party planning committee were working extra shifts on top of their extra shifts. Hundreds of yards of patriotic bunting had been stitched and assembled, and possibly several *miles* of paperchains had been painstakingly cut and glued, ready to decorate the pillars and supports. (And, if *that* wasn't a fire hazard, Milly didn't know what was.) And there was so much else to do. One end of the sorting hall had to be cleared so a temporary stage could be created. There was the Christmas tree to decorate, the trestle tables to assemble, the food arrangements to be finalised, duties for the day itself to be allocated . . . the list was never-ending.

Milly hardly had a second to herself and there was no time to see Jack, even had she wanted to.

She did find time, however, to pin a notice announcing the formation of the Army Post Office's Women's Group to the noticeboard outside the surgery. The inaugural meeting would be in the new year, but, in the meantime, interested parties were invited to enter their name on a list. The first to sign up were Nora and Liza – but over the subsequent days, the list grew longer and longer. Milly recognised many of the names – the girl from the canteen, the nurse from the surgery and, to her amazement, all of Team Incomparable – but many were strangers. Milly wasn't sure whether to be more excited or more petrified, and ended up being quite a bit of each. Thank goodness she had a few weeks to get used to the idea.

Outside the Home Depot, things were just as busy. Now everyone in the Woods household was fighting fit again, Christmas preparations could continue in earnest. Everyone was busy buying their Christmas presents and trying to keep them hidden from the other members of the family until they had a chance to wrap them. There were armfuls of holly and ivy to wrestle home from the Roman and festoon the house with, and Milly and Alice fashioned some into a huge wreath to hang on the front door. The gentle rhythms and routines of the festive season seemed to take on a special significance after all the drama and upset of the past couple of months, and Milly threw herself into the preparations wholeheartedly. On one of the many trips to the market, she spied Elsie and Hilda through the crowds and the girls all waved to each other cheerfully, good relations apparently restored. Maybe they could all have a drink together in early 1916. Goodness; how strange that sounded . . .

The day of the party dawned crisp and sunny.

Not that there was any time to admire the weather. The

royal party was arriving at 3 p.m. and there was so much to do. Milly and the rest of the committee had been excused from their regular duties for the day, but that didn't mean they could slacken off.

Far from it.

By half past one, Milly had finally fastened the last paper-chain between the last pillars. Her whole body ached from climbing up and down the stepladder dozens of times, and she was longing for a ciggie. No . . . she needed a ciggie – it was practically a medical emergency! Surely everyone could spare her for five minutes before she went to the lavvies to tidy herself up. Nora had brought in a smart, nearly-new, crisp white shirt for her to wear, and she might allow herself the hint of a lip colour and then . . .

Milly walked over to one of the entrances to the unloading bay and took a deep breath of London air. Then she lit up her ciggie. Strictly speaking, she was outside – sort of – and, anyway, everyone knew cigarettes were good for purifying the air and combatting disease. So, really, she was doing the royal family a favour . . .

The unloading area was a hive of activity. The lorries of mail were still arriving, of course – the Army Post Office stopped for no one – and even though it was officially past the last posting dates for Christmas, it seemed people hadn't stopped sending their letters and parcels. They probably never would. Last-minute deliveries were still arriving for the party as well, with members of the Christmas party planning committee – and strictly no one else – given special dispensation to sign for them. Over there, Nora was taking delivery of flowers from a smart blue florist's van and, on the other side of the bay, Liza was signing for something from Maison Gateaux. *That* would be the cake – the *pièce de résistance* – and thank goodness for that; everyone had been worried it wouldn't arrive on time and what a pity *that* would be. Milly stubbed out her cigarette and went to help Liza, staggering under the heavy box and putting it safely into a basket so Liza could wheel it over to where it needed to be. And now a young girl was pushing past her and running to sign for something from a van she couldn't see. Oh, all these comings and goings really were too exciting and, of course, there were photographers here, snapping away at the build-up to the big event. Milly wondered if Jack was somewhere around – he'd been allowed to bring his camera today – although the last time Milly had seen him, he'd been press-ganged into moving one of the great big piles of sacks. Hopefully he wouldn't fall this time . . .

As Milly turned to go back inside, she was struck by a sudden feeling of unease. Something, somewhere, didn't quite add up. Something, flickering at the edge of her consciousness, was wrong, but she was damned if she knew what it was. Shaking her head, she took a deep breath. It was the nerves, that was all.

After all, one didn't meet the royal family every day . . .

'There you are!'

It was Jack, appearing out of nowhere by her side. He looked so smart and so handsome, even though he'd obviously nicked himself a dozen times while shaving that morning. Milly resisted the temptation to brush the sack dust off his shoulder. It was too proprietary a gesture – and she wasn't officially his sweetheart.

At least, not yet.

'Miss Parker wants us,' Jack was saying. 'She's going to brief us on the postmarks we're presenting in case Their Majesties have any questions, and she also wants to do a last-minute run-through of proceedings now the stage is up. Sergeant Major Cunningham is going to stand in for the King.'

'I bet he is,' said Milly with a giggle. 'He'll be right in his element. Should we go now?'

'We've got ten minutes,' said Jack. 'I've got time to try and get some of this sack dust off me. See you by the stage at ten to?'

'I'll be there,' said Milly. She watched Jack as he headed away. Maybe today, after the presentation was over, he would ask her to take a stroll around the park. He would tuck her hand into the crook of his arm and, as they headed over to the lake, it would start snowing and he would gently lift her chin and . . .

Suddenly, Milly was tipped off balance. Before she could work out what was going on, an arm had clamped around her waist and another around her mouth, and she was being half pulled, half dragged back inside the Home Depot. Milly struggled desperately against her captor – trying to scream, trying to kick out, trying to wriggle free – but to no avail. Whoever it was was much stronger than her and clearly meant business. There was nothing Milly could do to stop herself being dragged out of sight behind the huge pile of sacks stacked inside the entrance to the Home Depot.

Icy fear ran down Milly's spine.

She was going to be attacked.

*Murdered.*

Her heart was hammering against her chest and her breath was coming in raggedy little gasps.

Stay calm, Milly. Stay calm.

Glancing down and behind as she struggled, Milly could see black trousers. Her assailant wasn't a soldier, then – or at least not one in uniform. Who on earth was he, then? He wasn't particularly tall, nor particularly bulky, but he was strong. Really strong. There was the mellow whiff of tobacco, the sharp tang of carbolic and something else, something she knew she should recognise but couldn't quite put her finger on . . .

Never mind that. Need to get away.

Milly carried on struggling, but still to no avail. The man

pushed her up against the sacks, her nose against the canvas, one arm twisted painfully behind her. Then he put his hand across her mouth.

She tensed as she felt breath on her ear.

'Where is it?' The voice was low, urgent, the hint of an accent. Something she should recognise . . .

Where was *what*?

For a wild moment, Milly thought her assailant must mean something to do with the party. After all, that was what today was all about. But that made no sense? Why would someone bundle her out of sight to ask her about a cake or Christmas bouquet?

'Where is it?' the voice repeated, more urgently this time. 'I don't want to hurt you. Just tell me where it is.'

Milly shook her head urgently. 'I don't know.' *I don't know what you're talking about.*

The man tightened his grip on Milly's wrist. '*Tell* me, Amelia!' he demanded.

Milly stopped struggling – it was futile and only making her arm hurt all the more – but her mind was going nineteen to the dozen. The man – whoever he was – *knew her name*. It wasn't a random, casual assault from an opportunistic stranger – it was a targeted attack by someone who knew her and wanted specific information. Moreover, it was someone who called her Amelia. There were very few people who called her that and precisely no one at the Home Depot.

Suddenly it all fell into place. The slight accent was German. The smell was yeast. Bread.

It was Mr Wildermuth!

Milly glanced down. Yes. She recognised his shoes.

Far from reassuring Milly, this sent her more into a panic. What on earth was Mr Wildermuth doing in the Home Depot? He couldn't be here for any innocent, law-abiding reason, that much was clear. But what exactly? And why?

Somehow, she had always known he was up to no good. Why, oh, why hadn't she listened to her instincts?

It didn't take long for the missing pieces to fall into place. Mr Wildermuth was part of the plan to bomb the Home Depot. Far from abandoning the plan when Milly had pulled out, Hilda and Elsie had simply found another way of making it happen. Milly remembered thinking at the time they had backed out almost too quickly, too readily, but how could she ever have imagined Mr Wildermuth would be involved? After all, Mr Wildermuth had said he barely recognised Elsie and then Elsie and Hilda had both warned Milly off Mr Wildermuth . . .

That must have been all a ruse.

They'd all been in it together and she had been too blind to see what had been under her nose all along.

And now Mr Wildermuth was going to bomb the Home Depot and there would be panic and disruption, and the destruction of any credibility the Army Post Office still enjoyed. Worse still, Mr Wildermuth might not be as determined to avoid any casualties as Hilda and Elsie had suggested. Maybe the King and Queen – who would be arriving within the next hour – were in mortal danger.

'Where is it, Amelia?' whispered Mr Wildermuth, jerking Milly's arm and her attention back to her present predicament.

Where was *what*? A specific van? The specific place he wanted to plant his bomb?

Or could Mr Wildermuth actually mean 'where is he'? Was he, God forbid, looking for the King? No, Mr Wildermuth's English was excellent; he wouldn't – even under pressure – make such an elemental mistake.

Milly felt herself being spun around and, for the first time, she came face to face with Mr Wildermuth. She hardly recognised him. Gone was the man who was so part of the furniture none of them even averted their eyes when he carried his chamber pot through the kitchen. In his place, a stranger.

A stranger with staring eyes, bulging forehead veins and an expression that was almost a snarl.

Milly's fear ratcheted up a gear.

In the meantime, she could only shake her head again.

'Be careful,' Mr Wildermuth growled. 'We are running out of time before I go out there and shout that there's a bomb in the building!'

Thank goodness for that!

Mr Wildermuth might have smuggled a bomb into the building, but at least he was going to give everyone a chance to evacuate.

Meanwhile, Mr Wildermuth momentarily loosened his grip on her mouth and Milly seized her chance. She positioned her mouth over his thumb and bit down as hard as she could. Mr Wildermuth pulled back with an exclamation of pain and Milly tried to make a bolt for it. Mr Wildermuth was far too fast for her. With a grunt of anger, he pushed her back against the sacks.

'What on earth is going on here?'

Milly and Mr Wildermuth swung round as one.

It was Jack.

Exquisite relief coursed through Milly. Thank goodness for that! Jack had saved the day and everything was going to be all right.

'Oh, Jack,' she gabbled, trying to push past Mr Wildermuth. 'I don't know what's going on . . .'

'You don't know what's going on?' echoed Jack coldly. 'I've been looking for you everywhere. You've missed the rehearsal, Miss Parker and Sergeant Major Cunningham are going spare and then I find you, brazen as anything, in here with *him*!'

For the first time, Milly registered the look on Jack's face and was suddenly aware of how she – it – must look. She was alone with a man behind a huge pile of sacks, breathing heavily and with – no doubt – her hair all over the place. No wonder Jack was putting two and two together and making five.

How could she get him to understand? To help her?

'Jack, this is Mr Wildermuth,' gabbled Milly. 'He's our lodger.'

Jack's brow furrowed still further. 'Your lodger?' he repeated incredulously. 'What's he doing here? Decided that having a fumble and seeing the King and Queen was too irresistible a combination to resist?'

Oh, Lordy. Time for more drastic action . . .

'There's a bomb in the Home Depot!' shouted Milly and Mr Wildermuth almost as one.

A short sharp silence.

Jack took a small step backwards. 'A bomb?' he echoed. 'How . . .? Who . . .?'

'He brought it in,' shouted Milly, jabbing a finger at Mr Wildermuth.

'She did it,' echoed Mr Wildermuth, pointing accusingly at Milly.

'It ain't nothing to do with me,' exploded Milly furiously.

'Nor me!' retorted Mr Wildermuth hotly.

Milly shook her head in disbelief. 'You just told me there's a bomb in here!' she said.

Had Mr Wildermuth gone quite mad?

Jack held his hands up and turned to Milly. 'You go first,' he said. 'Just the bare facts, please.'

Milly took a deep breath. 'I were about to go back inside after you left me and then Mr Wildermuth bundles me in here and starts shouting at me, and then he says there's a bloody bomb in here.' She took another deep breath. 'I know what I told you the other day, Jack, but I swear I've had nothing to do with . . . whatever's happened.'

'So, you do know about it!' interjected Mr Wildermuth. 'If

you don't tell me where it is, I'll march you out there and get them to evacuate the place . . .'

'Don't you dare lay a finger on her,' said Jack coolly. 'Now, before we all get them to evacuate the place, why don't you tell us why you think there's a bomb in the Home Depot and why you think Milly has something to do with it. Quickly now, there's a good chap. If there *is* a bomb in here, there's no time to lose.'

Suddenly Milly felt really frightened. She glanced around, suddenly petrified a bomb might go off any moment.

It could be anywhere.

In any of the parcels that shielded them from view . . . .

'I've had my suspicions for a while,' said Mr Wildermuth. 'There were rumours going round at the bakery that one of our drivers, Harry Watson, has links to an extreme suffragette movement through his fiancée. People were saying they were linked with the recent stone throwing and might be planning something bigger. I usually make it my business not to get involved in such matters, but then I discovered Miss Amelia here was a friend of Harry's fiancée, and I knew she'd taken to being out of the house at all hours. And then I overheard her saying she was in trouble with the police—'

'That were nothing to do with nothing,' interrupted Milly. 'That wasn't even about me.'

How *dare* Mr Wildermuth accuse her like that?

Jack held up a hand. 'Let Mr Wildermuth continue,' he said.

'Miss Amelia had already told me the King and Queen were visiting the Home Depot today,' said Mr Wildermuth. 'And then this afternoon, Harry Watson took the van to do the afternoon rounds. Only he hadn't been on the rota – and the chap who *had* been due to do the deliveries told me he'd been offered cigarettes to swap shifts – and that got my suspicions up. So, I jumped into our second van and followed him. The first few deliveries were legitimate – our regular customers – but then he stopped and picked up his fiancée and her friend over by King's Cross. One of them was carrying a big parcel and my doubts intensified. They drove straight here and I knew it wasn't on legitimate business – they're not one of our customers – so I knew there was something amiss. I could see the van getting waved into the compound but I didn't have any paperwork, so I parked, grabbed some bread from the back and Security waved me through. The van had disappeared from the exit by the time I got in, but I assumed, naturally, they had given the parcel to Miss Amelia. Indeed, I could see her standing by the entrance. So, I dumped the bread and pulled her in here to find out what she'd done with it . . .'

Milly looked wildly from one man to the other. 'I swear none of this were anything to do with me,' she said. 'I swear on the Bible; on my family's lives. They asked me – Jack, I *told* you they'd asked me – and when I refused, I thought that were the end of it. Please, Jack, you've got to believe me.'

Jack gave her a curt nod but Milly couldn't tell if he truly did.

Jack turned to Mr Wildermuth. 'If what you are saying is true, why didn't you run into the Home Depot screaming blue murder and get the whole place evacuated. Why waste time looking for Milly?'

Mr Wildermuth exhaled noisily. 'I should have done,' he said. 'I should have alerted one of the security guards outside. But it's not the best time to be German and bearing such a message, and, to be honest, I hoped it wouldn't come to that. I hoped we could move the thing. Maybe even disable it. Miss Amelia's family have been good to me and I have no wish to see her hang.'

*Hang!* Milly's blood ran cold.

Jack was frowning. 'How do we know you haven't smuggled

something in here and now you are trying to shift the blame onto Milly?'

Milly's breath caught in her throat.

Mr Wildermuth gave a hollow laugh. 'If I had delivered and planted something in here, don't you think I would have completed my task and got the hell out of here? I'm only here because I want to stop innocent bloodshed and to prevent Miss Amelia getting into trouble.'

There was a short, charged pause.

Mr Wildermuth *sounded* genuine. Could what he was saying possibly be true? In which case, there was no time to lose.

Milly swallowed hard. She suddenly felt quite light-headed.

'If there *is* a bomb in here, maybe Mr Wildermuth should alert the authorities and tell them what he saw,' she said, trying to keep a quaver out of her voice. 'We don't want anyone getting hurt and, even if suspicion does initially fall on me, I'm sure they wouldn't hang an innocent woman. But we need to act quickly. Elsie made it quite clear it would be a real bomb. Not a dummy.'

'What else did they say?' asked Jack.

Milly thought back, trying to remember. 'That it should be put somewhere to cause maximum disruption but no injuries. And it would be timed to coincide with the royal visit.'

Jack nodded. 'In that case, provided they've set it properly, we have a little time to play with. The royal party won't be arriving for a while. But these things can be unpredictable . . .'

'And the whole place could go sky-high at any moment,' Milly finished for him. 'Let's raise the alarm.'

Jack took her arm. 'If we do that now, they'll evacuate the building and disrupt the royal visit, and the publicity will be devastating for the Home Depot. It might never recover.'

'They know that,' said Milly. 'That's what they're banking on.'

'So, all the more reason for us to see if there's another option,' said Jack. 'We can't let them win. If this attack is a success, there will be many more, mark my words. So, think, Milly. And you too, Mr Wildermuth. Was there anything else you saw or overheard? Anything to give us a clue on who Hilda and Elsie might give the bomb to?'

Mr Wildermuth shook his head. 'I assumed they would be giving it to Miss Amelia,' he said. 'All I can tell you is that it was a parcel. A large parcel wrapped in brown paper.'

Jack gave a wry smile. 'Of course, it was,' he said. 'Just like everything else in this darn place.' He turned to Milly. '*Think*, Milly. You were standing by the doors to the unloading bay. Did you see anything out of the ordinary? Anything at all?'

Milly shut her eyes and tried to picture the scene. The bustle. The sense of excitement. All the lorries and vans being unloaded, the cameras popping. She hadn't seen a Clarkson's van; she was pretty sure of that. But there *had* been that feeling, that frisson of unease, the sense that something wasn't quite right.

What was it? What hadn't quite added up? She screwed her eyes up tighter . . .

*Yes!*

'I've remembered something,' she said. 'It might be nothing but . . .'

'You saw something?' asked Mr Wildermuth. He still, it had to be said, looked exceedingly doubtful about the whole thing.

'Not some*thing*,' said Milly. 'Some*one*.'

# 30

It was the red hair that had stuck in Milly's mind.

Not that there was any rule about people with red hair signing for deliveries, of course. But this particular person with red hair had no legitimate reason to be out near the unloading bays that afternoon. It was a long shot – there might well be an innocent explanation – but it was all that Milly had to go on.

'Well?' asked Jack, and Milly was aware that both men were staring at her.

'It was the girl from the surgery,' said Milly. 'I think her name is Sarah.'

'What of it?' asked Jack, a touch impatiently.

'She was signing for a parcel,' said Milly. 'There were that many vans that I didn't see where from, but she definitely came back into the depot carrying a bulky, brown parcel. The thing is, she's not on the party committee and, apart from the soldiers who are doing the regular unloading today, no one else is meant to be signing for parcels this afternoon.'

'But that could be anything,' said Jack. 'She could have been signing for medical equipment or—'

'Not this afternoon,' insisted Milly. 'And there's something else. I hadn't put two and two together before, but I'm pretty sure I saw Sarah at the ELFS mother-and-baby clinic. She was wearing a hat and I didn't really see her face, but I think I saw her carrying supplies. And she was with Elsie and Hilda.'

Milly finished with a flourish, working it all out herself for the first time.

'Right,' said Jack. 'Well done, Milly. It's a long shot, but there's only one thing for it. We'll have to go and confront her.' He turned to Mr Wildermuth. 'You can push off now, if you like? We can take it from here.'

'Certainly not,' said Mr Wildermuth. 'I am involved now and you may need my testimony.'

Milly nodded at him and then swallowed nervously. 'Shall we go, then?' she said.

'Yes,' said Jack. 'Quickly, now. And, Mr Wildermuth, probably best to say as little as possible.'

Milly smoothed her hair down and led the way out of their hiding place. She'd only been there a matter of minutes, yet, in that time, the whole world had turned on its axis. And it seemed she had changed too because, without really meaning to, she grabbed a hat hanging from a peg and crammed it on her head. Her new hairdo was so conspicuous and she really didn't want Miss Parker or Sergeant Major Cunningham catching sight of her and forcing her to deviate from her mission.

Milly, Jack and Mr Wildermuth made their way from the unloading bay over towards the surgery. They went the long way, round the outside of the building, to avoid recognition and confrontation. In Milly's mind, the surgery would be empty and Sarah would be sitting there alone, looking pensive, the package in question by her feet. From there, the fantasy would go one of two ways. Either Sarah would look genuinely surprised and show them the package contained nothing more than genuine medical supplies – or she would immediately crumble and admit all . . .

The surgery was packed!

The surgery was never this packed – the Home Depot was hardly a dangerous place to work – but today the door was open and there was a gaggle of people queuing in the corridor outside. Milly exchanged a panicked glance with Jack and Mr Wildermuth. What now? They could hardly burst into the surgery and ask Sarah if she'd smuggled a bomb into the building in front of everyone.

Jack turned to a soldier nursing his hand at the end of the queue. 'What's going on here, old chap?' he asked.

The soldier shrugged, looking singularly unimpressed. 'Several fainters, I gather,' he said. 'Quite overcome at the prospect of seeing the King.'

Milly puffed out her cheeks in frustration. She suspected many women had laced their corsets rather more tightly than usual that morning in an attempt to look their best. That combined with all the excitement and the physical work . . . and maybe it was no surprise so many had had an attack of the vapours. It wouldn't help the women's reputation within the Home Depot, though – and it certainly didn't help the matter at hand. Motioning for Jack and Mr Wildermuth to follow her, Milly started pushing her way up the queue, muttering apologies as she did so. 'I'm ever so sorry.' 'Excuse me.' 'An emergency, don't you know?'

Eventually, she managed to get through the door of the surgery and there was Sarah, right in front of her, tending to a woman with a bleeding finger. One of the infamous paper cuts, no doubt. The sister-in-charge – Milly couldn't remember her name – was bending over a prone figure on a bed, and there was another young nurse bustling around dispensing medication to a man who was clutching his head.

'Excuse me?' Milly said to Sarah.

Sarah looked up from her task. There was no flicker of recognition when she saw Milly.

'Can I help you?' she asked. She looked tired and there were high spots of colour in her cheeks, but she also looked calm – a young woman secure in the natural authority afforded by her role. Maybe Milly had got it all wrong. Maybe Sarah had picked up a perfectly innocent parcel. Or maybe she hadn't picked up a parcel at all. But Milly couldn't give up now.

After all, they hadn't anything else to go on.

Milly took a deep breath. 'I wonder if you could come with me,' she said, thinking on her feet. 'There's . . . a woman fainted over by the unloading bay and—'

'Goodness, not another one,' interrupted Sarah with a little laugh. 'The royals pay a visit and half the Army Post Office starts fainting! Can you get her over here and we'll give her the once over?'

'I would, of course,' said Milly, pursing her lips. 'But the lady is out cold and I think she's hit her head. I really don't like to move her.'

Milly held her breath.

It was worth a try.

Sarah narrowed her eyes. 'Should I call an ambulance?' she asked.

'Oh, no!' said Milly hastily. 'It's really not that bad, but better to be safe than sorry. Especially with the King and Queen about to arrive. We wouldn't want anything to disrupt their visit.'

Milly wasn't sure why she had said that. It didn't even really make sense! But Sarah finished bandaging her patient's finger and stood up.

'All right,' she said. 'I'll see if Sister can spare me. I could do with stretching my legs anyway.'

She disappeared over to the sister and then grabbed a leather bag. 'OK,' she said with a smile. 'Lead the way.'

Signalling for Jack and Mr Wildermuth to stay in the background, Milly led Sarah back around the outside of the Home Depot. It was quiet here on the park side of the building and Milly briefly wondered if they should confront Sarah here and save time. After all, surely it was only a matter of time before Sarah noticed Jack and Mr Wildermuth, and asked why they were being followed by a soldier with a patch over one eye and a man covered in flour! But the sentry soldiers were patrolling the perimeter fence as usual and Milly could see a couple of extra policemen over by the park entrance – to say nothing of the usual nannies and children catching the last of the winter sunshine in the park. No, it was far too risky. Far better to get back behind the huge pile of sacks where Mr Wildermuth had pulled her. That was assuming no one had starting shifting the sacks – or had taken refuge behind them themselves . . .

'Here we are,' said Milly, cheerfully leading the way behind the sacks. To her relief, the space was still empty. 'Oh, the lady isn't here anymore.'

Sarah had followed Milly inside. 'That's very annoying,' she said, before noticing Jack and Mr Wildermuth had blocked the only way out. 'What's going on?'

Despite everything, Milly felt a stab of guilt. Sarah looked *terrified*. She turned from one to the other, hands to her chest, pupils huge. Oh, how Milly hoped she hadn't effectively kidnapped an innocent woman under false pretences. But then again, Sarah's instinctive reaction seemed so extreme that *something* must be up . . .

'We want to know what you did with the package you were seen taking possession of about . . . forty minutes ago,' said Milly simply.

Goodness, how had all *that* happened in forty minutes?

'What package?' asked Sarah, green eyes widening. A stain began to flush her cheeks, joining her freckles together. 'I don't know what you're talking about.'

Surely her eye contact was too level to be truly convincing?

'We don't have time to mess around,' said Jack, stepping forward. 'You were seen by at least two people – who would swear an oath on it, by the way – taking possession of a parcel outside in the unloading bay. And we need to know what was in it and what you've done with it.'

Sarah transferred her unblinking gaze to Jack. 'Oh, *that* parcel,' she said with a light, tinkling laugh. 'Just medical supplies. Goodness me, we've been so busy this afternoon, I quite forgot nipping out to sign for it.'

'Would Sister be able to vouch for it?' persisted Jack.

'Sister doesn't know every package that comes into the surgery,' said Sarah defensively.

'I bet she does,' muttered Milly.

Sarah turned to Milly. 'If you don't let me go, I'll start screaming the place down,' she said.

'Be our guest,' said Milly. 'But I wouldn't if I were you. Because we all saw the package of "medical supplies" came out of the back of a Clarkson's bakery van so you aren't telling the truth, are you?'

Milly had been crossing her fingers behind her back as she said that because most of it was pure supposition. No one had actually seen where Sarah had got her parcel from, and they might be barking up totally the wrong tree. But the fact Sarah's skin had now turned alabaster white suggested they were on the right track.

'It's Sister's birthday,' blustered Sarah. 'And we thought we'd surprise her with a cake.'

It was a valiant attempt, but they all knew the game was up. Sarah suddenly tried to make a dash for it, but Jack and Mr Wildermuth were far too strong for her. They caught hold of her and pushed her back into the middle of their little circle. Sarah looked around her like a cornered cat surrounded by three starving dogs. Milly noticed she didn't shout for help, though. She remained completely quiet.

Jack stepped forward. 'Believe it or not, we want to help you,' he said. 'We think that package contains a bomb. If that's true and the police find out about it, you will go to prison for a very long time and you may even be hanged.'

'A bomb!' Sarah's laugh, for once, sounded quite genuine. 'Do you think I would be stupid enough to smuggle a bomb into the Home Depot? And who is this man?' she added, pointing at Mr Wildermuth. 'He hasn't said anything. What's he doing here?'

Mr Wildermuth opened his mouth to reply, but Jack held out a hand and stepped in front of him. 'Mr Wildsmith is a baker,' he said smoothly. 'He works for Clarkson's and he saw the package being loaded, and he became suspicious. He followed it here and saw you pick it up. So, you see, there are many witnesses to what you have done.'

Sarah swallowed hard, her eyes filling with tears.

'What do *you* believe is in the parcel?' asked Milly, pushing home her advantage.

'A jack-in-the-box,' said Sarah sulkily. 'In a giant Princess Mary Christmas tin.'

'A jack-in-the-box?' echoed Jack incredulously. He turned to Milly. 'Is that possible? All this for a jack-in-the-box!'

Milly shrugged. She didn't know what to believe – what to *think* – any more. 'Why would someone give you a jack-in-the-box to smuggle into the Home Depot?' she asked Sarah.

'To promote the fight for equality,' replied Sarah.

'But how would that help?'

Sarah took a deep breath and exhaled slowly. 'If you must know, the "jack" inside is actually a Jill – a female doll dressed in the suffragette colours, holding a sign saying "Votes for Women".'

Milly, Jack and Mr Wildermuth exchanged another glance. Could it be possible? Milly remembered Maggie telling her how creative Elsie was; how good she was at making toys. Could she and Hilda really have changed the plan from a bomb to a jack-in-the-box, to do nothing more than embarrass the royal family?

Milly had no way of knowing.

'Have you actually seen it?' Milly asked.

Sarah paused. 'No,' she admitted.

'And the plan was for you to present this box to the Queen?' Jack was saying.

'Not me,' said Sarah, shaking her head. 'My job was just to leave it by a pillar in the extension and someone else would pick it up and present it to the royal party.'

'Who?' persisted Jack.

'I don't know,' said Sarah. And then, with a defiant shake of her head, she added, 'By *kidnapping* me in here, you haven't achieved anything, have you? Everything will go ahead as planned.'

Oh, goodness.

This was awful.

Milly touched Sarah on the arm. 'Mr . . . Wildsmith has described the women he saw putting the package into your van. I know who they are and I think they've lied to you.'

'No!' said Sarah, shaking her arm free.

'I'm sorry, but it's true,' said Milly. 'I think there's some sort of explosive device in there that will cause a great deal of damage if not injury. I don't think there's a jack-in-the-box in there. I don't think anyone's going to pick it up. I think they're planning for it to go off where you left it.'

'Particularly if they asked you to leave it by one of the wooden pillars,' interjected Jack. 'That will cause structural damage and is likely to bring the whole roof down. You need to show us where the parcel is.'

'No!' said Sarah. 'It's all arranged. You can't stop it now . . .'

'If it is a bomb and it does go off, you will be in all sorts of trouble,' said Milly.

The defiance had gone and Sarah was openly crying now. 'If it doesn't happen as they want it to, they'll tell everyone what my sister did.'

'They've blackmailed you,' said Milly flatly.

It was a statement rather than a question. Of course they had.

When Milly had refused to go along with their plans, Elsie had simply changed tack. She had made up a more palatable reason for wanting to smuggle a package into the Home Depot, and had applied a little pressure as well.

Milly almost felt sorry for Sarah.

'You need to show us where you've hidden that parcel and you need to show us now!' said Jack. 'Either that or we'll go straight to the police and tell them what you've told us.'

Sarah didn't say anything.

'Actually, maybe we should just go to the police,' said Milly.

'I'll show you,' said Sarah hastily.

'Right,' said Jack. 'Let's head towards the extension. Sarah, you stay between me and Mr, er, Wildsmith. Heads down. Don't make any eye contact with anyone.'

'Luckily the extension is out of bounds today because of the visit, so we shouldn't be disturbed,' muttered Milly as they left the hiding place together and set off across the floor of the Home Depot. To her relief, Sarah kept to her place in the line – showing no desire to make a run for it. All around them, everyone's attention was on finishing their work before the imminent arrival of the royal party and no one took a blind bit of notice of the little group of four. Reaching the extension – with a huge *No Entry* sign tacked to the door – they slipped inside the warehouse unchallenged.

'Where is it, Sarah?' asked Milly. There were thousands of sacks in the extension – not perhaps stacked as high as they had been before the fire, but far, far too many to sort through by hand.

Sarah waved a hand. 'Over there,' she said, indicating an area to the left with the highest stacks of sacks – the very area Milly had rescued one of the Home Depot mousers from on

the night of the fire. Milly, Jack and Mr Wildermuth duly
turned and . . .

Out of the corner of her eye, Milly saw a blur of blue.

Sarah was making a dash for it!

Holding her skirts, the woman ran full pelt across the
extension, heading for a door in the far wall. Before anyone
had time to react, Sarah had wrestled open a bolt and disappeared outside.

Milly and the others stared at each other in shock.

'I'll go after her,' said Mr Wildermuth. 'You stay and look
for the parcel.'

Milly and Jack locked gazes. Should they let Mr Wildermuth
and Sarah disappear like that?

Either way, it was too late. Mr Wildermuth had disappeared.

'At least most of the parcels are in sacks,' said Milly, trying
to be positive. 'And Sarah did give us a clue by saying it was
at the base of one of the columns. I know there are dozens,
but at least it gives us somewhere to start.'

'True,' said Jack. 'Right, let's spread out and find the darn
thing.'

The two separated and started gingerly searching at the
base of each wooden column – most of which had a pile of
sacks stacked around them. Milly trod carefully, heart in
mouth, half expecting an explosion at any minute.

How had they got themselves into this mess?

'I'm assuming she won't have put it in a sack?' called Jack.
'If she's done that, we haven't got a hope in hell of finding it.'

'Let's hope she hasn't,' said Milly, moving on to another
pillar. And then she saw it! Slipped between two sacks and
facing the far wall was the package they were looking for!
And to Milly's eyes, it was so obvious there might as well
have been a large sign with an arrow pointing straight at it.
The package was addressed in Elsie's distinctive, loopy scrawl
and in her favourite purple ink. There was no stamp. The

recipient meant nothing to Milly – but the sender was one Nan Reid.

It was definitely *the* parcel.

It couldn't be anything else.

For the longest moment, Milly stood and stared at it. If she didn't move and she didn't tell Jack, then she didn't have to face what happened next. But that, of course, was ridiculous. Time was running out. They had to move now and they had to move quickly.

Milly walked over to Jack, who was circling another pillar, hands in pocket. She tapped him on the shoulder and he looked at her enquiringly, and, even given the gravitas of the situation, she couldn't help thinking how wonderful he looked.

'I've found it,' she whispered, and suddenly Jack was all ears, standing up straight, snapping to attention.

'Where?'

'Over there.'

Silently she led Jack over to the parcel.

'It's this one,' she said. 'The ink, the handwriting, no stamp . . .'

Jack gave a low whistle. 'The fact it's the only one not in a sack,' he finished for Milly. 'Stands out like a sore thumb, doesn't it?'

Milly nodded.

What next?

Jack crouched down beside the parcel. 'We need to open it,' he said. 'But it's hard to get at it where it is. While we're moving it, we might as well lift it onto something flat and stable.'

'There's a table over there,' said Milly, pointing back towards the door. She rushed across the extension and carried the little table over to the parcel.

'Let's take one side each and carefully slide it onto the surface,' said Jack. 'Keep it level and no sharp movements.'

Milly took a deep breath. It was difficult when her heart was threatening to burst out of her chest and every sense was on high alert, waiting for an explosion. Gingerly, she picked up her end of the parcel – telling herself that it was nothing more than a jill-in-the-box – and together she and Jack laid it gently on the table. Then – carefully, carefully – they stripped away the string and the brown-paper wrapping; a couple of months in the broken parcels department earlier in the year meant Milly had *that* down to a fine art. There was a box inside, but it looked nothing like the Princess Mary Christmas tin: no hint of brass; no embossed silhouette; no garland of laurel leaves. Just a roughly hewn wooden box – the type Ma said gave you splinters just looking at it.

'Maybe the tin box could be inside?' suggested Milly.

Was she clutching at straws?

'Let's see,' said Jack.

Gesturing for Milly to stand back, he opened the unfastened lid.

Inside, they could see a mustard tin, a clock, some coils of fuse and a battery. Milly knew next to nothing about bombs, but she knew enough to recognise what she was looking at. She edged further back, hand to heart, just as Jack stepped back with a whistle.

'It's not the most sophisticated beast,' he said. 'And definitely not the biggest. But it will make a hell of a noise and do a lot of damage. It's set to go off in about forty-five minutes.'

Suddenly there was the sound of running feet. Liza and Nora were rushing over to them.

'Milly! Jack! We've been looking everywhere for you,' said Liza, her face etched with frustration.

'Why the Dickens are you hiding in here?' added Nora. 'This really isn't the time to slope off for a smoke. Miss Parker is going *spare*.'

'Just a last-minute little hitch,' said Milly, urgently flapping them away.

It was too late.

Liza and Nora walked right up to them and looked in the box.

Irritation turned into horror.

'What on earth are you doing?' whispered Liza.

Nora clapped a hand to her chest. 'They've only bought a *bomb* into the Home Depot,' she said.

# 31

Milly's first thought was to wonder if Liza and Nora would immediately run for help.

Who would blame them for thinking the worst of her?

After all, it was barely two weeks since she'd told them about her stone-throwing activities and now, here she was, standing by a bomb in the Home Depot and just as the King and Queen were due to arrive. Milly might well have jumped to the same conclusion if the roles had been reversed.

'Oh, Milly,' said Liza. Her voice sounded almost sad.

'I promise it ain't what it looks like,' said Milly. 'It weren't—'

'But a *bomb*, Milly,' interrupted Nora. 'You've gone too far this time.'

Jack looked up from studying the bomb. 'Neither of you should need convincing,' he said coolly. 'But in case you do, let me reassure you your friend had absolutely nothing to do with smuggling this in. Neither did I, for that matter. More importantly, we have precisely thirty-seven minutes until it detonates and takes out most of the extension with it.'

In any other circumstances, Milly would have hugged him.

'We need to tell someone,' said Nora decisively. 'Uncle Alf. Sergeant Major Cunningham. This is too big for us to deal with alone.'

'If we tell them, they'll be forced to evacuate the building,' said Jack shortly. 'Far better we defuse it ourselves and let the royal visit go ahead as planned.'

'Defuse it?' said Liza. '*Us?*'

'Me,' clarified Jack. 'I spent my war disabling devices and I've seen bombs like this before; the suffragettes planted one very like it in St Paul's Cathedral. Trust me – I know what to do.'

'If we get the police involved, the Home Depot's reputation will never recover,' added Milly.

'But who brought it in?' asked Nora.

Right on cue, the outside door swung open and Mr Wildermuth pushed a red-faced and tear-stained Sarah back into the extension.

'Mr Wildermuth,' gasped Liza. 'What on earth are you doing here?'

'It's nothing to do with him, Liza,' said Milly quickly. 'In fact, he's rather saved the day.'

Mr Wildermuth pushed Sarah forwards. 'I found her hiding round the side of the building.' He pointed at the parcel. 'Ah, I see you've found the parcel. Is it a jack-in-the-box?'

'A jack-in-the-box?' echoed Nora incredulously.

'It's a bomb, I'm afraid,' said Jack. 'A crude one, but a bomb all the same.'

Sarah's eyes grew wide with horror. She started whimpering and the whimpers grew in volume until she looked like she was on the verge of complete hysterics. Milly stepped forward and grabbed her by the shoulders.

'Calm down,' she said, giving a little shake. 'Or the whole place will come running.'

'I swear they told me it was a jack-in-the-box,' said Sarah with a hiccup.

'I'm going to try and defuse it,' said Jack. 'The best thing you can do is stay quiet and out of the way.'

'I will keep an eye on her,' said Mr Wildermuth. He took hold of Sarah's arm and frogmarched her across the extension.

'The nurse from the surgery?' whispered Nora urgently, and Milly nodded in reply.

'She were blackmailed and didn't know it were a bomb. But there's no time for that now.'

'Yes,' said Liza. 'What do you need us to do?'

'A screwdriver and some wire-cutters,' said Jack. 'And bring my camera. You'll find it under the table in my station. Quick as you can.'

Liza and Nora were already on their way.

Left alone, Jack turned to Milly.

'I'd be more comfortable if you left,' he said. 'Just in case. Anyway, we need at least one of us to do the presentation.'

Milly hesitated. 'Do you really know how to disable it?' she asked.

She couldn't believe how calm they were both being.

Jack made a face. 'I know which wires to cut, if that's what you mean,' he said. 'But they're tangled underneath the clock and that makes it a bit more complicated because, with only one eye, it's difficult to judge distances.'

'Then I ain't going nowhere,' said Milly firmly. 'I know nothing about bombs but I've got a good eye and a steady hand and, if you show me what to do, I'm sure we'll make a grand team.'

'Are you sure?' asked Jack.

'Perfectly.'

There was no reason a woman couldn't cut a couple of wires as well as any man.

'You're a grand girl,' said Jack, and, despite the circumstances, Milly felt her cheeks flush with pleasure.

Sarah was still crying and her crying was getting louder. Milly went over to her.

'Honestly, Sarah,' she said. 'The best thing you can do is to go back on duty before they send a search party out for you and expose us all.'

Sarah started in surprise. 'Aren't you going to call the police?' she asked.

'No,' said Jack. 'Believe it or not, we're trying to save your bacon. And, if you really didn't know it was a bomb, then you'd go back on duty and make it seem like nothing is amiss.'

Sarah nodded. 'Thank you,' she said sincerely. 'I'll tidy myself up and then I'll go back to the surgery.'

'Tell them it took a long time to get the lady who had fainted back on her feet,' Milly suggested.

'I will. And thank you, again.'

She left as Nora and Liza came rushing back in.

'We're letting her go,' called Milly, in case there was any confusion, and the two girls nodded.

'Here's the camera,' said Nora, putting the box on the floor.

'And here are the tools,' added Liza, handing over wire-cutters, screwdriver and wrench. 'We've borrowed them from the workmen who assembled the temporary stage. Luckily they didn't ask any awkward questions.'

'And we've got your presentation postmarks too.'

'Thank you,' said Jack. 'We'd better get to work. We haven't got long. If one of you could stand guard . . .'

'I'll do it,' said Liza. 'Nora, you get ready for your presentation.'

'Shall I present your postmarks too, Milly and Jack?' asked Nora.

Milly considered this, head on one side. 'I think if we change plans at this late stage, it would only invite questions from the powers-that-be,' she said. 'There would be the most awful stink and Jack and I would probably both be sacked. I think we should both get up there to do our presentations if we possibly can.'

Jack looked up from scrutinising the bomb. 'Agreed,' he said.

'All right,' said Nora. 'I'll tell Miss Parker you're both feeling poorly – maybe the nerves, maybe something you ate – but you will both be there on time.'

'Off you go, Nora,' said Liza. 'If I stand by the door, I can just about see the stage,' she added. 'If needs be, I can signal to Nora and she can stall for time.'

Milly felt tears pricking at her eyelids. How wonderful her friends were. How could she ever have doubted them? But there was no time for that because, with a last look over their shoulders, the two were gone and she and Jack were alone again.

'Are you sure about this?' asked Jack softly, looking deeply into her eyes.

Milly nodded. She wished her hands were warmer – the extension was, of course, unheated and jolly parky – and her nerves were beginning to make them tremble to boot, but what other choice did they have?

She was probably still a safer bet than Jack.

'Good for you,' said Jack. 'Right. We need to cut the wires here and here.' He used the screwdriver to point to two wires which, as he had already pointed out, were partly hidden under the clock. 'It must be done smoothly and carefully without disturbing anything else too much. Reckon you're up for that?'

Milly nodded again. She wiped her palms on her skirts and took the proffered wire-cutters, trying not to think about what would happen if she failed in her mission. Her hands were clumsy, slightly numb.

Deep breaths, Milly. Stay calm.

Milly leaned over the bomb. One wire was more accessible than the other – she would cut that one first. She took the screwdriver in one hand and gently pulled the first wire away from the clock, every cell of her aware of Jack right beside her, and . . .

Suddenly there were loud cheers from outside.

Milly straightened up and exhaled a ragged breath, her concentration totally gone.

The royal party had arrived.

Liza poked her head around the door. 'They're here!' she whispered. 'Nora's about to go up to do her presentation. You haven't got long.'

Heart thumping, Milly bent back over the bomb. It was now or never. Never or now. The world closed in around her until it became just her, Jack and their shared task. As she gently, oh, so gently, teased the wire out again, concentrating too deeply to be truly scared, she thought how much she trusted Jack. She felt safe around him and knew he would never deliberately let her down.

'Easy does it,' he said reassuringly.

And it was more than that. More than her trusting him. He trusted her. Implicitly. He trusted her so much that he would stand by her side while she defused a bomb with numb and shaking fingers. No man had ever trusted her like that before, and she found she liked it.

She really liked it.

'Nora's presenting her flowers now,' said Liza. 'She's chatting to the royal family to waste time. You're due on *now*!'

Suddenly Milly felt suffused with confidence. With Jack by her side, she could do anything. Achieve anything. Be anything. Defusing a bomb was easy! Calmly, she reached out and cut the first wire. It parted with a satisfying *snip*. Then, feeling as if she was in a dream, she moved the cutters to the second wire.

Plenty of room.

Plenty of time.

*Snip!*

For a moment, Jack and Milly just stared at each other, slow grins spreading over their faces.

'I did it!' said Milly.

'You certainly did,' said Jack.

He bent his head towards her and . . . .

'Go!' called Liza. 'Go *now*.'

'I'll make sure no one sees the bomb,' Mr Wildermuth added.

And Milly and Jack went.

Snatching up their gifts, they ran helter-skelter past Liza, out of the extension and into the Home Depot proper. Slowing to a more circumspect walk – albeit the quickest one they could muster – they skirted the crowds and headed for the stage.

'Your hat,' muttered Jack, tapping Milly on the shoulder and Milly realised she'd been wearing the hat she'd 'borrowed' to disguise herself all this time. With a giggle, she whipped it off and hung it on a nail on the nearest pillar, hoping against hope her hair wasn't too messy. Phew! Imagine doing a presentation to the royal family in an outdoor hat. She might as well have had her coat on for good measure!

And there was the stage with the newly-fashioned steps on either side of it. And there – gulp – was the royal family and, behind them, Miss Parker fixing her with a steely gaze. Milly mounted the steps, bobbed her curtsey and handed over her presentation postmark. She'd missed her briefing and really had no idea what she was presenting, so fingers crossed there would be no awkward questions.

Hopefully there would be no questions at all.

The King and Queen both turned their attention to Jack, but Princess Mary was looking straight at Milly.

'Your hair,' she said.

Milly touched her curls self-consciously. Was it really that bad? That much of a mess? 'I'm sorry, Your Royal Highness,' she began, but Princess Mary raised a gloved hand.

'I think it's marvellous,' she said. 'I'd love to have mine cut like that, but goodness knows what my mother would say!'

'Oh, mine had a few choice words,' said Milly. 'And my sister said I would grow a moustache!'

The two young women laughed easily together and then

rincess Mary said, 'I think women here are proving they
don't need to grow a moustache to do the job as well as any
man! Keep up the good work!'

And Milly left the stage on cloud nine.

Milly's feeling of fizzing excitement stayed as she and Jack
stood together in the crowd to listen to the speeches.

The King was speaking. 'I hear from all quarters that the
women at the Home Depot have done work of great value,'
he said. 'I don't wish to inspire competition or disgruntlement,
but I gather none of the duties now performed by women
would be as well performed by men. Bravo. By all accounts,
you have shown marked aptitude for the work and have proved
both zealous and competent workers.'

'I'll say,' murmured Jack. 'It might not be the work His
Majesty is thinking of, but I'd say this woman has done work
of *great* value this afternoon and has displayed particular
competence.'

Milly smiled over her shoulder at him. The crowd around
them murmured and stirred, pushing the two closer together
until Milly was almost leaning back against Jack. He didn't
shift his weight and Milly decided she didn't mind. She didn't
mind at all. They stood there, part of the crowd, but somehow
apart. Alone. After a while, she felt Jack silently take her hand
in his and Milly decided she rather liked that too.

She liked it very much.

All too soon, the speeches were over and the royal party
departed for their tour to a chorus of cheers and a flurry of
flag waving.

Liza and Nora rushed over to join them.

'You did it!' said Liza. 'Well done, Milly!'

'I had an excellent teacher,' said Milly, smiling shyly u
Jack. 'But I'm not absolutely certain we got away with it
added. 'Miss Parker seems to be on the warpath!'

Indeed, Miss Parker was threading through the
heading in their direction, face like thunder.

'What do we do?' asked Liza desperately. 'Do we tell

'Yes,' said Nora, just as Milly and Jack said 'no'.

There was no time to think – let alone talk it through
because Miss Parker was upon them.

'You were cutting it very fine today, Miss Woods and
Private Archer,' she said. Her voice was pleasant enough,
but there was no mistaking the iciness in her tone – and the
fact she wasn't using their first names only served to underline her displeasure. 'And you both missed the rehearsal
earlier on, despite very clear instructions on where you
needed to be and when. I do hope you both have a good
explanation.'

Jack opened his mouth to reply, but Milly was faster. 'I'm
ever so sorry, Miss,' she said. 'Please believe there is a very
good explanation for what happened. It, er, came to our
attention that somebody was planning a . . . silly prank . . .
to disrupt the royal visit.'

'I see,' said Miss Parker, looking doubtful. 'Is this something
I should know about?'

'I don't think it's something you need to concern yourself
with,' said Jack. 'We were worried it might embarrass the royal
party, but luckily it was stopped in time.'

'Are there any injuries?' asked Miss Parker.

'No, nothing like that,' said Milly.

'Any damage to Army Post Office property?'

'None at all, Miss Parker,' said Jack.

'The . . . stunt . . . is not merely delayed and likely to
happen on another occasion?'

'That would be impossible, Miss,' said Milly firmly.

'And the would-be perpetrators?'

'Someone tried to smuggle something in that might embarrass the royal party,' said Milly. 'I was lucky enough to

intercept it. I can hazard a guess as to who it might be, but I didn't actually see them do it.'

Milly had her fingers crossed behind her back, but actually there was no need. Everything she had said was technically true.

'Very well then,' said Miss Parker. 'I have no wish to know about any silly flags or other paraphernalia that misguided people might have tried to smuggle in. That would only necessitate an investigation and take away from the success of the visit. So, I will just say thank you for helping the day to run smoothly and then pretend we haven't had this conversation.'

'Yes, Miss Parker,' said Milly, feeling the tension in her shoulders ease.

'And, Milly?'

'Yes, Miss Parker?'

'Always remember change is best coming from the inside.'

'Yes, Miss Parker.'

Miss Parker disappeared with a smile and a rustle of skirts.

'We'd better get back to the extension,' said Milly. 'We've left Mr Wildermuth standing guard over what's left of the bomb.' She stopped and made a face. 'I can't believe I've actually just said that. Can this day get any stranger?'

Suddenly, without warning, the incredulity of the situation hit them all and they started to giggle. Together, the four made their way back to the extension. Mr Wildermuth had moved behind some sacks so he couldn't be seen from the entrance, and visibly relaxed when he saw the four friends.

'I was worried I would be found,' he said. 'A German man. In here . . .'

Milly gave him a hug. 'How can we ever thank you enough?' she said. 'Without you, Sarah would have planted the bomb and none of us would have been any the wiser. And the bomb would have gone off, the whole building would have been evacuated and most of these sacks would be in smithereens.'

Mr Wildermuth gave a courtly little bow. 'It is my pleasure,' he said. 'I am fond of the country that has given me refuge, and I am fond of the family who has given me a home. I do not wish to see either suffer.' He paused. 'I'm only sorry I assumed you were somehow mixed up in this.'

Milly smiled and gave a little shrug. 'I don't blame you at all,' she said. 'And I'm so sorry for suspecting you.' She paused and then added, 'By the way, did I tell you about my sister Maggie?'

'No?'

'She discovered her husband has been killed at the front.'

There was a very long pause.

Then Mr Wildermuth said, 'I am very sorry to hear that,' and turned away, but not before Milly saw a flash of – something – in his blue eyes.

'What are we going to do with the bomb?' Nora was saying.

'Before we do anything, I am going to take some photographs of it,' said Jack, reaching for his camera. He snapped away at the contents of the box and then at the wrapper. 'Evidence,' he added, with a grin.

'My van is outside,' said Mr Wildermuth. 'I could take it away in that?'

'I've got a better idea,' said Milly. She looked round at the little group with a grin. '"Trust in God and keep your powder dry,"' she quoted. 'What say you we take a little trip to the Regent's Park lake? That way, we'll know the materials will never fall into the wrong hands again.'

They looked round at each other, faces lit with merriment. Moments later, they were dividing up the components into bags and pockets, grabbing coats and hats, and then they were off, walking brazenly past the sentry guard at the perimeter of the compound and out into the Regent's Park. It was dark by now – and bitterly cold – but the half-moon peered out through a gap in the heavy clouds and gave them plenty of light to navigate by. Milly found herself walking next to Jack and, in the gloaming, he took her hand and put it in her jacket pocket, holding it tightly with his own. The fizzing excitement Milly had felt all day only grew in intensity.

And then they were at the lakeside. They chose a quiet patch – far away from where the boats were launched – and then, without fanfare, slipped their offerings among the water-weeds. As the gunpowder in the open mustard tin slipped into its watery grave, Milly felt a stab of relief. If only all weapons could be disposed of as easily . . .

Back at 'their' side of the park, people were thronging out of the Home Depot full of high spirits and bonhomie. Judging by the shouts, it sounded like many were regrouping at the various hostelries on the Euston Road to continue their revelries.

Milly turned to the others with shining eyes. 'Shall we?' she said.

She really didn't want the afternoon to end.

'Rather,' said Jack, and her heart soared.

'Me too,' said Liza. 'Only I'm meeting James and . . .'

'And we'd love to see him,' finished Milly. 'What about you, Mr Wildermuth?'

'Please, call me Gus,' said Mr Wildermuth. 'And I thank you for your invitation but I must get my van back to the bakery – they've probably sent out a search party by now. Besides, there's a young lady I would rather like to pay a visit to.'

He touched his cap, smiled round at them all and was off. Milly looked after him, her heart full of happiness for Maggie.

'Right, troops?' said Jack. 'Shall we?'

They turned to leave and, as they did so, Milly suddenly caught sight of two incongruous faces. It was Elsie and Hilda standing over by the Outer Circle, both wearing thunderous expressions. They noticed Milly shortly after she saw them, and their expressions changed in the blink of an eye.

Confusion. Wariness.

For a moment, Milly was tempted to ignore them. But how could she? There were things that needed to be said and that needed to be said now.

'Wait,' she said to the others. 'The people who arranged to have the bomb smuggled in are over there. I'm going to go and talk to them.'

Liza followed Milly's line of sight. 'We'll all go over and give them a piece of our mind, if you like,' she said.

'I'd rather do it on my own,' said Milly. 'It seems almost unfair to outnumber them.'

'Understood,' said Jack. 'I'll be here if you need me.'

'I know you will.'

Their eyes met and, in that instant, Milly was rocked by the realisation that she loved him.

It was as simple as that.

Oh, how she loved him!

With a last glance over her shoulder at him, she walked up to Hilda and Elsie, trying to look more confident than she felt.

'Hello,' she said. 'Fancy seeing you here!'

Hilda and Elsie exchanged a glance.

'Hello,' said Elsie warily. 'We're just waiting here for a friend.'

Milly took a deep breath. 'I expect you're rather surprised there are no plumes of smoke and an emergency evacuation,' she said.

Another glance, more nervous this time.

'I don't know what you mean,' stammered Hilda.

'Oh, I think you do,' said Milly pleasantly. 'Let's just say you're very lucky I got to your unexpected present before the authorities did. In fact, if the powers-that-be ever find out that you smuggled a bomb into the Home Depot, I'd say you'd be in rather a lot of trouble, wouldn't you?'

Both Elsie and Hilda started with shock at the word 'bomb'.

'You've got no proof—' Elsie began.

'But you don't deny it?' interrupted Milly. 'You had no luck with me so you found someone else to help with your little scheme. And this time, rather than come clean, you made it more palatable by telling them the parcel contained a jack-in-the-box with a message from the suffragettes! Don't you think that was even more dangerous? Supposing that person had taken it into their own hands to present the box to the royal family and it blew up in their faces. What then?'

'What rubbish,' said Elsie dismissively.

Milly shrugged. 'It's been a very exciting day,' she said. 'Which, of course, is why you chose it. But it also means a lot of people have bought their cameras into work. You must have noticed all the flashes when you came into the compound. And it so happens that my friend over there, the one waving at us from under the plane tree, caught everything on film. Your arrival, handing over the package, your handwriting and Nan's address. The film is being developed at the moment and I'd rather say we have all the proof we need.'

Hilda and Elsie stared at Milly. For once, both were completely speechless.

'I know you've had a terrible time,' said Milly, injecting a conciliatory note into her voice. 'I understand what happened to Nan was dreadful. But it still doesn't excuse what you tried to do. And if you try anything like this again or if you carry out your threat to Sarah, I'll take the photographs to the police – even if it means all three of us go to prison.'

Suddenly, Hilda broke down and started to sob. 'Oh, thank you, Milly,' she said, the tears coursing down her cheeks. 'I don't know what came over us. I'm right glad that bomb didn't go off. But we were both so sad, so angry about Nan . . .'

'I know what came over *you*,' said Milly. 'You were too easily led by your sister. You should start standing on your own two feet and thinking for yourself. Elsie's got strong beliefs and I agree with her on lots of things, but she ain't right about everything.'

Elsie looked mutinous and for a moment she looked like she might launch herself at Milly. But then she took a deep breath and curled her hands into fists by her side.

'Look at you,' she said scornfully. 'You had a chance to make a difference and you took the coward's way out. You're nothing but a fraud. You and your fancy friends.'

Milly felt the colour rush to her cheeks, but forced herself to stay calm. 'That's rubbish,' she said firmly. 'Of course I'm going to continue to fight for our rights, but a terrorist campaign – a bomb – ain't the right way to go about it. What government would give in to that? From now on, I'm going to go about it the right way. And now, if you'll excuse me, me and my "fancy friends" are off down the pub.'

Then, with her head held high, she swept away from them and back to the others. Hilda and Elsie disappeared, and Milly, Nora and Liza collapsed against each other, hugging and laughing.

Then Liza nudged Nora. 'I've left something inside,' she said.

'What?' asked Nora blankly.

'Just something,' said Liza. 'Will you come back in with me?'

'Honestly,' said Milly indignantly. 'If I wanted to be alone with Jack, wouldn't I just say?'

'But if you really want to be helpful, we'll see you in the pub!' added Jack.

Everyone laughed and Nora and Liza disappeared.

Jack and Milly turned to each other.

'What a day,' said Jack. 'I'm all in a whirl, and it's nothing to do with the bomb.'

Milly smiled. 'I feel exactly the same,' she said.

Jack leaned down towards her. Milly tilted her head up to him and as their lips met, the first snowflakes of winter fell gently around them.

# *Epilogue*

## Christmas Eve, 1915

The snow was falling heavily by the time Milly arrived home from her lunch with Jack.

It had been a very special lunch.

A *wonderful* lunch.

A lunch where they had talked about everything and nothing, and yet, somehow, the space between the words had managed to be even more meaningful. The space between the words talked about the beginning of a story, two becoming one, maybe even the hint of a promise . . .

Afterwards, Jack had insisted upon accompanying her all the way home. He knew, he said, that Milly was perfectly capable of travelling around London on her own – that she did so every day – but he wanted to see her home. He didn't want the day to end, he wanted to meet her family and, besides, didn't he have a sheaf of photographs to share with them all?

And now, here he was, installed in the crowded family kitchen and looking perfectly at home.

Milly looked around at them all with affection. With love.

Jack was showing a thoroughly over-excited Charlie and Caroline the photos he had taken in Victoria Park while Boniface – who seemed to be spending more and more time indoors – took the opportunity to silently denude the Christmas tree of a gingerbread man. Over on the sofa, Maggie and Gus – who seemed to be spending more and more time with the family – were deep in conversation, while Arthur also took the opportunity to denude the tree of another gingerbread man. Alice, peeling tatties at the table with Ma, was sporting a new bob and trying not to look self-conscious. She glanced up and met Milly's eye with a characteristic scowl.

'Lovely hair,' said Milly with a warm smile. 'It really suits you.'

Alice looked totally nonplussed. Then her face relaxed.

'Thank you,' she said, turning back to her peeling, her cheeks slightly flushed.

Ma caught Milly's eye with a smile. 'Nice lunch?' she mouthed.

Milly nodded, her heart full. With her family, she had all she needed.

It was still true she, Milly Woods, absolutely, definitely didn't need a sweetheart.

But one thing was now just as certain. She absolutely and definitely wanted one.

But only if his name was Jack Archer.

# Acknowledgements

As ever, I have a host of people to thank, without whom A Post Office Christmas simply wouldn't have been written.

First of all, thank you to my wonderful agent, Felicity Trew, who makes all things possible. Thank you for your warmth, wisdom and unfailing support. Thank you to the marvellous team at Hodder for entrusting me with this series; to my fabulous editors - Thorne Ryan who helped to shape the story and to Olivia Barber who calmly and efficiently steered the book through the editing process with ne'er a ruffled feather. Thanks are also due to Laetitia Grant for her expert proofreading and to Lydia Blagden for the fabulously festive cover.

I've said it before and I'll say it again – writing can be a lonely old business, so thank heavens for lovely friends. Thank you to my writing buddies for keeping me sane whilst writing and editing A Post Office Christmas during lockdown. A big shout-out to the fabulous D20 authors - especially Jessica Ryn, Nicola Gill, Hannah Gold and Victoria Scott for going above and beyond - and another to the wonderful NaNas – Marilyn Groves, Frances Brindle, Gemma Allen, Kate G Smith, Sarah Edghill, Jan Baynham, Christina Lourens, Kate O' Sullivan, Miriam Landor and Anne Woodward. You guys have helped me more than you can know. Thanks to Jane Almey, Debbie Wermann, Fiona Print, Carol Richardson, Catherine Boardman, Sue Cook and Kim Bennett for always having my back. And thank you to all at the South Oxfordshire Archaeological Group for the fun and the 'helpful' ideas – although I fear 'The Post Office Girls Rock the Roman Dig' is unlikely to get through the acquisitions meeting!

A big shout-out to the DB clan – lovely Mum; Ingrid, David, Iain, Alexander and Anna Hamilton; Tonia, Richard, Matthew and Laura Lovell and, of course, UP. Thank you for your unwavering support in this saddest and most difficult of years. COYB!!

And to my immediate family - John, Tom and Charlotte, O and O - thank you for everything. You mean the world to me; I'm so proud of you all and I love you with all my heart.

# Bookends

## When one book ends, another begins...

Bookends is a vibrant new reading community to help you ensure you're never without a good book.

You'll find exclusive previews of the brilliant new books from your favourite authors as well as exciting debuts and past classics. Read our blog, check out our recommendations for your reading group, enter great competitions and much more!

Visit our website to see which great books we're recommending this month.

Join the Bookends community:
## www.welcometobookends.co.uk

 @Team Bookends    @WelcomeToBookends